SECRET CELEBRITY

The Cigarette Girl

SECRET CELEBRITY

Carol Wolper

RIVERHEAD BOOKS

A MEMBER OF PENGUIN PUTNAM INC.

NEW YORK | 2002

Riverhead Books
a member of
Penguin Putnam Inc.
375 Hudson Street
New York, NY 10014

Library of Congress Cataloging-in-Publication Data

Wolper, Carol.
Secret celebrity / Carol Wolper.
p. cm.
ISBN 1-57322-214-3
1. Women in the motion picture industry—Fiction.   2. Women—
California—Los Angeles—Fiction.   3. Motion picture industry—
Fiction.   4. Los Angeles (Calif.)—Fiction.
5. Celebrities—Fiction.   I. Title.
PS3573.O5678 S43 2002   2002016946
813'.54—dc21

Printed in the United States of America
1   3   5   7   9   10   8   6   4   2

This book is printed on acid-free paper. ∞

BOOK DESIGN BY JUDITH STAGNITTO ABBATE
AND CLAIRE NAYLON VACCARO

a c k n o w l e d g m e n t s

Thanks to . . .

Sean MacPherson for his inspiration.

Julie Grau, Owen Laster, Lindsay Sagnette, Angela Janklow Harrington, and Robert Lorenz for great advice and guidance.

Greg Pruss for the info and the laughs.

Nancy and Andrew Jarecki for their stories and party.

Don Henley and Glenn Frye for the use of their lyrics and permission to give the apocryphal Gault a writing credit.

Greg Dooley for his lyrics.

And the usual gang for their encouragement . . . Eric and Lisa, Peter and Barbara, Susan C., Ajay, my friends at Spring Creek Ranch, Dana, Jack, Hopkins, Chris B., Stace, Priscilla, Andy, Tom and Lisa, Kristen, Alan G., all the guys at Ago, and most of all—Sidney, for always keeping it interesting.

c h a p t e r   o n e

I'm sorry. I hate lists. You probably do, too. But some-times there's no other way to put it. So here it is—my "Are you having an interesting life?" checklist for people who live in L.A. and work in Hollywood. Or, with slight adjustments, for anyone else.

1. A secret passionate fling with a notorious lover. (No points for a public fling.)

2. A feast-famine-feast existence. (No points for all feast, no points for all famine.)

3. Time spent with one of your heroes (a director?) who proves to be boring.

4. A fascinating conversation with someone (FedEx guy?) you previously disregarded.

5. Access to a philosopher king who is not the leader of any cult . . . or agency.

6. At least one, but no more than three, formidable enemies.

7. At least one special project that's as compelling as a passionate fling with a notorious lover.

8. An ongoing friendly dialogue with your dark side . . . or Jim Morrison's ghost.

9. One friend who can unfailingly make you laugh even when that special project gets put into turn-around.

10. Enough temptation to keep things interesting . . . but not as much as can be found on location.

In the summer of '99, I did a lot of thinking about an interesting life because I wasn't having one. I don't know what I was having. A lull? A second reckoning? A slump? Disenchantment? It made sense. I was right on schedule. I was thirty-five years old. I'd put in ten years working in the business, always behind the camera. Writer. Set decorator. Producer—on a low-budget film and two music videos. And, most recently, aspiring director. Ten years was about what it took to go from feeling sporadically invincible and optimistic, to looking at people who felt sporadically invincible and optimistic as if they were in hyper-denial. This lull of mine wasn't helped by two issues that preoccupied me. I was obsessed with how obsessed people can get with celebrities. And on a more personal note, I was obsessed with this question: Can any girl in Hollywood trust her girlfriends not to fuck her boyfriend? Sadly, I was beginning to think the answer was probably not. Make that definitely not if the boyfriend's famous.

I did everything I could to bust out of the lull. I tried numerous solutions to shake things up including a homeopathic remedy that temporarily turned my skin yellow. I never expected to find the lull antidote at the Centerfold newsstand on Melrose and Fairfax. It was an unlikely place for a breakthrough. Jammed with newspapers and magazines, the place felt no bigger than a shack. It was also an exceptionally hot day. Hot and humid, which is not the way it's supposed to be in Los Angeles in August. Or ever. What are we, in Guam? What's with this humidity? As I stepped out of my apartment, I remembered that thunderstorms were in the forecast. Not that I would have minded one. Bring it on. Maybe a little electricity would shock me out of my coma. As it turned out, I didn't need a bolt of lightning. Instead, a name did it. That's all. A name. And the thing is if it wasn't for William, I wouldn't have stuck around long enough to even hear it.

William, also known as Magazine Guy, works the Centerfold's 6 A.M. to 1 P.M. shift, Tuesday through Saturday. He works the register, usually with his radio tuned to KCRW's "Morning Becomes Eclectic," a show that debuts cutting-edge music. He usually wears black jeans and a T-shirt, his blond hair always adorably messy. He

looks like he could have been a fine-arts major at Cal
Arts, but in fact did only one year at UCLA. He dropped
out to play drums in a band that had a decent run on the
local club scene before going bust a few years ago. We'd
gotten to be casual friends because I stopped in to buy
magazines at least three times a week. I'm an addict
when it comes to this stuff, which would make sense if
I believed anything I read. I don't. The only thing that
I take as truth are the sports scores. Everything else is
just bullshit, spin, more hype, and propaganda. So why
the addiction? I guess I want to keep track of the changes
and nuances of the fake world I live in. As does William.
We quickly worked our way up from "Have a good day"
to chatting about the headlines. The guy knows how to
get my attention.

"Is that a price tag I see hanging from her pussy?"

William was checking out the cover of one of the
weekly tabloids. The headlines announced the recent en-
gagement of an actress and her new boyfriend, a troll-
like, European, self-made billionaire. The photo showed
the two of them at some New York hot spot. I took a
good look at the tabloid cover, at the actress's bad plastic surgery. Eyelids pulled so high, her face bore a look
of perpetual surprise. "My God, look at her. She hardly
looks human anymore. She's beginning to look like an
inflatable doll."

William shrugged. "A very expensive inflatable doll.
She stays married to this guy for just one year, she'll
walk away with millions."

"Yeah, but she'll have to fuck him for a year," I said
as I handed him the stack of magazines and newspapers

that would feed my fix that day. A young guy brushed past me on his way to the music section. He went right for a copy of *SPIN*.

"Dude, check out the Afghan Whigs article," William called out before turning back to me. "Twelve dollars and sixty-eight cents."

I threw down a twenty.

"You want a bag for that?" he asked.

I laughed. "You usually only offer one when I buy *Penthouse Variations*."

"SOP. Standard operating procedure. Girl buys smut, we offer camouflage."

As William handed me my change, the guy perusing *SPIN* chuckled.

"You reading about the Whigs?" William asked.

The guy nodded. "You see them play the El Rey?"

"Yeah. How about that?"

The guy rolled the magazine and held it up to his mouth like a microphone and started to sing. "Come on, come on, come on little rabbit, show me what you got 'cause I know you got a habit." He wasn't a bad singer but he didn't continue. "Love that song." He smiled as he unrolled the magazine.

"Reminds me of something Richard Gault might have written," William said.

And there it was. That was it. The name that changed everything. *Richard Gault*. Not a particularly poetic name. It didn't roll off the tongue. It wasn't a movie-star name. The Gault being too close to fault to play in a town that believes in laying the blame else-where—no matter who pulls the trigger.

"Richard Gault. My God," I gushed. "I haven't thought about him in years. He was the greatest."

"Whatever happened to Richard Gault?" the young guy asked. "Hope he doesn't turn up on VH1's 'Where Are They Now' show."

William lowered the volume of the radio, a sure sign he was into the conversation. "I don't think VH1 gives a fuck about Richard Gault. His last and only record came out in 1975 and only sold three thousand, one hundred and fifteen copies. And his two movies were brilliant but did no business."

"Three thousand one hundred and fifteen," I repeated. I was astonished. "You know how many copies it sold?"

He shrugged and continued. "And since he never got fucked up on drugs or had some big sex scandal they could use for one of their behind-the-music things . . ." He shrugged again.

The young guy finished the thought for him. "No one gives a fuck where he is now."

The three of us grew silent, the way you do when you realize you miss something that until that moment you didn't know you missed.

"How old would he be now?" I asked.

"Fifty," William replied.

Suddenly the young guy got serious. "He's not dead, is he?"

"No," William said with conviction. And William would know. He's the authority. He's Mr. Information Man. Then looking at me with a smirk, he added, "Impressed you even know who he is."

"Know? Growing up, I wanted to be him."

"You must have been a precocious kid. Twenty-five years ago? What were you, five?"

"You were five," I guessed. "I was ten." Then I paused, thinking, Fuck, I just told him my age. But I couldn't dwell on that. "How did you hear about Richard Gault?"

"A few years ago, a friend gave me a cassette of his album. You can't hear it and not get interested."

★

AND IT WAS right then that I got my big idea. I grabbed my magazines. I think I said, "See you later." But I don't know for sure. Remembering Richard Gault shook everything up. What if? What if? What if? I thought excitedly as I headed outside. At the doorway, I almost bumped into a girl who was dressed in exercise clothes and carrying a cup of Starbucks. She wasn't so much in a hurry as she seemed distracted. I could tell William perked up at the sight of her by the sound of his voice. "Hey, Jennifer," he said. "What's going on?"

I made a mental note to ask William if this was the girl he'd been telling me about. But I couldn't concentrate on that right now. What if? What if? What if? I kept thinking as I unlocked my car, tossed the magazines on the passenger seat, and got inside. I turned on the ignition and put the air-conditioning on high. Adrenaline was ripping through my body. It had been a long time since I'd felt this way over an idea. It had been a long time since I'd even had an idea. And it felt like forever since I'd had an idea that didn't make me feel like a total sellout who was one step away from trying to become an inflatable doll with my own troll-like billionaire.

So I did what you're never supposed to do in Hollywood. I picked up the phone and called my agent, thinking my excitement would excite him. It didn't. And by the time I hung up I didn't care what he thought because I knew with or without his help, my life was about to get more interesting.

Thirty-five years old. Yes, I'm thirty-five. But I'm an L.A. thirty-five. In other places thirty-five generally means you're a grown-up. A lot of thirty-five-year-olds have kids. A lot of them have teenagers. They have serious jobs. They have life insurance. They can fill out the whole questionnaire. When asked who to call in case of an emergency, they have an immediate answer. But I'm not that kind of thirty-five-year-old. In Los Angeles you can be thirty-five and still find the Afghan Whigs more important than front-page news. Here it's not unusual to not feel or act grown-up. To not have kids. To have a job you're serious about rather than a serious job. To still think you're going to live forever.

And to be so unsettled that your "in case of emergency" person changes from week to week.

Living this way makes me, and people like me, a target for a lot of criticism, most often from people outside L.A. Real grown-ups look down on us as narcissists stuck in adult-escence. I was once accused of producing music videos that had no socially redeeming value. What?

But don't get me started on critics and how their reviews should come with a disclaimer. In this case it should have read . . . "I'm pissed off that my low-paying job requires me to spend eight hours a day in a cubicle watching other people have fun in million-dollar videos." And even though I have a couple of hideous cubicle jobs on my résumé, that doesn't keep me from wanting to take the critics on—which is further proof that I'm not a normal thirty-five-year-old.

Shouldn't I have more important things to fight over? Yes, I should. But I can't deny my get-even fantasy. I'd line up all those people who have criticized my life and work for being trite and say to them, Okay, let me explain something: The first seventeen years of my life were hell. I lived at the crossroads of depression and violence. All the grown-ups were like characters in a Eugene O'Neill play and every guy under twenty-five was a character out of *Reservoir Dogs*. Only not as cute.

Listen up, critics, you want me to get real? I've been real. It's overrated. You want me to make a contribution to society? Here's my contribution: Go west. Have fun. That doesn't mean I'm into a senseless life. I like sense. I like meaning. I just think you can get those things while walking with a light step and maneuvering with a delicate touch. Having lived through seventeen very dark, very long South Boston winters, I have great appreciation for L.A.'s almost endless summer.

Which is probably why I married my now, soon-to-be-ex husband. Met him six years ago, when he was twenty-five. We met on vacation up at Big Bear. One glimpse and I was hooked. They don't breed creatures like him in my hometown. His blond hair, sparkling green eyes, olive skin, and irrepressible zest appeared to be some blessed mix of Connecticut WASP and Mediterranean mojo. (I was close. His father was Pasadena WASP, his mother upper-class Italian—New York by way of Milan.) His two great talents at that time were skiing and smoothly popping open champagne bottles. I used to watch him fly down the mountain and think if he can do that, he can do anything. No logic there, but that's what love does. As for the champagne, he always ordered the best, generally on someone else's credit card. It was the first time in my life champagne didn't give me a headache. Quite the opposite. Even the next morning, I still felt all bubbly and happy. It was the first time in my life when the "what ifs" weren't worst-case scenarios.

My husband was like a Xanax for me. Any residual depression I'd been carrying around from my South Boston days was gone. *He made me laugh*. It felt good. It made me feel alive. He got me to believe the good times could indeed roll on and on. He delivered the right message at the right time. What can I say? I ended up marrying the delivery boy. And I do mean boy. I should have been tipped off when I discovered his favorite toothpaste was Aquafresh for Kids. But being in love, I found it adorable that his kisses tasted like bubble gum.

★

HE WAS LATE. He was always late. And of course he would be late for this lunch. The "let's talk about the terms of our divorce" lunch. I was sitting at an outside table at one of those Euro-trashy restaurants at the bottom of Sunset Plaza Drive. I'd already had an iced latte and had spent the last ten minutes eavesdropping on the guy at the next table's cell phone conversation. "Baby, you're hot. You're so hot, baby. Tell me how hot you are."

Suddenly, he was there. James (never Jimmy) Chase, my wayward husband. He kissed me on both cheeks, Euro style. It was an affectation that drove me increasingly crazy, seeing as he'd grown up in California. He sat down and immediately signaled over a waiter. "Oh my God, I think we're wearing the exact same glasses," I said. "Oliver Peoples. Black frames. Green lenses."

He took his off. "Not exactly," he replied, comparing them and then jokingly added, "You're always copying me."

"Yeah. Right." I smiled. It was one of those unfunny jokes. The kind couples who are divorcing laugh at for old times' sake, and as a way of rewriting personal history. The idea being that if we pretend an unfunny comment is funny maybe we can also pretend our marriage wasn't the cliché it turned out to be.

"Hey, bud." The waiter was standing next to James, grinning. "Haven't seen you around for a while."

Perfect, I thought. Of course the waiter knows James. That's the thing about my ex. He always knows and is on the best terms with all the waiters, bartenders, and maître d's, wherever he goes. Part of it comes with the territory. James is a personal manager—mostly actors and actresses—though probably no one you've heard of. Getting VIP treatment is a necessary part of his image. As important as his (our) Oliver Peoples sunglasses.

"I've been busy," James replied, implying by his tone that it was, at the very least, equal parts play and work.

"I bet you have," the waiter replied enthusiastically, as if living vicariously was a good thing.

I was tempted to say, What exactly do you mean by that? Does that mean you've seen James partying? Two girls and three Stoli martinis (his favorite drink) is the picture that came to mind. But before I could pursue that thought, James drew me into the conversation. Addressing the waiter, he said. "You know my . . ." He stopped. Stalled. What to say? You know my wife? You know my ex-wife? You know my friend? Which would it be? I know James. I knew he was weighing the pluses and minuses of each option. And I also knew he'd go for the easy way out. "You know Christine, don't you?"

The waiter looked at me, confused. "Ah . . . yeah. Great to see you again, Christine."

We'd never met but that seemed beside the point. I ordered another latte and James ordered a beer.

When we were left alone, I said, "'Wife' is still the technically correct term."

"I didn't see any reason to get into that with the waiter."

"You don't even have to get into it with your future wives," I said. "If you want, you can forget to even mention the first Mrs. Chase."

"If it was up to me," he sighed, "I'd never get married again."

He was serious. I couldn't believe it and I couldn't stop myself. "I've got a news flash for you, sweetheart. It *is* up to you."

★

I GUESS THIS is the time to tell you about James's girlfriend. I call her "Psycho Girl" and not because of anything she's done to me. I was on my way out of my marriage when she showed up. Or as my screenwriter friend, Elizabeth West, quipped, "You were climbing out the window and Psycho Girl just opened the door and made for an easier exit." I dubbed her Psycho Girl because of what she does to James. She has these sporadic ugly explosions. Screaming. Throwing things. A parody of a bratty diva rock star. Makes me want to say, Honey, don't worry about leaving your American Express card behind, just don't leave home without your medication.

But how about this? James doesn't seem to mind her psycho fits because he's convinced she could be the next Julie Christie. Based on what? She's had two small roles in obscure independent movies, and let me tell you, the girl cannot survive the close-up. Every time the camera zooms in on her face, all you see in those eyes is ambition. And as everyone knows, the real stars are the ones who show their soul. Or can at least fool you into thinking they are.

I also call her Psycho Girl 'cause she's a pathological liar. She loves to go on and on about her sexual fantasies. She says things like, "I don't know what it is about me, but I love whips." She'll tell you that she had five orgasms the night before when the truth is (according to James) she took an Excedrin P.M. and was asleep (in his bed) by ten. The girl would rather shop than fuck, but James is good at compartmentalization. I'm sure he's got a couple of other girls to play with when his faux sex symbol is at Gucci.

I wish I didn't feel this way about her. I wish I could say, So what? Not my problem. But because she appears to get away with her bad behavior, at times, the injustice of it all weighs on me. There have been moments when I've felt as if she's violated my equilibrium, my sacred space. To put it in exaggerated TV-sound-bite lingo, I've felt like a victim of a home invasion.

But I can't dispute Psycho Girl has some major assets. The perfect blond hair, short and sexy, that frames a face of angelic innocence. And those legs of hers, that can and often do stop traffic. Watching this girl cross Sunset Boulevard in a short skirt is a true experience. Oh, and did I mention she's only twenty-two?

★

JAMES AND I managed to avoid the divorce topic for the first half of the meal. Instead we talked about our friends and what they were up to. So-and-so just got back from London. So-and-so just went AA. So-and-so has gotten so boring and earnest since joining AA that friends are tempted to spike his iced tea. We talked about his cousin, a successful businessman who lives in La Jolla and was now dating a San Diego Chargers cheerleader.

"My cousin has the worst taste in women," James said.

"I think he'd say the same about you," I replied. "He certainly doesn't like me."

"My cousin doesn't get women like you."

"What kind of woman am I?"

"The kind that gets me," he laughed. "I'm kidding. His problem is he can't figure you out. You're prettier than the smart girls, and smarter than the pretty girls."

"I think you meant that as a compliment, so why does that make me feel incredibly mediocre?"

"Oh come on, sweetheart. You know how great I think you are."

I gave him my best cynical stare.

"Don't you believe me?" he asked.

"It's not that I don't believe you, James. It's just that at the end of the day, it doesn't mean a whole lot."

He pretended to be hurt. "My feelings don't mean anything?"

"Of course your feelings mean something," I replied. "But what you *say* doesn't necessarily mean anything, or at least it doesn't mean what any sane person might expect it to mean."

He took another sip of his beer. He was enjoying this. He loved being told he wasn't like everyone else.

Even if that meant he had a problem. "But it does mean *something?*"

I should have let it go but I wasn't that healthy. "Here's what it means. December twenty-eighth, 1998. Dinner at Indochine. You, drink in hand, stand up and announce to the whole restaurant that you are madly in love with your wife."

"And you loved it."

"It embarrassed me, and I loved it."

James was beaming now as if amnesia had taken hold and he had no idea what was coming.

"Three days later," I continued, "a mere seventy-two hours later, you announce in the privacy of our apartment that marriage doesn't work for you. Now, a sane person would not expect that madly in love was a prelude to rejection. Therefore what you say usually demands an interpreter. Not that that's my concern anymore."

"But I did love you. I do love you. I just don't want to be married."

"Just cut down on the martinis, honey."

Now he was really loving this. His favorite role, the charming, irresistible guy who has to win over the disapproving, aloof woman. If I could have stayed aloof and disapproving, we'd still be married. "Remember," he said, "you're the one who insisted we get married. Not that I didn't want to."

"I did? I insisted?" James excelled at selective memory. No point in correcting him so I just moved on. "Did I also insist you fuck Remy—my best friend?"

"I can't help it if she couldn't control herself. What was I supposed to do?"

A typical Jamesian response. It wasn't his fault. It never was. He acted as if he wasn't the one who unzipped.

"She was my best friend," I reminded him. "She was, at least, supposed to try to resist." I paused for a second as it hit me that I still irrationally blamed her more than him. Probably because I had higher expectations of the female gender when it came to loyalty and returning calls in a timely fashion. "The whole Remy thing threw me into a crisis with all my girlfriends," I continued. "I still don't feel comfortable trusting any of them."

"It's good for you."

I shook my head. That's what James always said about anything difficult that I had to deal with. It was as if it were a gift he was giving me. And then when it worked, when in fact it did make me stronger, he gloated as if it were all his doing. Why, I asked myself, why were we even talking about this? I really didn't care all that much anymore. And I was afraid that if I thought about any of this for too long a new "what if" would take hold, one that had been steadily growing over the last year. What if men were a lot weaker than advertised? Or at least the men who crossed my path. It was a thought that could inspire a momentary urge to end it all, to throw myself in the path of the next speeding Ferrari.

"Let's face it, James," I said. "You got married for the bachelor party."

It was a line I enjoyed saying and he enjoyed hearing. And I knew that of all the things that had happened in our six years together, somehow this would be the line that got the most attention in our book of memories.

★

BY THE TIME we got down to the dollars and cents of it, James was bored. "Look," I said. I pushed a piece of paper in front of him. "Here are all our assets."

"We're rich," he said, smiling.

I handed him another piece of paper. "And these are all our debts."

"We're broke," he joked. His smile didn't diminish one watt. He didn't have to worry. He had a trust fund and family money that had nothing to do with our shared resources. He may not have cash flow but he always had access. He finished off his beer. "*Our* debts?" he teased. "Ours?"

"Don't make me do this," I said. "Don't make me break this down. Don't make me start counting up all the bottles of Cristal you put on my credit card when you were entertaining your friends." Not that I would have or could have counted. Truth is, that stuff never bothered me.

"Oh, so they're *our* debts but now they're *my* friends?" He was leaning across the table as if at any moment he might kiss me. I swear if someone were watching us they'd think he was flirting. If he was, he was on auto-flirt. But I couldn't afford auto-flirt or any other kind of flirting. This was a serious matter.

"You can have seventy-five percent of the equity in the condo. I'll move out by the end of the month. And

I'll be responsible for seventy-five percent of our debts. But in return I need thirty-five thousand in cash. Now. This week."

It was a bad deal for me and he knew it. He'd probably come to this lunch hoping he could get away cheap, and now he was being offered a deal that would earn him money. Not that he'd admit that.

"Thirty-five thousand? You're robbing me." But he was beyond delighted. That 100-watt smile of his got even brighter.

"And, you don't even have to pay any legal fees. In fact," I said, as I pulled out a document I'd had prepared, "if we both sign this now, we can file it at the court today and six months from now, we'll be divorced. The notice will come in the mail. Someday when you least expect it, it'll be sitting there with the rest of the junk mail. It'll be like—surprise—you're divorced."

"Thirty-five thousand," he repeated. "Why do you need thirty-five thousand? You owe money to some drug dealer or something?"

"Yeah," I laughed. "Those two quaaludes I bought six months ago really got me into deep financial trouble."

He looked away. I thought it was to check out a gorgeous girl who strolled by, but his gaze remained fixed even after she passed. It occurred to me that he might be stalling for time. Now that the divorce he wanted was within reach, he seemed in no hurry to cross the finish line. It was a character trait I'd observed often over our years together. James wasn't a "closer"—that's Hollywood's word for it. But he was one hell of an opener. And we'd "always have Big Bear."

"So why do you need the thirty-five thousand?" he asked seriously, as if asserting his matrimonial right to know what his wife did with her money. I could have spent an hour discussing the absurdity of James's "right to know," but I wasn't that sick.

"Look," I said. "It's a great deal for you. Do you want it or not?"

"Is this about some guy? Are you trying to make me jealous?"

"No and no," I said. And then because I was curious and also because I knew it would drive him just a little bit crazy, I said, "You ever hear of Richard Gault?"

"No. Why?"

"Never mind."

Jennifer came in the other day. Usual deal. After working out. Sipping hard on the straw of her iced mocha. She looked like she was in a hurry. Always does. I wanted to say, "Ease down, you're just grinding metal." A line from *Aliens*. But what's the point? She's probably just another L.A. case of A.D.D. I'm beginning to think no one can focus on anything for more than thirty seconds anymore—except, of course, themselves.

She stopped in front of the tabloids, zeroed in on the latest gossip. "You into that stuff?" I asked her.

"Just seeing if my friend is in there this week."

Translated that means boyfriend. Translated further—famous boyfriend. Any guy who's been in L.A. for more than a few days can figure that out.

"Who's your friend?"

"Oh, just somebody," she said.

I know her type. Celebrity obsessed. The Hollywood virus. Stick around a little while and she'll be dropping clues about mystery guy. If I took her out for a drink I might get her to cough up his name after a few sips. Or, at least his initials. For most of these girls, there's no point in fucking a celebrity unless people know you're fucking a celebrity. "So is he in there?" I asked her.

She was scanning the *Star*'s two-page gossip page. Scanning the names in bold type. "Nope. Thank God," she said. She folded the paper closed and put it back on the rack. "Not that they ever get it right." She then picked up a copy of *People* and went right to Startracks. I wondered what she'd do if she saw a photo of mystery guy with another girl. She might want to rip it out and throw it away or rip it out and save it. When you've got the Hollywood virus these things are always a toss-up.

So why am I into this girl? Yeah, she's pretty. Nice body. But so what. Lots of those around. And I'm not one of those guys who likes a girl more 'cause she's bonking some big shot. I do have a weakness for girls who are trouble though and Jennifer is a walking T-zone. But this is more than a weakness. I know the girl's license plate number. I hate to admit this, but I started paying attention to her the day she came in with her dog. I'm not a dog person. I couldn't tell you what kind of dog it was. But she was like another person with that dog. She was playing with it and talking to it and kissing it, like she might actually have a heart underneath those fake tits.

Christine would be able to figure Jennifer out in a minute.

They were both at the newsstand the other day, but Christine was on her way out when Jennifer got there. Got to get them together though 'cause Christine's radar when it comes to girls, when it comes to anyone, is awesome. She denies it. She says, "To tell you the truth, I don't always know where intuition ends and paranoia begins."

Which reminds me, I got to tell Christine I found some interesting stuff on the Internet on Richard Gault. I'll tell her Thursday. *Vogue* and the new weeklies arrive then. She'll be there. Wait till she sees the cover of this new magazine that just arrived. The big headline is "Hillary Clinton Opens Up." Yeah, like that's ever gonna happen. She's a fucking politician. Then they've got an article about Gwyneth Paltrow and they got her to pose all decked out in this leather getup that's supposed to be, what? Dominatrix? Yeah, I want to meet the person who came up with that idea. Here's my idea: Why don't they get a dominatrix to dress up like a dominatrix. Or, better idea: Why doesn't someone start a magazine called *Lies*. A civilian's opinion—for whatever it's worth.

Christine laughs when I go off on this stuff. We both get into it. I like her. I had a dream about her last night. She was wearing this tiny kilt and a T-shirt that said "caliente." I wonder if she's got a boyfriend. Even if she doesn't, I bet she's unavailable. It's like she's living in some parallel reality. No wonder she loves Richard Gault.

The Ridgeley Apartment complex is the real Melrose Place. The tenants are mostly young and have enough sex and melodrama in their lives to keep a nighttime soap opera running into syndication. Its former and present residents include a professional ice skater who attempted suicide. The ex-girlfriend of a major TV star. A British video director who was rumored to have had an affair with Madonna years ago. A New York journalist who knows everyone who is anyone on both coasts. The heir to a cosmetics fortune. (He lived in the only expensive apartment—the penthouse.) An agent. A struggling fashion designer. And, Waz.

Waz was the reason I knew about the place. Warren Zubrowsky was the name on his passport but no one called him that. He was forty-two, a painter but he made his living as a DP for videos and commercials. We'd met on a job and had become close because we were both going through an obsession with Paul Auster novels. The obsession passed but the friendship remained. Every few weeks we'd talk on the phone or get together for lunch. Usually to talk about how *not* to get sucked into the vortex of a spiritually bankrupt culture. That, and who was fucking who. But this was the first time I'd visited him at his apartment. It was also the first time I'd called with a specific request.

★

WAZ AND I sat in his living room, drinking Hansen's lemonade out of the bottle. I sat in the leather armchair that faced one of his paintings—a luminously lit staircase that led nowhere. Waz sat across from me on the couch. The TV, set in a custom-built wall unit, was on with the volume off. The windows, which faced the courtyard, were open. The grass had recently been cut and the flowers—mostly bird-of-paradise—were in full bloom.

"Does anyone ever sit out there?" I asked.

"Nope. Never. Well, one guy did. Once. Dickey Johnson. Apartment 101. One Sunday afternoon, he dragged a lounge chair out there and parked himself on it with the Sunday paper. Everyone looked at him like he was crazy." Waz paused. "Actually, he is. But I like him."

"What does he do?"

"I don't know. Probably won't know. He's very private. And he's moving back to Philadelphia. Says he doesn't like the weather out here."

"Sunshine doesn't do it for him?"

"He hates the Santa Anas. Only he calls them Santanas. The other day he said, 'Don't want to be around for those Santanas. Those winds are spooky.'"

"Well, they are."

"Yeah, but they beat being in Philadelphia."

"What do we know? L.A. is probably the only city in the world you and I could live in. What does that say about us?"

★

"HEY, WAZ MAN." The person calling out was walking through the courtyard. He stopped in front of the apartment's open windows. He was a young man in his late twenties, dressed in a suit, carrying a Filofax and wearing Persol sunglasses. For a second I thought it might be Dickey Johnson but it didn't fit my image of a guy who'd make a spectacle of himself by camping out in a drugstore lounge chair in *this* courtyard.

"Hey, Jeffrey," Waz said. "You're getting a late start, aren't you? I thought agents were at their desks and on the phone to New York by eight A.M.?"

"Seven A.M.," he replied sharply.

I noted that it was now 11:30. Not that I cared what time anyone got to the office. Especially not an agent, since they weren't placing those early-morning calls on my behalf.

"You have a late night?" Waz asked.

Jeffrey acted as if he didn't hear the question. He looked away for a moment and then turned back. "I'm thinking of getting a new car. Are you happy with your Bronco?"

Waz grinned. A grin halfway between amusement and discomfort. "The Bronco's great, man. But doesn't strike me as your set of wheels."

"Let me guess," I jumped in. "You're a BMW guy."

Jeffrey studied me carefully. "I know you, don't I?"

"We might have met. Christine Chase."

"Actress?"

"Uh . . . no."

I didn't volunteer any further career information and he didn't ask. Instead he said, "So, what do *you* think of *his* Bronco?"

"I like it. I like a rough ride." I was trying to be cute, but Jeffrey either didn't notice or didn't care. He seemed completely lost in thought. Completely. As if he'd left the planet. I was tempted to let loose with one of my high-pitched hail-a-cab whistles, but after ten or so seconds he returned to earth.

"Maybe I'll give my car guy a call today," he said and then drifted away without saying goodbye.

After he left, I turned to Waz. "Notice how many guys everybody has? My car guy. My phone guy. My sound-system guy. My cable guy. My computer guy. My security-system guy. The list is fucking endless. This is why I feel like a misfit. I have no guys in my life."

"You really are a loser."

"But tell me something. Was I right? Does Jeffrey drive a BMW?"

"Of course."

"What would make a guy like that want to switch to a Bronco? Armani suit. Three-hundred-dollar Filofax. And a Bronco. Doesn't quite go together."

Waz looked out at the empty, quiet courtyard. "Maybe that's good," he said.

"Maybe," I replied. My intuition said otherwise. But then it was possible I'd once again crossed over into paranoia.

★

I WENT THROUGH two lemonades before I had the courage to blurt out what I'd come there to say. "Want to do something that could be interesting?"

"That covers a wide field," Waz said. "Lots of interesting things you and I could do together."

I looked at him with surprise. That was the most flirtatious thing he'd ever said to me. And even though Waz had a look about him that suggested he knew how to put the x back in sex, I didn't pursue it.You see it was also possible he wasn't flirting at all. I swear I'm losing my ability to recognize the difference between a wall and a door.

"A work thing," I explained, playing it safe.

"Well, that cuts the field in half." He was looking particularly appealing with the sun hitting his slightly weathered face and that winning smile of his. The one that had helped him charm his way out of two speeding tickets. No easy feat when you're dealing with the LAPD.

"A work thing that might go nowhere and probably won't make a dime."

"Gee, where do I sign?"

I ignored the playful sarcasm. "I want to make a documentary on Richard Gault."

He thought for a moment and then it came to him. "*Strange Days*. Was it directed by Oscar Davies? Released when? In the mid-seventies?"

"I knew you'd know him."

"He quoted one of my favorite lines in a movie. 'We never really know how much or how little space we take up in someone's life.'"

"His lines off the screen are even better."

Waz waited for proof and I was prepared. "*Esquire* magazine interview. 1975. 'Travel light. Be heavy.'"

"That one's a little too fortune cookie for my taste but I get what you mean." Waz polished off the all-natural lemonade and reached for his favorite toxin. A Marlboro Red. He lit up. "What's he doing now?"

"I don't know. That's the idea for the documentary. It'll be about finding him. Meeting him. Getting him to talk to us."

"Very yellow brick road."

"Gault's not Oz."

"How do you know?"

"Because I can't take one more disappointment."

"Oh, in that case." He reached over and affectionately messed up my hair. Was that a yes? A maybe?

Suddenly his attention fixed on the TV screen. He leaned over and upped the sound. It was a hard-core news piece about Kosovo. A shot of refugees stuck in dismal, crowded camps. "Look at that," he said. "Look at what that guy's wearing."

One of the refugees who looked like he'd been through hell was dressed in a Backstreet Boys T-shirt. It was surreal. VH1 meets genocide. When the news anchor went to a commercial break, Waz lowered the sound back down.

"It's going to be a weird millennium," he said.

He was right, and though I didn't want to get into it with him, it was probably another explanation as to why I was in a depressing lull and one of the reasons I was hoping Richard Gault would lead me out of it. I hated talking about the millennium, hated thinking about it. The media had been fixated on it for so long it had become just another overhyped holiday. All the attention and talk just seemed designed to get you to spend money. A lot of people were loading up their closets with disaster supplies for the worst-Y2K-case scenario. Then there were all those people planning some mega celebration to usher in "2000." According to the media, disaster or expensive celebrations seemed to be the only options. I didn't buy it. Waz didn't buy it. But you've got to buy something. You can't just go through life not buying all the bullshit. Eventually you've got to find something worthwhile, which is how I really wanted to sell the whole Richard Gault idea. What if there's still someone out there worth buying? But instead I built a case for its potential profitability. I told Waz I had enough money to get started and figured once I had some edited footage I could take it to HBO. If they liked it, they'd put up the money for the rest. I started to tell the story of a friend of mine who did just that with her documentary on rodeo girls and . . .

"Stop," he said. "I don't care about all that. Just tell me this. What's the chance of you actually getting to Richard Gault?"

Of course, he asked the only question I feared answering. "It's not impossible."

He laughed. "If you had said no problem, I'd say pass. But not impossible. Okay, sounds good."

"Really? You'll do it?"

"Why not?"

Oh my God, I thought, is he in the lull, too? Are we all stuck in the summer-of-'99 lull? The pre-millennium lull. Stuck in the middle of the kind of chaos where everything changes but nothing is new. Are we all looking for something, anything, to wake us up? To challenge us? To get us excited? To take us to the next (and let's hope there is one) frontier? And then Waz added something that seemed to have nothing to do with anything but I knew exactly what he meant. "I think I'm going to miss Dickey Johnson," he said.

chapter five

I met Jennifer. In a sentence, she's an H and D girl. Hint and deny. I know a lot of girls in Hollywood like her. They love to hint about some famous guy they're friends with or were friends with. Or are sleeping with or did sleep with years ago. Some will even go so far as to mention the movie he was in back in the seventies. Some will even say it was a big movie. About a boxer. And that it won an Oscar. They'll admit that there were many sequels. And if you say, "You mean *Rocky*. You mean Stallone," they'll say, "No, no, no." Hint and deny. It's a way of flying with the A-list without actually having to show the boarding pass you don't actually have. Jennifer wasn't name-dropping Sly. She wasn't exactly name-dropping at all. But she was carrying the latest issue of *Rolling Stone* with her and kept saying, "My friend is in here this week."

We (Jennifer, William, and I) were at the Coffee Bean on Sunset. You could cast the next "Friends" clone from the crowd hanging around there. So many Lisa Kudrow and Matthew Perry wannabes. As well as a real working actor in his twenties. No name came to mind but his face was familiar because he had a small part in one of WB's highly promoted prime-time teen dramas. There were also a few misfits in the mix. A man in his forties who'd brought his computer and sat there gulping coffee and working on his (let me guess) Hollywood dream. As well as an older man wearing a suit and carrying a gym bag. He shuffled past us before hunkering down at a table in the back.

★

WILLIAM HAD ARRANGED this meeting by telling Jennifer I might be able to give her a job on my documentary. "And what job might that be?" I'd asked. He also jokingly played the guilt card, arguing that I owed him since he'd gotten me some good Internet leads on Richard Gault. I would have done it anyway because I considered William a friend. I'd also recently started entertaining the theory that success demands a certain amount of discomfort, and I guessed that this girl would be good practice. From everything William told me I figured she'd take me out of my comfort zone by reinforcing the very values I was struggling to overthrow. I imagined her to be the kind of girl who could be at a table, seated across from the person who had just discovered the cure for cancer, and her opening remark would be: "I love scientists. I hear Russell Crowe might play one in his next movie."

★

"WHAT PAGE is 'your friend' on?" I asked.

"I can't tell you that," she giggled. She did have a great giggle. It made you want to giggle, too. That's the thing about these girls. They generally operate with high levels of contagious energy.

"It's not Leonardo, is it?" William looked concerned.

"No," she said. And this time her denial seemed authentic. "But," she added, "I did meet him once in New York. At 'Bond Street.' I love him. He's sweet."

My guess was that she was one of those L.A. girls who overused the word "love." Second only to "the" in frequent usage.

"You spend a lot of time in New York?" I asked.

"I've got lots of friends there," she said. "Friends everywhere." She looked across the room, trying to catch the eye of the twentysomething working actor.

"You're a friendly girl," William commented dryly.

"Yes, I am," she said, flirtatiously touching his arm.

Oh God, William, I thought. What are you doing? Of course I could see what he liked about her. She was young and, though not gorgeous, she was attractive with dark curly hair and lively blue eyes. She also had the kind of body that could wear a twenty-five-dollar dress from The Limited and look as good as a supermodel wearing D&G. But inside that package was a scrappy poacher. She'd poach anyone's territory. She'd poach your guy, your best friend, your contacts. Anything that one way or another would bring her closer to celebrity limelight. This girl was on a mission.

She reached for William's blueberry scone. He didn't seem to mind. She took the tiniest bite.

"I love the blueberry ones," she said.

He pushed the scone over to her side of the table. "Finish it," he said, thrilled to have something to offer.

"All I needed was a bite," she replied, seductively licking a few crumbs off her fingers.

Well, a bite and a job, judging by how she abruptly got down to business. She looked at me with all seriousness and said, "You should hire me because I'm very coordinated."

"You are?" My face showed no emotion. No reaction. I had no idea what to say to that.

Then she giggled again. "I mean I'm very organized. Why did I say coordinated? Well, I'm that, too. Oh God, don't you hate when you do that?"

"Yeah," William said to appear supportive, but I took it as another case of a guy willing to dumb down in order to score.

"How old are you?" Jennifer suddenly asked, turning her full attention my way.

The question threw me not only because it was a total non sequitur but it was also a question I found incredibly rude. I considered it as personal as asking someone how much money they have in the bank. Or asking a guy the size of his dick. Or in Jennifer's case, who's paying her rent.

"How old am I?" I repeated, my tone suggesting she might want to rethink her approach to this job interview.

"I'm just curious," she said. "I'm really bad at figuring out ages between twenty-five and forty. But I'm trying to get better at it."

"Am I your homework assignment?"

She giggled. "No, no. I'm sorry. I didn't mean it that way. You look great and I was just wondering."

I didn't buy the compliment, but as part of *my* own homework (learn how to be comfortable being uncomfortable), I decided to answer. Besides, William already knew.

"I'm thirty-five."

"Thirty-five?" She might as well have screamed "Yikes!" And then she quickly added, "Good for you." Whatever that meant.

Two sips of coffee and Jennifer took over, launching into a pitch for a job on my *imaginary* documentary. Let's face it. At that point, all I had was *my* Hollywood dream. Jennifer saw herself as some kind of assistant/researcher/script supervisor.

"There is no script," I explained. "It's a documentary. Camera rolls and people say what they say."

"Huh?" she replied, slack-jawed.

I was about to write her off as stupid and naive when she followed up that sluggish "huh" with a little more bite. "A friend of mine made a documentary and a lot of it was scripted," she said. "Most of it. And he ended up winning an award at the Sundance Film Festival." She spoke with confidence, making it sound as if, in her world, no one expected a documentary not to be choreographed fiction made to look spontaneous and real. To expect anything else was to be written off as stupid and naive.

It was a topic I would have loved to pursue, but William started acting odd. He had totally checked out of the conversation and was no longer looking at Jennifer adoringly, or looking at her at all. His eyes darted around the room and he kept turning around to the table behind us. Abruptly, he got up and dashed over to talk to the kid working the cash register. I couldn't hear what was being said but it was obvious something was going on. A couple of other Coffee Bean employees had joined William and they huddled together talking conspiratorially. It was strange, but then again strange encounters happen in L.A. all the time.

Since people are always reinventing themselves, it's not unusual to run into someone you knew from one of your previous incarnations. And if they, too, have moved on into another reinvention then it's almost as if there are two of you talking to two of them. It can go beyond strange. And it can get crowded. And then if a couple of others join in as well, it gets even harder to figure out what's going on, if anything. Which is a long way of saying I had no idea what inspired William's little huddle. But it occurred to me that he might be having some kind of reunion with some altered piece of his past. Something had to explain the intensity and awkwardness of that little grouping.

"What do you think that's about?" I asked Jennifer.

She glanced over at him, "Life, The Movie," she replied. "It's a book," she added nonchalantly. "That's the title, *Life, The Movie*. You know it?"

"No. What's it about?"

"Haven't read it," she replied, "but I heard Bono liked it." She then broke off another, even tinier piece of William's scone and popped it in her mouth.

Whatever reinvention Jennifer was up to, it didn't include actually reading books, nor did it include curiosity about a newsstand guy and a bunch of caffeine addicts.

Suddenly William's huddle broke up, and two of the store employees walked in our direction. Behind them I could see William on his cell phone.

"I'm going to find out." I stood up as the employees passed me by. They both looked extremely serious, far more serious than is appropriate for anything that generally goes on in a "Friends"-type haunt on the good end of Sunset. They stopped in front of the older man in the suit who was still sitting alone, hunkered down at the table in the back corner. Their bodies blocked my view but I could see that the man's gym bag was now on a chair and it was open.

I turned back to William, who was walking toward the side exit, his Nokia pressed to his ear. Something told me this wasn't his hourly check-in with his voice mail. As I walked up to him, his tension was obvious. His free hand nervously pulled at the hair on the back of his head.

"What's going on?" I asked.

"Fuck," he said. He walked a few more paces, trying to find a clear patch. "Can you hear me now? Can you hear me now?" he shouted into the phone.

An employee ran up to us, flushed and perspiring. "They're on their way."

Relieved, William powered off his phone and turned to me. "Where'd Jennifer go?"

"Nowhere. What's going on?"

He looked over to Jennifer, who was back to perusing her magazine. "Jennifer," he shouted. "Jennifer."

She glanced up. "What?"

"Come here."

"Why?"

"Just come over here." There was an urgency in his voice that seemed to shock her. She didn't appear to be the kind of girl who normally responded to orders from guys like William. But I guess she decided to humor him because she got up, still clutching her copy of *Rolling Stone,* and sauntered over. Or maybe she just wanted an excuse to parade by the TV actor who was doing what Elizabeth West would call his PDP thing— public display of privacy. There he was sitting in plain view in a very public place, acting like the last thing he wanted was attention. Yeah, right. But he was doing a pretty good job of pretending. His eyes were fixed on the Calendar section of the L.A. *Times* and not even Jennifer's sexy sashaying could tempt him away.

It was only then that I began to notice that, with the exception of the actor, a quiet hysteria was (don't bust me on this) brewing. The line of people who had been waiting to put in their coffee orders had dispersed. They'd broken into groups of twos and threes, whispering to each other while keeping an eye on that back table.

"Okay," Jennifer said, addressing William. "So what's over here that's so important?"

Protectively he pulled her closer. "That old man back there has an ax."

"What?" I couldn't believe it. An old man with an ax at the Coffee Bean was like a scene in some bad youth-oriented horror flick.

"He does?" Jennifer tried to get a better look.

Right then, two black-and-whites pulled up outside. Four cops got out. Two of them stayed at the door while the other two moved inside. A customer quickly pointed them in the right direction. Now even the young actor had to come out of his PDP celebrity cloud. He watched the action accelerate as the cops stepped in front of the two employees who had been quietly talking to the now (in my mind) would-be ax murderer. The sight of the uniforms kicked everything into "NYPD Blue" gear. All those actor wannabes who moments before were checking out the trades, probably dreaming of being cast as the courageous hero in the next Jerry Bruckheimer blockbuster, quickly moved away from the action. Ambushed by real life.

The old man was now clinging to his ax as if it were his dick.

One of the cops spoke to him nicely. "Put it down on the table."

"I'm not breaking any law," the old man snapped back.

"You've got a fucking ax in your hand," one of the Bean employees said. "I think there might be a law or two against that."

The other cop put his hand in front of the employee's face like he was stopping traffic at an intersection. "Let us take care of this," he said testily. Getting back to the old man he said, "I'm ordering you to put it down."

The old man peered at him as if he were straining to read something on the cop's expressionless face. "You know I needed help once. Know how long it took for the police to get there? Forty-five minutes."

"I'm sorry that happened. I can't answer for that. I wasn't there," the nice cop said. "But right now, you have to cooperate with us so we can help you."

"Help me?" The old man let out a clipped shrill laugh that made Jennifer jump. William stroked the back of her neck. I swear she started to purr.

"You're here to help me?" The old man was standing now. His eyes bulging. "Do I look like an idiot? 'Cause if I do, tell me and I'll change how I look. Is it the shirt? Is it too yellow? Is that a sign of dementia? Tell me. I'll change to a nice sky-blue so you don't mistake me for an idiot again."

The tough cop put his hand on his gun.

"For the last time," the nice cop said calmly, "I'm asking you to . . ." And then before he even finished his sentence, he pounced. The old man was caught completely off guard. He'd been waiting for the cop to finish his thought. He was counting on a couple more seconds. A few more words. Or at least a few more syllables. But no. Turns out nice cop was also fast cop. He twisted that ax out of the old man's hand with one move. As it fell to the floor, a girl in the crowd screamed.

"Everything's okay. Everything's okay," the tough cop yelled. In a flash, the perpetrator was cuffed and it was all over.

For a moment there was an eerie silence. Until a customer spoke up. "Don't bother changing the shirt."

A few people chuckled. The old man looked at the jokester and said, "Whatever your problem is, it's not me."

★

AFTER THE AX man had been taken away, we were back at our table. The mood in the place had changed considerably. Though the whole incident had lasted only about five minutes, it forged a bond with everyone present. It was as if we'd been on location together for six months. A long, arduous shoot during which we all, out of necessity, became family. The man in his forties had even shut off his computer and was involved in conversation with two young girls who earlier wouldn't have given him even a first look. The incident made me feel as if William, Jennifer, and I had skipped steps in our tentative threesome friendship. The fact that I could use the word "friendship" at all is proof of that. Jennifer? A friend of mine? Inconceivable when we all first sat down. Now we were one step away from sharing lipsticks.

"Did you see that? Did you see that?" Jennifer kept saying excitedly. Of course we saw it. William and I were standing right next to her. "Did you see those two cops who stood at the door?"

"Yeah," I said in my friendliest tone.

"Did you see what they did? They went up to that actor who was sitting there and offered to walk him out. Like they were his personal security guards or something."

"They did?" I turned around and saw that his table was vacant. "Just him?"

"Yeah, just him."

"Why?"

"Duh. Because he's a celebrity. That's why."

"How do you know that's why?" William asked.

"'Cause I heard what they said. The cops went up to the actor and they knew his name and all and said, 'Would you like some assistance in getting out of here?'"

She leaned back in her chair and crossed her arms. "That's what happens when you're famous. You get extra protection."

"A 'celebrity' may be overstating what that guy is," I argued gently. "C'mon, Jennifer, even you didn't know his name."

She remained adamant. "He's enough of a celebrity to get the special treatment." She bit her bottom lip and then sighed. "That's what I want. To be under the big protective umbrella of celebrity."

William looked like he'd just been kicked in the stomach.

"Somehow I don't think it's that simple," I said.

She looked at me, guileless, and replied, "Oh yes it is."

That's when I decided to hire her. Not because I needed an assistant. Or a researcher. (I had William.)

And I definitely didn't need a script supervisor. I decided to hire her because I wanted to be around someone whose indefatigable optimism might help keep me from slipping back into another one of my "what if" worst-case scenarios. I also thought it'd be interesting to get a twenty-three-year-old's perspective on Richard Gault. A twenty-three-year-old, celebrity-obsessed poacher-on-a-mission's perspective. It might make my life worse but it would make my documentary better. Besides, what could she poach from me? A question I should have spent a little more time contemplating.

"By the way, do you know anything about Richard Gault?" I asked.

"William played me his record."

"And?"

"I love his songs. They made me want to fuck."

William brightened a bit and got up to order another scone.

chapter six

I think I should explain why a ten-year-old girl would become so fascinated with a twenty-five-year-old Richard Gault that she would want to be him. Picture this: It's a rainy Friday afternoon in my South Boston neighborhood. I'm walking home from school but I don't really want to go home. But what are my choices? It seems on every other block there's a church. Doors unlocked. Everyone welcome. But I'm already too jaded by the whole religion thing. Easy to be when your parish priest is known for trying, and failing, to get kids to kiss the cross he wears on a very long chain around his neck. Very long. So long the cross falls right on top of his dick. We might have been young but we weren't stupid. I keep walking.

On every corner there's a bar. Off limits for a kid, not that any of it looks very appealing. The doorways are so dingy and depressing it makes me think I'll never want to go into one of those joints, no matter what magical spirits they might offer. The only place left is the movies.

Maybe six people are at the four o'clock show. It's a futuristic movie about roving bands of rebels carousing through the streets of some nameless U.S. city. Richard Gault plays the leader of the good-guys group. Occasionally he's on a motorcycle but mostly he just walks around dressed in black, protecting his turf. He looks a little like Brandon Lee, but he doesn't do any martial arts stuff. He doesn't have to. People know not to fuck with him. If anyone tries to bullshit him, he nails them on it. He gets what the deal is. You can't fool him. You can't manipulate him. But he isn't robotic or anything. He has his weaknesses. He lost the girl he loved (I don't remember this part too well. Did she die? Disappear?) and it's made him see life as terminally chaotic and senseless. The irony being that his very presence brings order and sense wherever he goes.

I couldn't (unlike Waz) tell you any of the dialogue from the film. But I wanted to be able to be that cool and move through the streets of South Boston the way he moved through futuristic USA. However, even though I wanted to be him, I also wanted to be *with* him. I wanted to be his new girl. I wanted to be walking around, hanging out with him, hanging on his arm. And even though I didn't really know what a blow job was all about when I was ten, I did know that if Richard Gault had been wearing a cross on a long chain, I wouldn't have minded kissing that. So there you have it. Richard Gault—my first role model and my first sexual fantasy. You don't forget those things—even twenty-five years later.

★

THE AFTERNOON TALK show host has just finished crooning a stage tune to his audience of mostly middle-aged women. It's about halfway through his show and it's time to bring out a new face. "I'm thrilled to introduce you to my next guest. It's his very first television appearance. You may not recognize his name but he stars in *Smashland,* a new movie opening this Friday. And, he has just finished his first album for A&M records. Please join me in welcoming Richard Gault."

A breathtakingly handsome man in his mid-twenties walks out on the set. He seems embarrassed by the applause. He shakes the hand of the talk show host and sits in the designated guest chair. The host looks at him like he could fall in love. Like he is falling in love, taken in by Richard's green eyes, high cheekbones, and longish thick dark hair.

"So this must be an exciting time for you," the host says, getting excited himself.

"It's weird," Richard replies, slumping in his seat. "There's a lot going on. It's easy to get hooked on the velocity. You know what I mean?"

"Well, you're in the fast lane now," the talk show host says, as if bestowing Richard membership into an illustrious club.

Richard nods as if he agrees but then unexpectedly switches gears. "Thing about the fast lane," he says, "is it's fine as long as you don't veer on over into the suicide lane. And in this business that's an occupational hazard."

For a second the talk show host is thrown off guard, as if the name of his *boyfriend* had just been announced on the air. He quickly recovers. "So tell me about your movie," he says.

★

I HIT the pause button on the videotape player. Richard Gault's face was in freeze-frame. A close-up. It was the eyes and smile that killed me. The eyes that said this guy had done a lot of living. And the smile that said he was ready for more. Bring it on. There are certain men who are catnip for women and Richard Gault was one of them. Just looking at him you knew this guy could get wild, but he also seemed solid and strong. Taurus the bull with the soul of an Irish poet. I imagined him to be the kind of guy I could take chances with. I could go as close to the edge as I wanted and he'd never let me fall. He was a mentor. A satyr. Playboy. Child. Rebel. A God. Uh-oh. I was moving into idol worship territory and I'd never even met the man. So what? I watched the clip again. I loved how casually subversive he was. He wasn't smashing guitars like The Who or burning them like Hendrix. He'd simply pissed on the fantasy of celebrity by suggesting its dark, suicidal side. If Richard had said it as a joke, or tossed it off, that would have been one thing. But he said it seriously. Very seriously.

As if he'd been thinking about it for a long time. That was a no-no. He was supposed to be thinking about lights, cameras, and action. Or cash, cars, and girls. He broke the covenant. Thou shalt not get real on a talk show.

★

I CHECKED my watch. Damn, Jennifer was twenty minutes late. I'd already viewed this same bit of footage six times. What was her problem, and why hadn't she called? She couldn't have gotten lost. The Museum of Television and Broadcasting was located right on the corner of Beverly and Santa Monica Boulevard in Beverly Hills. In a large white building. Impossible to miss. What credible excuse could she come up with? Of course, I knew she'd have one. Girls like Jennifer always do.

To kill time, I pulled out my phone and checked my voice mail again. Thank God, I had at least one new message. It was from my soon-to-be-ex-husband, teasing me by saying he had something for me. Knowing him, that could be anything from a hot tip on a new Andrew Blake porno (the Helmut Newton of the porno world) to a piece of my junk mail that mistakenly got sent to his address. I was about to call him back when Jennifer suddenly showed up in a frenzy.

"Sorry I'm late. The traffic on Santa Monica is nuts. What are they doing with that street? All those road crews. And you can't make a left turn for, like, a mile. What are they thinking? And what's the deal with parking in Beverly Hills? Two hours' free parking if you get your fucking car there at eight in the morning. You can never find a spot in one of those lots at a normal time." She threw down her Louis Vuitton knapsack and pulled up a chair. She took a deep breath, slowed down, and glanced around. "I like museums," she said.

She said this as if she were saying she liked chocolate cake. Sometimes her comments seemed so generic they bordered on inane. But once again, just when I was silently wondering how unoriginal this girl really was, she came back with a thought that not only made sense but was more interesting than anything I'd said lately.

"I feel safe in museums," she said. "It's one of the few places in Hollywood where you can feel the creative forces outnumber the destructive ones." And then in a one-two punch she said, "Love those pants. Who makes them? Tark?"

Of course she was right. Jennifer knows her labels. "Yeah," I replied as I cued up the tape to the start of the segment. Jennifer could probably have spent a good fifteen minutes discussing Tark pants and every style they'd made over the last couple of years, but I cut the conversation short.

"You ready to see the man?"

"Sure," she said and then broke into song. "'City girls just seem to find out early. How to open doors with just a smile.' Richard Gault wrote that line," she said, flashing her own charming city-girl smile.

"No he didn't. That's an Eagles song."

"Richard Gault was an uncredited writer on it."

"Says who?"

"Says William."

She had me on that one and she knew it.

★

TEN MINUTES LATER, we were back on the street. All Jennifer said after viewing the tape twice was "someone that hot could have been a big star." I needed something more. More from her. More from me. I felt on the verge of panic. No wonder. I had no idea what my next move was, the summer heat was oppressive and I was spending the only money I had on a project that had less chance of succeeding than Jennifer's shot of marrying a big celebrity. And her odds were staggering, considering there were about ten thousand girls competing for the same five guys. Maybe I wasn't cut out to be entrepreneurial. I wasn't good at tapping into the battle mentality needed to negotiate an independent career in Hollywood. I could be gutsy in my own well-decorated climate-controlled world but I didn't want to have to go off to war. I'm the kind of girl who can't even handle going camping.

★

YOU NEED to shop," Jennifer said, correctly observing that I was floundering. "Shopping and a coffee Frappuccino will improve your mood. And your posture," she added with an air of authority. She guided me toward Rodeo Drive and then south toward Wilshire.

Maybe it's the South Boston girl in me, but I always feel out of place in Beverly Hills—and have no desire to feel in place. It'll never be my kind of neighborhood. If being rich enough to live and shop here is the apotheosis of the American dream, it is also the perfect example of the American void. No matter how crowded the streets, how jammed the traffic, it always feels formless. More movie set than an actual movie set.

As we walked by the designer stores, Jennifer suddenly got very animated. At first I thought this is good. Maybe a little of her effusive energy will rub off on me. I never expected it to kick into manic gear so quickly.

As she jumped from story to story I became aware that she was living proof of the def con four system. Def con one is when someone drops the name of a B-list celebrity for no reason whatsoever. Def con two is when they drop the name of a B-list celebrity for no reason but act like they're completely uninterested in that celebrity. Def con three is when they drop the name of an *A-list* celebrity for no reason at all. And def con four is when they drop the name of an A-list celebrity for no reason, and make it sound as if they're not only not interested in that celebrity but burdened by having to mention them at all.

Here's Jennifer's version: As we strolled past Hermés, she suddenly said, "When I was up in Vancouver watching the Grizzlies play the Lakers and Jean-Claude van Damme was talking about the play-offs . . ."

I forget the rest of the story but I took note of this. Jennifer didn't exactly say whether or not Jean-Claude was talking to her, to someone else, or even to himself. She could have been sitting in a row behind him and eavesdropped. He may have said it to a reporter. She may have read it in the newspaper. And beyond that, there was no reason even to mention it. It pertained to nothing. She was definitely in def con one territory.

A few minutes later, she scored def con two points when she blurted out that Rosanna Arquette wanted to know where she got her shoes. She rolled her eyes as if this were the biggest inconvenience in the world.

Def con three kicked in when she segued from that to mentioning that Matt Damon really liked her Indian bracelet. She said this as if I knew which bracelet she was talking about and implied that Matt went out of his way to compliment her. Maybe, I thought, he was stuck next to her at a party and was just being nice. Maybe he was thinking he'd like to get a bracelet like that for his girlfriend.

Jennifer didn't get to def con four until a few blocks later when she said, apropos of absolutely nothing, "So I'm at the chiropractor and George Clooney is there and I just wasn't in the mood to have to talk to a movie star." This coming from a girl who lives to talk to movie stars. By the way, I found out later she doesn't even know George Clooney. And who knows if he was even interested in talking to her.

Anyway, it brought me to the point where I was about to scream, Enough! And just then, Jennifer with her uncanny ability to sense when you're just about to write her off, rallied back. This time she used her most intoxicating quality—her ability to have and create a good time. She grabbed my arm, almost giddy with excitement, and said, "I got it. I know where we're going first. You are so going to thank me for this."

★

ACACIA IS a store that, though located in Beverly Hills, feels like it belongs in West Hollywood. Its customers are not the rich bitches who shop along Rodeo for the designer duds that'll make them feel better about their bad marriages but instead fun-loving girls who are looking for something to wear to the next party. Jennifer knew that you can always find something at Acacia to lift your spirits. Some little top designed to make your tits look great. Or a simple black skirt with a sexy side slit. Or moving over to the jewelry case, a faux diamond toe ring. A turquoise ankle bracelet. The perfect hoop earrings.

Like my ex, James, who seemed to know every maître d' in town, Jennifer seemed to know everyone in retail. Karen the owner of the shop gave her a big hug, and the girls who worked there started pulling stuff off the racks as soon as she walked in. "Wait till you see the halter dress that came in this morning," one said. Another held up a drop-waist floral skirt. "You've got to see this on."

"What I've got to do is get some coffee," Jennifer announced. "Christine and I both need some caffeine. Immediately."

"I'll go get them," one of the cute salesgirls said.

"That is so sweet of you," Jennifer said, giving her a kiss on the mouth, which caught my and everyone else in the store's attention.

"You want a tall or grande?" the kissed girl asked.

"Grande, with foam," Jennifer said. "Christine and I have work to do."

I kept thinking about that kiss while waiting for the coffees. Not that girls kissing in public surprises me. It's a very L.A. thing. And though girls kissing on the mouth may not be the norm for everyone, it is for enough girls so that it's no big deal. Some do it because they like kissing girls. Others because they think that having a bisexual persona will make them more attractive to some of Hollywood's most desirable men. I didn't know Jennifer well enough to know if the kiss was about one or both those things and I didn't care. What caught me off guard was that it appeared to be a delicious kiss. The equivalent of a small bite of a juicy peach.

My mental faculties were suddenly ambushed by the reminder of a world of sensual delights. For weeks now I'd been focused on work and methodically getting through all the mundane things I compelled myself to do. My only gratification came with crossing another completed errand off the list. My only satisfaction came from a good night's sleep. But that kiss woke me up. Made me remember and yearn for the kind of satisfaction and gratification that can only come from sex, sex, and more sex. If only I had a boyfriend. If I did, at that moment, I would have called him and suggested a wild afternoon interlude. But instead I just made a mental note to go fruit shopping.

Twenty minutes and one mocha Frappuccino later I was in the dressing room looking at myself in a black leather halter dress. It had sexcapade written all over it. Suddenly the curtain to the dressing room was pulled open and Jennifer stepped inside with a half-dozen items over her arm.

"You don't mind sharing a room, do you?" Without

waiting for an answer she plopped her stuff down and pulled off her shirt. This girl didn't need some simple top designed to make one's tits look great. Hers were already astonishingly beautiful. At that moment I understood the source of her confidence. Or at least, I thought I did. It wasn't until she stepped out of her skirt and stood there wearing absolutely nothing that I really got it. Jennifer had the perfect pussy. It was a concept that had never entered my brain until that moment. Why would it? Except for those gorgeous girls who parade around naked in four-inch high heels in all of Andrew Blake's porno videos, I'd never before seen a girl who had what I now call a pashmina pussy. The trim patch of hair between Jennifer's legs was so fine and soft, it looked like something you'd only find on the hides of the newborns of some about-to-be-extinct Tibetan animal. If William ever got close to this, I thought, he'd be worshiping at that altar for a long, long time.

"Look at how beautiful you are," I said, which you can say to girls in L.A. without being considered a lesbian. Jennifer smiled knowingly. I'm sure she got this all the time, especially when she got naked.

She slipped on a slinky red dress that was so slinky, underwear was not an option. "I once had a boyfriend who always wanted me to wear red," she said, as she examined the back view of herself in the mirror. Pleased, she then glanced at the price tag. "What am I thinking?" She laughed. "I can't afford to go shopping for real. Not that that will stop me," she added nonchalantly, as if somehow she'd been granted immunity from reality. "The first red dress I ever owned came from here," she continued. "My ex-boyfriend bought it for me as a present but he got the wrong size so I had to exchange it. That's when I met Karen and I've been coming here ever since."

"What happened to the guy?" I asked.

"Oh, him? How about this? I only went out with him for a few months. I liked him but I wasn't in love with him or anything. But I am very passionate when it comes to sex, which some guys misunderstand. One night he gets out of bed after we've been fucking for, like, an hour. He sits down in a chair, looking really upset. I asked him what was wrong and he said, 'This is what's wrong. You fuck me like you have expectations and I'm not comfortable with that.' I couldn't believe it. Expectations of what? If anyone had been pushing for a more serious relationship it was him. So I said, 'Yeah, I do have expectations. I expect you NOT to be an asshole.'"

She took another sip of her coffee, sucking on that straw like it was, well, not a straw. "Anyway he was my link to Karen and Acacia and started my passion for red dresses, so it wasn't a total waste," she giggled.

As she spoke I tried to remember if, when I was twenty-three, I'd felt as resilient as she appeared to be. But more important was the way I felt at that moment. Carefree. A gigantic thing for someone who has been walking around in a burdensome lull. Suddenly, there I was, with a Frappuccino in me and a black halter dress on me, feeling all charged up by hanging out with a girl who knew how to suck every last drop of sunlight out of an L.A. afternoon. And of course just when I didn't want any distractions and had stopped thinking about the fact that my cell phone never rings, it rang. It was James, my ex-husband.

"So what's up?" I asked, fast-forwarding to the point.

"I know someone who knew Richard Gault back in the seventies. You want to meet her?"

Leave it to James to not only find out who Richard Gault is but figure out that a connection to him would be of value. James—the consummate networker and facilitator. He'd make a natural politician if he wasn't so hooked on public displays of debauchery with crazy girls and Stoli martinis.

"Can you arrange that?" I asked.

"Done," he said. "But you've got to do something for me."

"Oh, and what might that be?" I said, expecting something that would leave him, once again, with the better end of the trade.

"My girlfriend is doing a play at the Coronet and I want you to come see it and bring some of your friends. It's one night only and I've got to make sure it's a packed, friendly house."

Did I want to see Psycho Girl in a play? Or subject my friends to bad theater? No. And again, just so this is clear, it's not because she's my ex's current girl. 'Cause when I'm over a guy, I'm over him. When that steel door comes down, it's down. But I did want the Gault connection, and even without it, I'm a sucker when it comes to doing favors for an ex. Besides, I was having a carefree moment, so carefree, I hung up the phone, turned to Jennifer, and said, "What are you doing Saturday night?"

The other day Jennifer and Christine stopped by the Center-fold. I never would have figured them to be hanging out to-gether. But there they were. Sounds like they've been hanging a lot. I noticed Jennifer has started talking like Christine. Us-ing words like "hideous." One of Christine's favorites. And "obviously." Things are always very obvious to Christine and half of what she reads in magazines she calls hideous. I also noticed, well, Jennifer made a point of showing me, that Christine's now wearing a toe ring that is exactly like the one she always wears. It's the symbiotic thing that girls get into. I don't know what it means but I'm not complaining.

The other funny thing is Jennifer's turned into "career girl." Talks about it all the time. Called herself a consultant until she decided that didn't sound sexy so now she's settled on associate producer. Though she hasn't brought it up around Christine yet. Like Christine cares. Like she doesn't have other things stressing her out. She was in here the other day in the worst mood. When I called her on it, she said, "Oh sorry, am I being a bitch?" I said, "No, you've got the chip to be a bitch but you're not." That made her laugh. Then she got into a whole thing about how everything in her life is in such flux she was thinking of renaming her production company Flux. But then she walked into Skylight Books and noticed the cashier had "flux" tattooed on his arm and she figured that if it's on his arm it's probably already been appropriated by the pop culture. She got on this whole thing about how it's probably already the name of a new L.A. band. Or one of those new clothing stores in Los Feliz. Or maybe another hideous new magazine soon to hit your local newsstands. "Relax," I told her. I was going to say you need to fuck more. But for all I know maybe she's fucking all the time. But if she is, the guy's not making her happy.

★

I WAS THINKING of writing a song about Christine. You know, an L.A.-woman-in-flux kind of song. But Jennifer's still got the muse position. I was thinking about her and her famous boyfriend, whoever he is, and I was thinking this—I hope she's actually fucking him because nothing is worse than a failed Hollywood star fucker. And as soon as I thought that, I got the idea for a song about all the sad, desperate L.A. girls who are failed star fuckers. See what I mean about Jennifer being my inspiration? She inspires even when she's not the girl in the song.

Her name was Marilyn. Back in the seventies she had a small part in Richard Gault's first movie and they became friends. That's it. That and her phone number were all the information James had. William took over, hitting the Internet and getting her bio, credits, and even photos of her taken from an E! Entertainment's research file. One of William's ex–band members was now a music reporter there and since E! is notoriously cheap when it comes to salaries, ex–band member didn't mind earning an extra hundred bucks to steal a few old 8-by-10 glossies.

On the drive over to Marilyn's, I handed the photos to Jennifer, who was in the backseat of Waz's Bronco.

He was driving. I was up front fanning myself with a copy of the latest issue of *Harper's Bazaar*. William was stuck at his job, but at least he wasn't stuck in a hideous oven, which is what the Bronco felt like. God, it was hot. And since Jennifer claimed air conditioning made her sick and Waz seconded that emotion, I was outvoted and sweaty. I was beginning to hate summer. I considered the possibility that summer is only fun if you're under thirty-five. Doesn't matter that I work out all the time and an objective eye would say I'm in good shape. Subjectivity rules and I'm acutely aware of all flaws. I'd never feel confident wearing that little slip of a dress Jennifer had on.

"She certainly had seventies hair," Jennifer said as she handed me back Marilyn's head shot. "Kind of like the Farrah wing thing."

"Has anyone ever seen a really good head shot?" I said as I took another glance at Marilyn's attempt to look like a desirable ingenue. "I don't think they exist. They all look so fake. I'm not saying a lot of these people don't look attractive in these shots, I'm just saying they never look *interesting*."

"Maybe, sweetcakes, it's because there's a real shortage of interesting people around," Waz replied, doing his best Robert Mitchum as Philip Marlowe impersonation.

"You guys," Jennifer said, giving the back of the front seat a playful kick. "That's your scar tissue talking. Give it up." There was something about the way she delivered that piece of advice that made me think that

somewhere along the line she'd been to one of those mo-
ronic self-help seminars.

"There are lots of interesting people around," she
lectured. "Just the other day, when I was at Barney's, I
ran into . . ."

She then dropped the name of some celebrity, which
provoked Waz to pull a twenty out of his pocket and
hand it to me.

"Thanks," I said, with a self-satisfied smile.

Jennifer was either oblivious or uninterested in this
monetary transaction. Not that I would have explained
even if she'd asked. What could I say? I bet Waz twenty
bucks that before we passed three traffic lights, you'd
name-drop? Although it's possible Jennifer would have
had no problem with that. It's possible she'd just laugh
and say, "Not exactly a high roller, are you?"

She'd be right about that. Although I guess a case
could be made that I was taking a big risk in my life.
Taking a steady job in production at some big company
was a safer choice. Lusting after men I'd actually met
and who were available and appropriate would be a
saner choice. But no, I chose the path that had me waking up at 4 A.M., with so much anxiety I could hardly
breathe. Even with the windows open and the smell
of my neighbor's garden—freesia, honeysuckle, garde-
nias—I felt as if I were experiencing one of Ingmar
Bergman's darkest Swedish nights. I worried that if I
fell back asleep I would find myself playing chess with
death, a terrifying nightmare for a girl who doesn't
know the difference between a knight and a rook.

★

AS WE TURNED right off Sunset to head north up the canyon, Jennifer remembered she had a Richard Gault story for us. She offered this up as if knowing about Richard Gault wasn't part of her job. As if this were just another of many stories that she'd amassed from one of her recent late-night outings and she was now sharing it with a couple of close friends.

"There's this guy I know in the music business. He's sort of famous." She paused. Waiting for what? Neither Waz nor I said a word. Without twenty bucks at stake we didn't care who she did or didn't name-drop.

"Anyway," she continued, "we were all hanging out at Mr. Chow's and I asked him if he'd ever heard of Richard Gault. And he told me that when he was a teenager he'd smoked a joint with him once at a party in Topanga. He said the stuff was unbelievably strong. Like one hit and you're a mess. So anyhow, there was this other guest at the party who'd also smoked some and was wrecked. Totally wrecked. And the guest is trying to *back* out of a parking spot—and he's parked on one of those narrow roads up in the hills."

Jennifer was leaning over the front seat now, making sure we caught every word. "But the car's in drive and he doesn't know it till he hits the accelerator and practically drives off a cliff." She put a hand on Waz's shoulder even though she was facing me. Obviously, Jennifer's not shy about getting physical even if she's only known someone for five minutes. I could be wrong, but I think she even gave Waz a little extra squeeze as she upped the volume on her story.

"The front wheels were actually in the air. Can you imagine? In the air. Everybody's going crazy. But Richard Gault, even though he's wrecked, too, calmly talks the driver—who is so scared he can't move—into slowly climbing over the seat so he can be helped out through the back door. And then they both celebrated by taking another hit of the joint. Isn't that a great story?"

"Let's get that one on record," Waz said.

Jennifer dropped her hand from his shoulder and assumed a sultry pose in the backseat. "Uh . . . not going to happen," she said. "This guy doesn't do documentaries."

"Who's your friend, again?" Waz asked, looking at me with a twinkle in his eye.

"Uh, can't really say," Jennifer replied coyly. And then realizing that Waz and I were getting bored with her hint-and-deny routine, she coughed something up. "I also asked him if he knew Marilyn."

I turned around. "Did he?"

"Yeah, he did. When I mentioned her name, he laughed and said, 'Yeah, sure, I remember her. She fucked half the guys in the Players Directory.'"

★

MARILYN LIVED in a small yellow house at the top of Laurel Canyon. The place was what a real estate agent might describe as a charming fixer-upper. Most of the charm coming from the array of tall golden and purple wildflowers that leaned over the front walkway like a perpetual greeting committee.

When Marilyn opened the door my first thought was she was exactly what I expected. A middle-aged woman who had the demeanor of someone half her age. It was the norm among actresses and ex-actresses, especially the ones still living in Laurel Canyon. She was dressed in a T-shirt, jeans, and was wearing three-inch-high platform sandals. In any place other than L.A., she might pass for thirty-five. But looking at her through my well-trained L.A. eyes, I would have guessed mid-forties even if I hadn't gotten her birth date from her E! Entertainment file. I know how to scan a face. What I saw in Marilyn was a woman who probably didn't have the money to afford top-of-the-line plastic surgery so she was getting by with a combination of good moisturizers, good genes, and the occasional Botox injections. No forty-five-year-old has a perfectly natural-looking wrinkle-free forehead—unless they're getting a little help from Dr. Klein or they're Dorian Gray.

We followed her into the living room. From the looks of the place, Marilyn was a collector. Books. Decorative baskets. Pottery. Crystals. Photographs. Needlepoint pillows. And a bright blue yoga mat, rolled up in a corner beneath a framed mandala. It was all a little too granola for my taste, but I guess some people would call it homey. There was so much stuff everywhere, I could have easily suffered an attack of claustrophobia had it not been for the expansive view. Almost a wall of windows looked out over an underdeveloped part of the canyon and beyond that, in the distance, the overdeveloped boulevards of Hollywood.

"Can I get anyone anything to drink? Water? Snapple? Diet Coke?" She looked at Waz. "A beer?"

"No thanks, not for me," he replied.

"I'm fine," I said, holding up the bottle of Evian I'd brought with me.

"Do you have Peach Diet Snapple?" Jennifer asked.

"I wish," Marilyn said. "I'm all out. I should buy that stuff by the case."

"I do," Jennifer giggled, inspiring a giggle out of Marilyn.

And just like that, the two of them began to bond as if they were both twelve and this was the first day of junior high. Jennifer's good, I thought. This girl knows how to work it. The more time I spent around her the more I was beginning to see that she had a genius for networking. She probably would have made a great agent, but girls like Jennifer are not going to give up their interesting life for a ten-hour-a-day trainee's program and a cubicle at William Morris.

We were eventually ushered outside onto the patio, which was obviously the selling point of the house. Its redwood deck, potted plants, and lounge chairs with bright blue cushions seemed the only part of the place that had been updated in the last few decades. An observation confirmed when Marilyn launched into the history of her and the house. It was a typical Hollywood story. Twenty-five years ago she was making a decent living as an actress and bungalows like this one could be had for fifty thousand. To her credit she didn't dwell long down that memory lane and was quick to say she gave up acting years ago and was now a portrait photographer. Which I think meant she was making a lot less money doing head shots for the new crop of girls trying to look like desirable ingenues.

From the second she started talking, Waz turned on the camera. I could tell Marilyn loved talking about herself, which is a habit anyone who has ever had a brush with fame seems to acquire. I once knew a guy who got co-writing credit on one song on a record that made it into *Billboard*'s Top 100 (#82) and his whole speech pattern changed. Suddenly everything he said sounded like he was saying it for posterity. He started acting as if his life were fodder for the celebrity files at "Entertainment Tonight." Sometimes I think I live in a city filled with people who are, at all times, ready for their close-ups *and* their sound bites.

For an hour, between not very interesting anecdotes about Richard Gault, Marilyn digressed to talk about acupuncture, mystery novels, and her fondness for fig and tangerine candles. I was a beat away from calling it a wrap when she got into the good stuff. Why she waited an hour, I don't know. Wait. Of course I know. It's like a girl who won't let a guy fuck her until he's put in at least an hour of foreplay. But now that Marilyn had received the requisite amount of attention, she was ready to let us in.

"Everyone had a crush on Richard Gault," she said, suddenly dropping her innocuous tone. "Even guys. Not in a sexual way, though of course some did. But I'm talking about the straight men who loved hanging out with him 'cause he was such a guy's guy."

She paused, gently tugging at her bottom lip as she searched for the right way to put it. "He was the center of his group. A Robin Hood, spurring more cautious souls into action. And he was very funny," she laughed. "I remember at this one party there was this girl who had been checking him out all night. Finally she goes up to him and says, 'Richard, do you want to dance?' 'Wrong verb, darling,' he said. 'Wrong verb.'"

★

FOR THE NEXT twenty minutes, Marilyn told stories about Richard in the studio recording. Richard on location. Richard playing pool at Barney's Beanery. Richard's girlfriends. His ex-girlfriends. His future girlfriends. But even after all that storytelling, she couldn't stop. Not until she was sure we understood his special place in Hollywood lore.

"I once went to a premiere with him," she continued. "And this was before his movie had come out. The press was there, tripping all over each other to get to the big stars, and the big stars were tripping all over each other to get to Richard."

"They were?" Jennifer asked and then gasped when she saw that Waz had stopped shooting. "Oops. I'm not supposed to ask questions while the camera's rolling, am I?" She looked to him, not me, for forgiveness. And he readily gave it.

"Only one 'oops' per day," he said sweetly, as he took this opportunity to step into the shade for a few seconds of relief.

"Got it," Jennifer said apologetically. "It's just that I've only seen big stars trip over themselves to get to bigger stars."

Marilyn chuckled. "Not to sound like I'm a thousand years old, but it was different back then."

I made Marilyn stop. I didn't want her to say another word till Waz was back on the job. This was exactly what we needed. I wanted to know what it was like back in the seventies because I knew the world that informed Richard Gault was as important a part of this documentary as the man himself. And this was my chance to hear about it from a witness. Someone smart. Someone who was, if not in the middle of the action, close enough to describe the scenery.

"Look," she said, as she shifted in the lounge chair to showcase her body at a more flattering angle, "Richard Gault grew up in the sixties. Back then it was important to be able to know the difference between what was cool and what was bullshit. He was one of those guys who had a sixth sense about all that. What he didn't see coming was, as the seventies progressed to the eighties, people still thought it was important to know the difference between cool and bullshit, but it was because bullshit paid better and they wanted to get on the money train."

She paused and took a sip of water, sucking on an ice cube as she pondered her next thought. While we all anxiously waited for her to suck it down and spit it out, I found myself becoming increasingly aware of the effort she'd put into this moment. It wasn't just making sure Waz shot her from her best side. It was the time she chose to be interviewed. Late afternoon. Light enough to shoot but not too bright. We could have been inside in the air-conditioned living room but we were outside in the heat. I assumed this was because Marilyn knew that the light that hit the patio at this time of day would be the most flattering. If there's one thing women in Hollywood are masters at, it's lighting.

Finally when that cube was nothing but a sliver, she picked up the story. "But for a while there," she said wistfully, "Richard was not only in sync with the times, he was ahead of them."

Suddenly she sat up straight and looked over at Jennifer. "What do you think people in Hollywood want most of all?"

Jennifer looked to Waz to see if it was okay to answer but I, finally asserting myself as director, gave her the nod. I decided to stop worrying about whether asking questions off camera was going to make assembling the documentary more difficult. "We'll figure it out in editing" was becoming my motto. Besides, I didn't want anything to interrupt Marilyn's performance.

"Fame," Jennifer said quickly.

"Well, yes," Marilyn agreed, "but there's something even bigger. What people want most of all is to be part of the next new thing." She stared off over the canyons for a moment. A dramatic gesture from a one-time actress but one that worked nevertheless. When she finally turned back toward us I could tell she was ready for her finale. She spoke slowly now, as if weighed down by the profundity of what she was sharing. "The biggest fear for a lot of Hollywood people is that they'll become passé. Old news. Used and ultimately refused. No matter their past glory days. Richard understood that. He used to say, '*Any* culture that only worships youth is ultimately a culture of suicide.'"

Jennifer looked a little depressed. This was not part of her vision of life in the fame lane. Where was the big protective umbrella of celebrity? But Marilyn didn't pick up on the little dark cloud over Jennifer's head. She was about to bring her point to a climax and nothing was going to interfere with her big moment. I swear her breathing got heavier as she approached her crescendo. Waz zoomed in tighter. Marilyn's close-up was getting closer. She'd timed it beautifully. The lighting was perfect. The gentlest, most forgiving light of the day. So gentle and forgiving, years had been erased from her face. Though twenty-two years older than Jennifer, at that moment Marilyn could easily have passed for her big sister. And in one of those epiphanies you can get when you're up in the canyons right before the sun sets, I realized that, in a way, these two *were* sisters. At twenty-three, Marilyn was probably a lot like Jennifer. Maybe more articulate. Maybe more promiscuous. I doubt Jennifer was working her way through the Players Directory. But both of them were girls with no discernible talent, trying for the big Hollywood score. Some things may have changed since Marilyn was trying to fill her scorecard. Houses with great views couldn't be bought for fifty thousand anymore. But how much else had really changed? That question would have to be pondered later because Marilyn's crescendo was now.

"Richard was always into things way before anyone else. Music. Art. Books. Ideas. People. Richard was always onto it and into it way before anyone had a clue. You'd see him with someone who looked crazy and weird and it would turn out, a year later, this guy was Jaco Pastorius, an amazing jazz musician. Jaco played the bass like Hendrix played his guitar. Passionately. And he was sexy. Some called him the Mick Jagger of the jazz world." She put her hand on her heart, a cheesy gesture that for some reason touched me. "But, Jaco, and even Mick, were nothing compared to Richard."

She took a long, deep breath and threw her head back. For a couple of minutes she didn't move. It was an act worthy of an opera star. When she finally turned her attention back to us, she was smiling, pleased with her delivery. But I wasn't completely pleased. We hadn't gone all the way down this road only to stop short of the destination.

"Did you ever fuck him?"

Marilyn laughed, delighted with the question. "Can you say that on air?"

"It's HBO," I lied. Not a total lie. It was my master plan. "So, did you?"

She moaned softly. "Let me put it this way. When you're forty-five and you're still talking about a guy the way I'm talking about Richard Gault, it can only mean one of three things. One—you're a loser, living in the past." She boldly looked right into the camera. "You're going to have to take my word on this one—but I'm not. Two—the guy was the messiah. Not the case. Richard was no saint. Thank God. Or three—not only did you fuck him but the sex still figures into the top-three experiences of your life." She then shrugged. "It's just a fact," she concluded. "Not an obsession, just a fact."

And now it was Waz who piped up. "Ever think that maybe you're projecting all over this guy? A lot of girls do that. They swoop down on your life and put you up on their pedestal because it works for them. You ever consider that?"

Marilyn was nonplussed by this thought. She calmly got up and picked up a copy of the latest issue of *Vanity Fair* that was lying by one of the lounge chairs. She opened it up and pulled out a photograph that she'd tucked inside. If her opera diva moment was her finale, then this was her encore. She handed it to me. "You can't have it but you can shoot it," which Waz was doing at that very moment. "If you find him, you come back and tell me if I'm projecting."

I stared at the Polaroid, which was dated 1980. A photo of three people, Marilyn looking exuberant, Richard Gault looking handsomely pensive, a look that could spur my cautious soul into action. And there was a third guy.

"Who's he?"

"R.D. Swanson."

"Who?"

"R.D. A songwriter and Richard's best friend. He lives in Aspen. I'm sure you can find him. Everyone knows everyone in Aspen."

I had only one question left. "How come you didn't try to find Richard yourself?"

"Because," she said matter-of-factly, "if he wanted to see me, he'd be here."

As I said, the woman was smart.

★

ON THE WAY BACK, even though Jennifer rattled on about how she had to get ready to meet up with her mysterious famous friend, I made Waz drive by a building where there was an apartment for lease. I had to find a place to move to—soon. But nothing makes me feel more like I can't cope than trying to find a new home. Maybe if I had lots of money and my pick of the best apartments in any one of my favorite buildings, I would feel like I was in charge of my life. Instead I was seriously contemplating going to a tarot card reader in the hopes that she would tell me my apartment-hunting karma was about to improve. If it was, it wasn't changing fast enough.

When Waz pulled up in front of a hideous two-story faux-Tudor-style apartment house, a car was pulling out of the adjacent driveway. It was a red Camaro, driven by a man in his thirties. Why I looked at the bumper sticker, I don't know. But once I did, I couldn't imagine living in that apartment house, on that block, or maybe even in that zip code. Here's what he had plastered on his fender: "Bite the pillow, sweetheart, I'm on my way home." What kind of weirdo guy rides around with a sticker like that—an advertisement for what I guessed was a big ego and a small dick. My least favorite combination.

"Okay, forget it." I sighed as soon as I caught a glimpse of that Camaro. "I'd rather check into the Motor Court Motel than live here."

"Never apartment-hunt on an empty stomach," Jennifer announced as if a bowl of pasta would change everything. Not that she was a girl who ever ate a whole bowl of pasta. Twirling one linguini around a fork for half an hour was more her style.

Waz made a U-turn and headed east toward my street. "I might be working on a commercial for a couple of weeks starting Tuesday," he said.

"And next month, I might be going to New York for a few days," Jennifer announced.

Oh good, I thought, my whole team is falling apart. What am I, their hobby? But I couldn't get too nuts. Not only because I was paying them so little but because the only thing on the agenda was tracking down R.D. Swanson. So, I said nothing. I just looked out the window, grateful to catch a breeze whenever we crossed an intersection.

Waz dropped me off first so I didn't have a chance to ask him what he thought of Jennifer. Had we been alone I'm sure he would have said, What's her story. And that was a good question. Just what is her story? Where does she get the cash to fly off to New York? How does that girl pay for her life? "Who someone fucks and how they make their money tells you everything you need to know about them." That's a quote from Richard Gault that ran in a 1976 issue of *Esquire*. I loved the quote except when I applied it to myself. I used to think it was my friend Elizabeth West's line. She uses it constantly. I think she even used it in a script. When I read William's Internet research on Gault, I was surprised to see who the real author was. When I confronted Elizabeth, she said, "I thought you knew. It's like not knowing who wrote 'to be or not to be.' Well, not exactly," she laughed. "Only in my world."

★

AS I GOT out of the Bronco, Jennifer gleefully leaped over to the front seat. For a second I wondered if she and Waz had hatched some secret plan and the two of them were off somewhere together. Maybe a get-to-know-each-other drink at The Formosa? Intuition or paranoia? I was too tired to figure it out.

"We got some good stuff today," Waz said as he waved goodbye. As he pulled away from the curb, Jennifer leaned out the window and said, "Love you."

Love me? How could she love me, she hardly knew me.

"And you know what else?" she shouted. "Your posture's improving."

If it was, it was a fucking miracle.

chapter nine

Nobody wants to go to the theater in L.A. Nobody I know, anyway. That doesn't mean they don't go—reluctantly. Doesn't mean there isn't some good theater going on somewhere. But, I haven't found it. My friends haven't found it. Okay—one exception, Eddie Izzard's one-man show at the Tiffany. But mostly what passes for theater around here is a bunch of actors performing in showcases in the hopes that a casting agent will see them and cast them in the next episode of "Dharma and Greg."

James was holding court at the front door of the Coronet Theater acting like he was the mayor of Hollywood. He greeted me with Euro kisses and then did the same to Jennifer, though they'd never met. Guess he'd dropped handshakes from his repertoire. Is a simple hello no longer an option? Not that Jennifer minded. James was a cutie, and she had no way of knowing he wasn't the mayor of something.

"So glad you could come," he said as if he were sponsoring the event. Then it struck me. He *is* sponsoring the event. He's playing big manager guy promoting his latest discovery. It was a page from the Hollywood Handbook.

"Is it just the two of you?" he asked, looking around. Did he expect me to bring a busload?

"Three. My friend William is meeting us here," I said.

"I think you're really going to enjoy the show," he said, looking directly at Jennifer.

"I am? What's it about?"

He smiled as if she'd just asked the most brilliant question. "Some people would say sex and alibis."

"And what would the other people say?" She was standing in her slinky pose. Her body rubbing (note: not leaning) against the doorway. Her head down slightly and cocked to one side. Her eyes looking right at James suggesting that the two of them shared some private landscape and language. James was thrown by her response. Computer overload. He had a girlfriend backstage, a soon-to-be-ex-wife in front of him, along with a young girl who had "possibly available" practically written on her forehead. I could see that he was scrambling to come up with a noteworthy line to keep her attention. Scrambling and getting nowhere until a guy who'd been standing nearby answered for him. It was Jeffrey, Waz's neighbor. The CAA agent.

"Alibis and sex," Jeffrey quipped.

James chuckled politely. Jennifer gave the guy nothing. Had she known he was a CAA agent, she might have been a bit more friendly. But she was working James, and I was beginning to see she was a serial monogamist when it came to networking. If I gave her the benefit of the doubt, I'd say it was because a single agenda was a classier way to go. However, it was also possible that Jennifer worked better one-on-one. Split the attention, split the effect.

Jeffrey nervously shifted back and forth on the balls of his feet.

"Hey, did you ever get a Bronco?" I asked, hoping a change in conversation would afford us all a quick way out of a moment that was beginning to feel as heavy as the air before a monsoon.

He stared at me curiously. "How do you know about that?"

"We talked about it. Remember? I was visiting Waz, and you were on your way to work and you stopped to talk to us."

He mulled that for a moment before responding, sadly, "Oh that. Yeah, that. That all seems like a long time ago."

"It was two weeks ago."

"Two weeks?" He seemed surprised.

"A lot can happen in two weeks," Jennifer said.

"In two hours," James added, as the courtyard lights started blinking, the cue that the show was about to begin. The crowd began to make their way inside. Jeffrey, who appeared to be alone, turned off his cell phone and quickly moved ahead.

★

"TWO HOURS? Is this thing two hours long?" Jennifer whispered in my ear. "I've got to meet some friends at ten-thirty and I can't be late."

She started to fill me in on the details. Who was going to be waiting for her at what trendy restaurant or party, but I didn't bother to listen or answer. I was thinking about the agent and how from the first time I met him I knew there was something strange about him, though I still couldn't say what it was. As we moved into the theater, Jennifer went on and on about wasn't that so-and-so sitting in the back row. She was just so obsessed with anyone who had a modicum of fame. And then I remembered a line from a Richard Gault song that William had quoted the other day. It was something about "Beware of crazy women, beware of weak men." But I couldn't remember if the weak men made the women crazy or the crazy women made the men weak or if they were all that way to start with. But it did make me think that there were far too many crazy women in my life and there had been far too many weak men in my bed and I should do something about that before I became crazier and weaker than I already was.

★

WILLIAM HAD SAVED us seats. Good ones. In the middle, five rows back. I made sure Jennifer sat next to him because anyone could see that he was beyond smitten with her and being that close to his lust object would make his night.

I settled in my seat, prepared to appear as if I were enjoying this performance, no matter what. I figured it was part of my deal with James. He needed an enthusiastic audience and I was ready to enthuse. But let me tell you, it wasn't that easy.

Curtain goes up and there's Psycho Girl on the stage alone. She's sitting on a chair wearing a short skirt and a push-up bra. Nothing else. And I mean nothing. We were sitting close enough and the lighting was designed so that when she occasionally uncrossed her legs, she flashed the audience. Nothing more than what Sharon Stone did in *Basic Instinct,* which was part of the problem. The gimmick was dated. These things come with a shelf life and this one had 1992 stamped on it. But maybe the whole point was that this was an homage to a piece of memorable celluloid history. At least she's not going for a part on "Dharma and Greg." I had to give her that.

The first ten minutes of the show belonged to her. It was her opportunity to seduce the audience. Problem is she wasn't a great actress, which distracted from her God-given natural seductive charms. She was supposed to be playing a character who could fuck like a guy—which is to say she could fuck without attachment. A character who is so into sex, so good at sex and so good at leaving after sex, that she inspires a gender reversal. Uncharacteristically, it's the guys who become attached and wait by the phone.

Let me just say, I get around and I've never met a girl who can fuck with the same level of detachment as a guy. Especially if she's doing a guy she really likes. It goes against a woman's DNA. And secondly, I knew too much about Psycho Girl's personal life to find her portrayal of a sex machine believable. James once joked that she was a pleasure anorexic, which, by the way, he found intriguing. And even if James hadn't shared these bedtime secrets with me, the girl had downer energy. Everything about her said Valium, Valium, Valium. Or worse. I'm not talking addiction, just the usual Hollywood dabbling. My guess is if the choice was lie around in bed in a self-medicated zone or work up a sweat getting laid, she'd go for the sweat-free option. So, sitting there listening to her talk dirty and sassy and saucy was like getting sex tips from a heroin addict. Uh . . . no thanks. I'll take my sex tips from someone whose idea of a good time doesn't involve throwing up and nodding out.

But I did listen and did so with a look of great interest on my face. I laughed when anything remotely funny was said and made sure I didn't shift in my seat or look around or do anything that could be construed as boredom. Not simply because of some twisted loyalty to James but because for some reason, and I have no idea where this comes from, I do have empathy for struggling actresses. I'm moved by their efforts to deliver something that often isn't there. It's courageous even if at times it must feel as unfulfilling as a fake orgasm.

Occasionally I glanced over to see if Jennifer and William were hating me for having dragged them along. Not the case. They were both watching attentively, especially when Psycho Girl flashed. Though later William would say that flashing three times was a bad move. "Once is interesting. Twice is suspect. And three times is a cry for help."

I noticed that intermittently Jennifer's knee touched William's leg. She did it in a casual way, as if they were old friends and she was just stretching to get a little more legroom. But of course that's not the effect it had on William. Or me, as she stretched in my direction. I was beginning to see that nothing Jennifer did was devoid of sexual innuendo. It was, I realized, her trademark. The way that Oliver Peoples black-frame sunglasses with green lenses was mine.

Meanwhile, the sexual charade on stage continued, but now a second actor had made an entrance. I immediately pegged him to be his generation's Tab Hunter. Good looking. Could deliver a straightforward line. But wasn't ever going to have Hamlet on his résumé. The plot did get a little more interesting, and I could feel the audience, as one entity, raise its attention a notch. It may not have been great theater, but it was distracting and, maybe more to the point, it was professionally packaged. Lighting. Directing. Set Design. Music. All accomplished by pros working with a decent budget. My ex must be in a generous mood, I thought. Must be all that money he saved on the divorce. Or, maybe he's in love.

★

RIGHT BEFORE the end of the first act, Psycho Girl did something that pulled me in. She delivered a line with the right witty touch, and the audience laughed heartily. So did I. But it wasn't that line that pulled me in. Instead it was the look of relief that crossed her face on hearing the audience's response. It wasn't the right emotion for the character, but it said everything about what she, the aspiring actress, was feeling. It was as if until that moment she wasn't sure any of this was working but now she knew it was all going to be okay. In that moment, she revealed her vulnerability as a person trying to do something she wasn't sure she was any good at. How could I not relate and be moved by that? Which is probably too long and too detailed an explanation as to why, when the curtain came down, I was enthusiastically applauding. And I wasn't even faking.

★

"HOW LONG IS this intermission?" Jennifer asked as she checked her watch.

"The usual. Ten minutes. Fifteen."

She took out her cell phone and checked her messages while I checked out the people milling around the theater's courtyard. Everyone and everything seemed so civilized. So soft-spoken and polite. It was all very Chardonnay. The only person who seemed out of the white-wine loop was Jeffrey. He was standing alone in the shadows, looking like a guy in desperate need of a shot of very strong whiskey. An agent not doing the room? Something was definitely off here. Approaching S.O.S. time.

There was also a gossip columnist in the crowd and a photographer who worked for the same local publication. I'm sure James had charmed them into coming. Maybe fed them a couple of juicy items. Sent champagne. Whatever it took.

It was no secret that Psycho Girl loved being written about. She boasted that she loved it all. Call her wild. Spread rumors of her torrid past. Describe her as volatile. Crazy. The person most likely to be the subject of a future "E! True Hollywood Story." She'd laugh it off. As long as the photo that ran with the item was a good one. Get her from a bad angle and she'd go into a two-week depression.

★

"FUCK." Jennifer snapped closed her phone.

"What?"

"Oh nothing. It's just that I'm waiting for a message from 'the guy,' and I hate waiting for messages. And he knows I hate waiting and . . ." She stopped as she caught sight of the gossip columnist. "What's that loser doing here?"

It was out of character for Jennifer to be so overtly bitchy.

"Looking for something or someone to write about," I said. "And it's not going to be easy."

Part of James's full-court press, when it came to getting a client print, involved the false promise of a high-profile crowd. I'd often seen him rattle off names to a reporter to lure her out and then send flowers the next day to apologize for all the no-shows. He'd have to send a huge bouquet this time because there wasn't one celebrity in the audience. Unless you count an actress known for a shampoo commercial and her date, a reporter for a local news station. My sympathies were entirely with James on this one. He was going to end up with nothing but a few lines written about his girlfriend, while the reporter would walk away with Veuve Cliquot, orchids, and sellable gossip.

"Why doesn't she just make up some shit, like she usually does?" Jennifer kept staring at the columnist, as if daring her to come closer. "A couple of weeks ago, she wrote about 'the guy' and one of his 'model girlfriends' at a premiere. She described them as lovey-dovey. Okay, they weren't even speaking to each other that night. They were in a huge fight. I know other people who were at the party, and they said they looked like they wanted to kill each other. Does that sound lovey-dovey? By the way, who says 'lovey-dovey'?"

And then as suddenly as she cranked it up, Jennifer shut it down and looked elsewhere. "Where's William?"

I spotted him in animated conversation with James. "Over there, talking to my ex."

Jennifer and I watched as the two of them laughed together like old buddies.

"What do you think that's about?" Jennifer asked.

"Well, it's been my experience that, when men instantly bond and they look very serious, it's all about career. But when they're doing that lighthearted bonding thing, practically high-fiving each other, it's either sports or pussy. And since James is not big on sports—he only goes to Lakers games to socialize—I guess that leaves pussy."

Jennifer laughed. "I like the way you think."

It was a nice compliment, one that I managed to enjoy for a second until she nonchalantly added, "A lot of guys like that smart, older-woman thing."

★

THE SECOND ACT was better and worse. The better part was that it was shorter and that "Tab" had some funny bits. The worse part was that the playwright veered off into a whole thing about how women have to become sexual warriors. War analogies don't fit into my concept of a good relationship or of good sex. I want to fuck an Alpha male, not be one. But at least it beat sitting through another production of *The Vagina Monologues*.

In the end, Psycho Girl and "Tab" had a mock-sex scene, where she straddled him while holding a big, black water pistol and wearing a leather miniskirt and combat boots. Don't ask. But at least it was over. Well, over except for the obligatory trip backstage where everyone gets to say how much they liked the show when all they're really thinking about is where to eat and whether or not they can still get a table at Dan Tana's or Ago's.

★

THE ROOM WAS too small, too hot, and too crowded. Psycho Girl was standing in the corner, a bottle of Evian in her hand. She was surrounded by an entourage of paid friends. You know the type. Not as pretty or even as

moderately successful as she is, which is the require-
ment. It's a straightforward deal. Psycho Girl has access
and always picks up the check, and in return they play
the dual role of cheerleader/bodyguard.

Absent from that little backstage grouping was
James, who was across the room, heavy into another
bonding moment. This time with Jeffrey. And it was a
serious bonding moment. Definitely about career. Someone must have tipped James off that Jeffrey was a CAA
agent. James is supposed to know all that stuff. If he did
his homework, he should know every agent (instead of
every maître d') at every big agency in town. But James
is not the kind of guy who ever does that kind of homework, which I have to admit is one of the things I've always liked about him.

As he and Jeffrey talked, Jeffrey did his best to keep
from having anyone brush up against him. When someone did, he got a pained look on his face as if they'd
touched an invisible wound. I noticed his forehead was
sweaty and that he stood with both hands thrust deeply
in his pockets. Although he had a glazed look on his
face, he would occasionally nod at whatever line James
was trying to sell him.

★

"DO YOU THINK I have to say something to Psycho
Girl?" I asked Jennifer. "Or can we get out of here? Now."

"I'd say something."

"I guess I could do the polite lie—'Thank you for
that. You were great.'"

"That'll work."

"Maybe the quasi-honest approach is better—'Quite a show.'"

"I've got one," Jennifer said. "Foolproof. You can say this to any actress and she'll be thrilled. Just go up to her with a big smile on your face and say, *'Sexy!'*. That's it. That's all you need. One word and you're out of there. Always, always works."

"That's a good one," I laughed as it occurred to me that Jennifer was turning out to be a better "date" than expected. She could be amusing as long as I didn't get offended by her backhanded compliments and didn't dwell on her inconsistencies. Earlier she was in a frenzy about how she had to be somewhere at 10:30. Could not be one second late. It was now 10:45 and she hadn't mentioned a thing since intermission. Must have something to do with not getting the right message from "the guy." She did keep her cell phone clutched in her hand. God forbid she should have to search for it in her purse and possibly miss the call. But that was understandable. What girl isn't a slave to her cell phone when expecting the call that can take her evening from backstage claustrophobia to wild sex? But her next move was completely unexpected. There she was standing next to me, planning our escape, and then in a heartbeat she bolted across the room. Like a Beverly Hills prima donna who just spotted a prime parking spot in front of Gucci, she pushed ahead of everyone in her path to squeeze into a slot that opened up near Psycho Girl. How she got past the barricade of paid friends, I don't know. But there she was, talking away to "the star" as if she were her biggest fan. She may have used *sexy!* as her opening remark, but she followed it up with an impromptu testimonial that had Psycho Girl almost teary. Within minutes they were whispering to each other in that conspiratorial way that makes you think that at any minute they might sneak off together and do a couple of lines.

Thinking about it now, it made perfect sense that they would hit it off. They were about the same age, they were both fiercely ambitious, and they made each other look good. Jennifer made Psycho Girl appear more normal, and Psycho Girl made Jennifer appear more complex. And since how you look in Hollywood is what it's all about, I speculated that I could be witnessing the beginning of a beautiful friendship. Probably not a long one, though. It was only a matter of time before the two had a falling out. Fact is, neither could be trusted *not* to fuck the other's boyfriend. But until that schism occurred, I imagined there'd be a lot of parties and shopping in their future.

★

WILLIAM AND I waited outside. We had a cigarette while we stood on La Cienega watching the Saturday night traffic whiz by. A bus with a clogged tailpipe nearly asphyxiated us.

"Why are we waiting around inhaling carbon monoxide? Don't we have better things to do on a Saturday night?" As I said this it occurred to me that I *should* have something better to do and that William probably did.

The guy was even better looking outside the Centerfold newsstand. Nighttime became him.

"Let's get Jennifer and get out of here," he said.

"Yeah," I agreed, but I didn't move. Couldn't. I was momentarily catatonic when I realized that I was staring at William's mouth and imagining it all over my body.

He was leaning against the theater front's fence. The ornate ironwork made me think of New Orleans. And there was something about the way he looked under the streetlight. He had a slightly decadent air about him. His blond hair looking especially messy and adorable. An old Grace Jones song came to mind. "Love Is the Drug." But I was thinking of the Roxy Music version. And I think the connection was that at that moment William reminded me of the kind of guys I used to go for back when that song first came out—southern versions of Bryan Ferry. And if I were still in my twenties, I'd probably have my tongue down his throat. But I was thirty-five and nearly divorced, and I knew too much to be pulled into a season of lust. I needed a push.

★

WILLIAM BROKE a small floral branch off the vine that was dripping over the courtyard's trellis. Whatever it was, it reinforced my French Quarter fantasy. Even from a few feet away, the floral scent was heavily sweet.

"Love that smell," William said, as he held it up to me.

"Me too." I took a step back. "But I can't. Allergies," I explained.

"Everybody in L.A. has allergies," he said. "Except me."

"Allergies. Chronic fatigue syndrome. Reflux. I'm a Hollywood cliché. Actually, I don't have chronic fatigue. I'm not even sure it exists."

He laughed. "I've got to see this."

"See what?"

"Promise me that when you finally track down Richard Gault, I'll be there."

"What do you think you're going to see?"

"I don't know. I just have a feeling about the two of you."

"Track him down? What am I, a documentary film-maker or a stalker?"

"We stalk ourselves." He tossed the floral branch back up on the trellis. "It's another Richard Gault line. From his song 'Get Me Out of Here.'" William then turned toward the theater. I could see he was a little annoyed that Jennifer was taking so long. He might be smitten, but he was a guy. Impatience came with the testosterone.

"I don't even know why we're waiting for her," he said. "Doesn't she have to be somewhere?"

I checked my watch. It was after eleven. "I think she had a plan. Probably has a new one by now," I replied.

"Probably more than one." He shrugged, knowing that none of them involved him.

The door to the theater opened, and a few people emerged. We got a glimpse of a few others hanging in the lobby. Jennifer was nowhere in sight.

"Fuck it. I'm leaving," William said.

"Yeah, me too."

But neither of us made a move to leave. A slight awkwardness prevailed. It was the first time he and I had been around each other outside the Centerfold newsstand.

"Want to go over to El Carmen?" He threw out the suggestion like it was no big thing.

"Okay. But I should let Jennifer know we're leaving."

He took his keys out of his pocket. "Meet you there."

I took a step toward the theater but stopped to watch him walk away. Don't know why. And for whatever reason, he looked back, caught me looking at him, and smiled.

"By the way, nice dress," he said.

I was wearing the short, black leather halter dress I'd bought at Acacia. "Thanks."

"See you in a minute," he called out as he darted across the street.

★

WHAT WAS THAT? I wondered. The compliment. The awkwardness. And most of all, that look he usually reserved for Jennifer. It's nothing, I decided, chalking it up to the distortion that comes with being out on a Saturday night. It's the way guys get sometimes. It's the "can't be with the one you love then love the one you're with" kind of thing. Maybe the day should be renamed Satyrday. Don't get me wrong; I'm not complaining.

chapter ten

El Carmen is a Mexican bar on Third Street that serves tacos, mainly so their customers don't get too drunk on their excellent margaritas. There are a couple of other things worth noting about the place. The walls are adorned with imported velvet paintings of Mexican wrestlers, which tells you the second you walk in, this is no Taco Bell with a liquor license. The other thing is the seating. There are the usual bar stools, often filled with girls who like to flirt with the sexy bartenders. Then there are the tables that run along the wall, opposite the bar. Perfectly fine, but not a lot of privacy. The real VIP table, though the bar doesn't cater to that way of thinking, is the booth in the back corner.

I loved that booth but even more I loved the

whole philosophy that went into creating the place. Sean MacPherson, the young owner of the bar, once explained that when he opens a new place he doesn't do it hoping it'll attract celebrities. What he hopes is that the secret celebrities will show up.

"What's a 'secret celebrity'?" I asked.

"You know," he explained, "someone who is famous only in his own exclusive circle—set design, photography, interior decorating—not to the *People* magazine–perusing masses." I loved that Sean celebrated the currency that comes with not being glossy-magazine famous. He was one of the few people in Hollywood who didn't buy into the notion that status comes with publicity. If he had made an appearance at El Carmen that night, I would have christened him his generation's Richard Gault, and I'm sure he'd get the reference. That's the thing about Richard Gault. I was starting to see that the people who were aware of him and his fans were all people I liked. It was the new litmus test. Hi, I'm Christine Chase. Nice to meet you. By the way, ever hear of a guy named Richard Gault?

★

WHEN I ARRIVED at the bar, William was already there. He'd managed to snag the back booth and was sipping a margarita with another one waiting for me. "I took a wild guess. If you don't want it, I'll drink it."

"Good guess," I said as I settled in and took a "let the games begin"–size sip. It occurred to me that the only three things we'd ever discussed were magazines, Jennifer, and Richard Gault. I wondered if a "one-on-one" with William over margaritas was a bad idea but he wasted no time introducing a fourth topic.

"So I see your ex-husband has a thing for crazy women."

I looked at him confused until my memory kicked in. "Oh, is that what you two were bonding over back at the theater?"

"We both went out with this girl Tisa a few years ago."

I snickered. Something I don't do very often. It's not very attractive. But it was the only possible response to hearing something that would have once caused considerable pain and now just felt like another footnote to the big joke.

"Do you know her?" he asked.

"No, but James and I were still married a few years ago. Still, supposedly, in love."

"Well, a little Tisa goes a long way. She actually was hospitalized for a while. For observation. She checked herself in."

"Lovely."

"And now this one. His new girlfriend. The crazy actress."

"Pulled a little tight, don't you think?"

"A little tight? Dating that girl is like playing Russian roulette with a fully-loaded gun."

That line inspired the first allergy attack (maybe ever) brought on by laughing. What was I allergic to? A good time?

"He says he's in love," I said.

"Round of applause," he replied with a smirk.

"What? You don't believe he is?"

"Maybe he is, maybe they all are."

"They?"

"You know. All the people who tell you they're in love. Then they wait for you to tell them how great that is and how lucky they are and if you don't, 'cause you don't necessarily believe it—I mean how many more blondes is Rod Stewart going to declare his undying love for in this lifetime?—they look at you like you're anti-life. Like you should be expelled from the human collective and have your oxygen supply cut in half."

Obviously drinking margaritas brought out the loquacious cynic in William, and I liked it. He wasn't a preacher on some soapbox, he was a lounge lizard living out loud in the privacy of a back booth.

"I hear you," I said as I inched closer. "Guys may get the anti-life label but you know what happens to me if I don't get all excited because some girl—who has a new boyfriend every three months—tells me she's in love? You know what label I get? I get the bitter label. Nothing is worse than that. The 'B' word is the Scarlet Letter of the new millennium."

"You're not anywhere close to bitter," he said.

"Thank you. In fact, I'm actually very romantic."

He polished off his drink. "Don't have to convince me."

"And I don't mean Lionel Ritchie kind of romantic," I added.

"You're probably more into a Lenny Kravitz kind of love."

"Exactly," I said, pleased he'd nailed it so perfectly, and then I started sneezing again.

★

A WAITRESS STOPPED by the table. "Are you okay?"

"I'm fine. You wouldn't happen to have any Claritin on you?"

"Not on me, but . . ." She glanced around the room. "But maybe I can find you one."

Claritin. Prevacid. Xanax. As common as aspirin in Hollywood. There was a fifty-fifty chance she'd come back with a pill.

"Are you okay?" William asked.

"I'm fine."

"You got a good sneeze. I hate those little delicate sneezes some girls have."

"Yeah, well, I lucked out in the sneeze department. I may not be five-nine with the body of a model, but I have a good sneeze."

A drop of water slid off the outside of my margarita glass and landed on my leg, right below the hemline of my dress, which, when I was sitting, rose to mid-thigh. In normal light, I'd be self-conscious. But this was lounge-lizard lighting and I was even tempted to yank that hemline higher.

William wiped up the drop of water with the cuff of his shirt. "You have a lot more than that."

Lines were definitely being crossed here and I needed a second to slow things down. "And I'm not one of the crazy ones," I added. "Though some people would think that what I'm doing with my life is completely nuts."

"It's interesting, not crazy."

"Interesting? Really?"

"Yeah."

It was the right thing to say. It was the perfect thing to say. Damn.

★

IT WAS ABOUT 1 A.M. and William and I had expanded our conversational skills to seven or eight topics when the margarita groove we were in got considerably less groovy. Jennifer showed up and slid into the booth as if we'd not only been expecting her but had been patiently awaiting her arrival.

"Somebody's going to have to learn how to give a good party. What's with people leaving at midnight? Things should be just getting started. But this was a party in Brentwood. I should have known. That place is way too suburban for me."

"Did you see mystery guy?" I asked.

Judging by her pout, it was the wrong question to ask.

"Something came up," she said, mimicking his message. She signaled to the waitress for a margarita and while waiting took a sip of mine. "I hate when people say that." She pulled out a cigarette and lit up even though we were in the non-smoking section. "And I really, really hate it when they tell you that just as they're driving up into the canyon. Like they don't know they're going to lose the call. Bullshit." She laughed as if she had fully recovered from the disappointment.

"S.O.P.," William said. "Standard Operating Procedure for the quick exit. Place the call as you hit Beverly and Coldwater. At best you've got thirty, forty-five seconds before the cell cuts out."

"I really don't want to talk about it," Jennifer said. "In fact, watch this." She reached for her cell phone and powered off. "I am officially out of range." She chucked the Nokia in her bag and smiled.

I wasn't buying her laughs and smiles. My intuition told me this girl was a sad little unit, and to my surprise I felt compelled to make her feel better. I went to the one thing that always seemed to crank up her spirits a notch or two—an opportunity to name-drop.

"Whose party was it?"

She got right into it, running the names. The producer who gave the party. His wife who is the sister of an actress who's married to an actor who used to have a big TV career in the mid nineties but was now . . .

This party recap was halted by the presence of the waitress, who arrived with Jennifer's drink and the latest drug report. "Sorry, couldn't find any Claritin."

"That's all right. I'll survive."

"I have Claritin," Jennifer said, digging in her purse. She pulled out a medicine container, handed it to me. "Take as many as you want, I have unlimited refills."

"Thanks."

I took one and was about to put it back when she said, "Uh . . . maybe I should take one, too. It works as an anti-inflammatory and I think this spot on my face is a little swollen." She put her finger on what appeared to be a flawless complexion, perfectly smooth, perfectly clear. But she downed the pill anyway and took a sip of her margarita as a chaser.

★

THIS IS ALL I remember. Shortly, five, maybe ten minutes after taking the pill, I decided I should leave. I wanted to get up early and work out the next day, and I also thought I should give William a break and let him spend some quality, after-hours time alone with Jennifer. From that point on it got very hazy. More drinks were brought to the table. The music got amazing. It was as if every song was appropriate to exactly what was being said at that moment—with most of the talking being done by Jennifer and me. We discovered we really liked each other. We discovered we adored each other. I remember touching the skin on her arm and telling her it was smoother than anything I'd ever touched in my life. She became obsessed with my hands, declaring them the hands of an artist. We drank another margarita and concluded that it was the best margarita either of us had ever had. Ever. And then we turned our attention to William, who was fidgeting with the container of Claritin. I told him he had the sex appeal of Jude Law in *Ripley*. Jennifer decided his hair was the cutest thing since Johnny Rzeznik of the Goo Goo Dolls. We started to call him our Goo Goo Doll.

At some point the check was dropped on the table.

William picked it up immediately and handed it to the waitress with his credit card. Jennifer and I applauded his chivalry. We got into a whole thing about how women love to nurture the men who protect us. And when a man picks up the check for no reason other than that it's the polite thing to do, we feel very protected. And since nurturing makes us feel very female, which in turn makes us feel very sexy, it triggers the urge to find a great guy to fuck. A great, protective, kind, funny, sexy guy to fuck. All of which William appeared to be, even if he had to flirt with his credit limit, which is what I'm sure he was doing when he slapped down his MasterCard. We told him all this and more until he interrupted.

"Uh . . . girls, what's this?" He was holding up a tiny pill.

"It's Claritin," I said.

He opened his other fist to reveal a larger pill. "No, *this* is Claritin." He held the tiny pill and looked at Jennifer. "And this would be . . . ?"

Jennifer didn't answer right away or even compute the question, but when she did, a big goofy smile broke across her face. "Oh no, oh no." She started laughing.

"What? What?" I looked over at William, who seemed to understand what was going on. "What is it?" I took the tiny pill out of William's hand and examined it closely as if doing so would solve the mystery.

"It's ecstasy," Jennifer said. "A friend gave me three tabs and I put them in this Claritin bottle and forgot that I . . ." She stopped and pushed my face closer to William's. "You two look so beautiful right now."

"X. I'm on X? Really? I've never done ecstasy before."

Jennifer took William's hand—the one with the tiny pill in it—and gently put it up to his mouth. "Take it," she said.

I remember looking at his face at that moment. I remember I wanted to lick it.

Jennifer draped an arm around me as we waited for William to join us on the E-train. But he didn't. What he did do—and what I'll never forget—is he waved over the little old man who was peddling roses from table to table and bought the whole bunch. He split the huge bouquet and gave Jennifer and me each a half. They were the most exquisite roses I'd ever seen. Velvet ruby roses. And then the three of us walked out of there, Jennifer and I like two beauty pageant queens. Both winners, no runners-up. Ah . . . the charm of X. And William, who was going to make sure we didn't fall off our stage.

★

HE TOOK US to a twenty-four-hour diner and made us drink lots of water. "You do know you're not supposed to drink alcohol with ecstasy. You do know that?" he asked Jennifer.

"Of course I know it. De-hy-dra-tion. I once got it so bad I woke up with a line, right here." She touched William's forehead to show him the exact spot. "I freaked. I thought it was going to be there forever."

"Why are we here?" I asked as I looked around the place, which seemed to be in a 1970 time warp and in fact reminded me of the diner in *Five Easy Pieces*. "There's water at my apartment. We could all go there." At that point I felt surgically attached to Jennifer, so it was going to have to be a group move.

"I don't think you girls should drive."

"You could drive us. You drove us here. You're our designated savior."

"Uh . . . yeah. Well. I can drop you off there if that's where you want to go."

"Drop us off?" Jennifer was astonished. "Two girls on X and an invitation to come home with us and you're going to drop us off? Oh, sweetie," she said, leaning over and giving him a kiss, "you are being way too chivalrous."

William is the kind of guy who wears his lust on his sleeve, and anyone could see he wanted to leap over the table and pounce on Jennifer. Christ, even the old man at the cash register was watching the show expecting to see some action. But William just sat there with a cock-eyed grin. "You girls are great."

I knew right then that he was out of there. "Great" was his way of saying good night. Guys often say that, or something equally complimentary and noncommittal, right before they disappoint you. It's gotten to the point where as soon as I hear a guy say "you're great" I prepare for the worst. But since I was on X, worst was not a concept I was entertaining.

★

AFTER WILLIAM LEFT, Jennifer and I settled into a back booth at the diner, drinking water and falling in deep like with each other. We confessed our fantasies and our fears, which, thanks to the X, seemed so much less formidable than they'd been just hours before.

"I was at the dry cleaners the other day and this customer, a guy, about fifty," I guessed, "is talking to a woman who works there. The woman asks him if he's seeing anyone special. He says, 'No, I wish. I keep meeting all these women in their thirties who are living in tiny apartments with their cats.' Then he laughs like it's hilarious to even think about going out with one of those losers. And I'm standing there thinking, Fuck, I'm just one Siamese away from being one of those women."

Jennifer giggled. "No you're not. Those women don't have your thing."

"My thing?"

"Yeah. You're always going to have something going on. A documentary. Something. That mind of yours is always going."

★

SHE LEANED over and rubbed my head affectionately.

The old man working the cash register looked so happy watching us, you'd think we'd just left him a hundred-dollar tip.

"Sometimes, almost never," Jennifer was quick to add, "but sometimes I worry that I could end up being one of the ones who disappear."

She lost me on that one, but I nodded as if I understood and continued to look deep into her beseeching blue eyes.

"I went to an AA meeting with a friend," she continued, "to be supportive, you know? And this other woman got up and started talking about how in Hollywood by the time you're thirty-two you can't afford to stumble. Because by the time you're back on your feet, you're thirty-five and it's too late and you have no choice but to leave town. She said women disappear all the time. They go back to their hometowns and you never hear from them again."

"That's an actress thing," I said. "You're not going to disappear."

"You sure?" Jennifer wasn't in need of reassurance as much as she was flirting. And she was very, very good at it.

"My intuition tells me you've got nothing to worry about. I'm more likely to disappear than you are," I said. "Except I don't have a home to go back to."

"Me neither. And that's the good news," Jennifer laughed. "We won't be tempted."

I love this girl, I decided. I may even have told her that but I can't remember.

★

EL CARMEN WAS CLOSED. I don't even know what time it was when Jennifer and I took a taxi back to the scene of the crime. We hugged like sisters before going off in our separate cars, each clutching our half of the bouquet of velvet ruby roses.

I could drive okay. I was alert. Sort of. Alert enough

to obey all traffic laws, but that probably had more to do with the automatic pilot in my brain than anything else. Because the first thing to happen that fell outside of standard operating procedure didn't register. And it was a pretty big thing not to register. It was explosive. Literally. Just as I was passing the Beverly Cinema, where Ingmar Bergman's *Wild Strawberries* was playing, I noticed that my Jeep Cherokee was lopsided. My first thought was how cute. My car's a little lopsided. How perfect, because I feel lopsided, too. I went with that thought, fascinated by all it implied, until I became aware of an unusual sound coming from beneath my car. I was now at the intersection of Beverly and La Brea. Normally very busy but at that hour only two other cars were on the street. Both drivers stared at me as they passed, one even shouting something out his window, though I couldn't hear what he said. The noise was getting louder and an odd burning smell permeated the air. I decided I should pull over. I got out and went over to the passenger side, the lopsided side of the car. I looked down at where the wheel *WAS*. It was gone. Nothing left but tire shreds and a medal rim. The smell of burnt rubber and wafts of smoke coming from under the car made it look as if the IRA had planted a bomb. But my paranoia was held in check by the X so not only did I not jump to any terrorist conclusion, I didn't even panic. Oh, how cute. My tire blew out and I didn't even hear it. Oh well, how great that it happened so conveniently, just a couple of blocks from my apartment.

And then I did something I'd only do on X: I proceeded as if everything was going to be all right. I got back in, and with the smoke and the screeching noise of metal on granite, drove my lopsided car the two blocks home. I calmly parked it in the garage and decided I'd think about it tomorrow. Ecstasy had turned me into a twenty-first-century Scarlett O'Hara.

chapter eleven

Bad Luck. It's like the old blues song: "If it wasn't for bad luck I wouldn't have no luck at all." What kind of luck is it to be hanging out with Jennifer and Christine when they're on X, a third little pill right there with my name on it, and I have to pass? But I had to because of this girl, Sarah. She and I have had this very cool thing going on for a couple of years now. We get together every so often and have a good time. No questions asked. It's the best sex I've ever had. No one gets me the way she does. She's also a very cool girl. And we had a plan. She was doing backup vocals at the studio till one, one-thirty. So the plan was 2 A.M. Talk about chivalry. Chivalry is not getting home late when the girl who delivers classic rock-and-roll groupie sex is com- ing over. And Sarah wouldn't be into me on some trippy

X thing when she's looking for some serious Marvin Gaye sexual healing.

The more I'm around Jennifer the more I see how fucked up she is when it comes to her so-called boyfriend. She's always complaining that he's so fucking vague. No kidding he's vague. It's called lying. What's he supposed to do? Tell her the truth? No upside.

It's not like girls don't lie all the time, too. It's in their wiring. What about all the women all over Hollywood manipulating their guy by saying, "I love you." You tell me what's the bigger lie? Cheating or manipulating? I don't know. I can only think about this stuff for so long before I want to bang out a thirty-minute drum solo that would have the cops all over me for disturbing the peace.

★

DOESN'T MEAN I didn't think about a threesome with Christine and Jennifer. Maybe my number will come up again or maybe it won't. I think Jennifer talks a good game, but I bet if we got right down to it, she'd talk her way right out the door. She's probably the kind of girl who only gets wild with a big-name guy who can do something for her. Some guy who can elevate her game a notch or two. Sounds skanky but it doesn't bother me. So getting notched up turns her on. Hey, everybody has their thing.

Christine's another story. She might be able to get into sex for sex. Just a hunch. But she's also got this fucked-up thing going with Richard Gault. When I told her I had a good feeling about the two of them meeting, she got all charged up. Here we go. Another girl falling for a guy she only knows on paper. But whatever. I like these girls. And I like them together. Hanging out with the two of them is awesome 'cause Jennifer stimulates me and Christine calms me down. Together they're like a speedball minus the day-after dues.

Waz came through. He got me a one-bedroom apartment in his building. I moved in right across the courtyard from him. I'm in Dickey Johnson's old apartment and Dickey even left behind his old drugstore lawn chair.

I decided to use the occasion of this big move, the beginning of my life as a divorcée (love that word, sounds so fifties), to change my whole style of living. I adopted the minimalist look. A bed. Books. A table and two chairs. A desk. A computer and a CD player. That's all. And of course three phones. Regular. Cordless. And cell. Not that any of them were ringing all that often. And none rang with the only call I was waiting for, the one from R.D. Swanson, Richard Gault's songwriting friend and our best access to the star of my would-be documentary. Correction. Only access. William had dug up some leads on the Internet and we actually located a phone number for R.D. in Aspen. I'd left a message two days earlier. My only move now was to give him a little more time and then try again.

I'm not good at waiting, especially when the waiting takes place in late August, my least favorite month in Los Angeles. Although I could never go back to living in a place with real seasons, August is the only time I need a break from L.A. It's the only time of year when the days feel oppressively identical. The same light. The same heat. The same lethargy. I feel cut off from all action. Waiting for a phone call on one of these days can make me feel as if I'm stuck on a deserted island with no bridge to the mainland. Which, ironically, was exactly the way I used to feel sitting through one of South Boston's blinding blizzards.

Logically I understood why the phone was quiet. Half of Hollywood was in the Hamptons or Tuscany. The other half, out in Malibu. Waz was shooting a commercial in San Francisco and Jennifer was in New York City doing whatever it is that she does. William was putting in his usual time at the Centerfold when he wasn't off in some canyon hideaway trying to write songs with some girl named Sarah. For weeks, my best friend, Elizabeth West, had been stuck in Vancouver reworking another action movie. Her approach to those high-pressure jobs was to drop out and power through. The most she could handle was an e-mail. So I was spending a lot of time in my sparse but well-air-conditioned apartment sitting by silent phones and reading magazines.

This is all such bullshit, I thought as I checked out a "What's in and what's out" list in *W* magazine. How can crabcakes be out? They're crabcakes. You either like them or you don't. You don't eat them because they're deemed in one year and then move on to eating mussels the next. Who would do that?

But my favorite bullshit of the day was found in the tabloids. Pick any one. They all use exactly the same phrase. If covering a Hollywood couple rumored to be splitting up, they inevitably report, "The couple's friends are praying they work out their differences."

Like people in Hollywood pray for stuff like that. When Hollywood people get down on their knees, it's rarely to pray. And if they do, chances are they're not asking God to save someone else's relationship. Truth is, most people are relieved to hear that a relationship is breaking up, especially a high-profile one. It makes them feel better about their own flawed unions.

I know this sounds cynical, maybe even bitter, but it's actually a good thing. Even a healthy thing. When you live in a world filled with people who are constantly flaunting their togetherness—Melanie and Antonio, Michael and Catherine, Angelina and Billy Bob—it gets to you. What these people put out for public consumption is all their bliss. What any person over twelve understands is that that's bogus. Nobody gets a stress-free relationship. Of course we all understand why these people don't want to reveal the real deal. It's an invasion of their privacy. But if they're just going to dole out the good stuff and hide the bad, they should understand this: WE'RE GOING TO RESENT YOU. We might admire and adore you. We might envy you. We might masochistically buy these magazines to read more about your perfect life but we will also deeply resent you because we know it's a lie—a lie that makes us feel bad about ourselves. And we will also resent all the magazine editors, writers, and photographers who perpetuate the lie. So we're relieved when one of these high-profile perfect relationships falls apart because it makes the rest of us feel that now we're at least getting a little truth and a little relief. If things aren't so perfect with them, maybe that also means they aren't so imperfect with us.

I've never prayed for one of these movie-star couples to resolve their differences but on occasion have wished they'd crash and burn. However, being so uncharitable is not where I want to live. To counteract the less-than-generous attitude that reading the tabloids arouses, I put on a Gram Parsons CD—a seventies jewel Elizabeth West turned me on to—for a dose of his soulful cosmic American music. Parsons was a genius at taking the high road and making it sexy. Actually the CD was a tribute to Parsons—his songs lovingly performed by a variety of artists. I listened over and over again to the Mavericks do "Hot Burrito #1" and was so seduced by the vulnerable romanticism of the song that I didn't care whether or not the phone ever rang. So, of course, it did.

"Hi. It's Jennifer."

"Jennifer. Are you back?"

"Not yet. But I will be on Thursday, and we're going to have a party Saturday night. You have to come."

"Who's we?"

"Me and Frankie."

Lately Jennifer has picked up the habit of talking about people in her life as if everyone knows who she's talking about. It's the first sign of second-stage narcissism. I had no idea who Frankie was. Girl? Guy? Supermodel? Super-something? I just played along with it. "You and Frankie. Great."

"I'll give you the details when I get back, just wanted to get you on the list."

"Ah, so it's a list party?"

"Of course. Oh, and one more thing and then I've got to go, call waiting. I think you and William should date."

★

I HUNG UP wondering if I was ready for a "list party." There are two kinds of parties in Hollywood: a normal party and a list party. A normal party is someone calling to say, You're invited, Saturday night, nine o'clock, blah blah blah. Usual stuff. A list party is not just a party, it's a fundamental Hollywood equation. Girls plus celebrities plus power equals list. First you invite a lot of hot young girls. Once the girls are in place, you can lure a few famous actors or musicians to show up. And once you've got the celebrities committed, the big agents and studio executives begin to harass you for an invite. And with that kind of lineup, a list becomes essential. It's the party throwers' attempt to discourage interlopers and reassure the VIPs that they're in a protected environment. But let's face it, if someone wanted to pretend to be Christine Chase it's not as if the standard bouncer, armed with clipboard and list, would know the difference.

★

AS I SAT there in my spartan apartment, surrounded by research material on Richard Gault, I found it hard to be too critical of Jennifer's bad values. Yes, she was chasing celebrities. But how different was that from me chasing Richard Gault? I could justify my pursuit by claiming he wasn't a celebrity and it was all about work, but it was more than that. It started that way. "Whatever became of Richard Gault?" was the question that launched the search. But as I began to fill in some of the blanks, it was as if I were painting a canvas. With each piece of information on his life, the canvas got a little more detailed. Lately, I had come to see that I was painting myself into the picture. I imagined myself meeting him and connecting to him in a way that warranted my appearance in his tableau. Was that any different from Jennifer imagining herself snagging Heath Ledger or Russell Crowe? I may walk in through the work door and she may walk in through the party-girl door, but weren't we both ending up in the same fantasy room?

★

MUCH LATER, as I continued working my way through my weekly stack of magazines, I stopped when I came to

Us Weekly. Who's that girl on the cover? I wondered. This is *Us Weekly.* Their covers are reserved for those who are name-brand famous. This girl was an unknown. Or at least I thought she was until I saw her name beneath the sexy cover shot. This singer-actress was bigtime famous but the photo had been retouched until she was unrecognizable. In real life she's attractive (saw her at Starbucks) but so are millions of other women. And I guess that's the problem. Somebody decided this star had to look like one in a million so they turned her into an updated Barbarella with computer-enchanced cleavage on top of her already surgically enchanced cleavage. They then took an airbrush to her for such extensive "refining" that she appeared to have no pores and hardly any nostrils. Obviously, sweating and breathing weren't part of this makeover. I tossed the magazine and missed the trash can. It landed on the floor next to my beat-up old Nikes, a reminder that I hadn't been to the gym all week. I knew I should get up that second and get my butt on a StairMaster but I didn't move. Without inane reading material to distract me, Jennifer's suggestion that William and I date now grabbed my attention.

I wondered if William had said something to her but quickly dismissed that possibility. If he did it was only to inspire some jealousy on her part. It was the PDD technique. Public Display of Detachment. By appearing detached from the object of his affections William would have a better chance of snaring his dream girl.

Even if William had a modicum of interest in me, it wouldn't matter anyway, because I couldn't date him. I could fuck him, maybe, but not date him. I was in a lull.

I needed something big to pull me out. William was smart, cute, sexy, a decent, caring person, but I needed a bigger-than-life experience to return to the playing field. I was T.S. Eliot's "patient etherized upon a table" in need of some powerful jolts to get the heart pumping again. It did occur to me that this same rationalization could be used by every aspiring Barbarella, star-fucking, fame-chasing girl. Integrity? Uh . . . sorry, don't have any 'cause I'm too busy trying to get my heart rate up. That thought scared me enough to reach for my Nikes. Forget the gym. I needed a long hike way up in the hills away from Hollywood's fast lanes and dead ends.

★

SUDDENLY MY ATTENTION was drawn to the court-yard. I looked out the window to see Jeffrey, the agent, standing there. What was he doing? He wasn't out there sunbathing in a drugstore lounge chair. Not in that Hugo Boss suit. He wasn't checking out the birds-of-paradise. His gaze seemed to be fixed on some distant spot. It's unsettling to see someone simply standing in the middle of a courtyard, in the middle of the day, for no apparent reason. I opened the window and stuck my head out.

"Hi, Jeffrey. Remember me? Christine? I just moved in."

He looked over in my direction, no expression on his face. "Apartment 101."

"Yeah, that's me. Maybe you, me, and Waz can get together for a neighborly drink one of these days."

"A neighborly drink," he repeated, as if it were a brand-new concept, one he'd have to spend some time getting used to.

At that moment my phone rang. "Hold on a minute, let me get this." I found the cordless under a stack of papers. I prayed it was R.D. Swanson but it was a caller from the *L.A. Times*. "Are you interested in home delivery?"

"No." I slammed down the phone. "I think there should be a law against unsolicited phone calls, don't you?" I said as I came back to the window. But I was talking to myself. Jeffrey was gone. No sign of him anywhere.

Frankie is a guy. So I'm told. A producer. I never actually met him. When the party is for two hundred, meeting the host is something that happens by chance, if it happens at all. But you can get a pretty good sense of someone from where they live.

Frankie had a Mulholland Drive address. Lucky him. Mulholland is my favorite meditation drive. Joan Didion may have mythologized L.A.'s freeways as a place of solace, but for me, it's a ride along this slower rural road. I love the gentle curves that follow the crest of the hills that separate L.A. from the Valley. Usually, I turn left at the top of Nichols Canyon and head west with no plan or destination in mind. I've often thought that the intersection of Coldwater Canyon and Mulholland is the ultimate in central location. It's like being on Fifth Avenue and Fifty-seventh Street minus the noise and people. For a couple of miles on this stretch of Mulholland the traffic never jams and the drive feels almost like a cruise down a country road. And yet the street feels racy. How could it not? Some of the town's most charmingly incorrigible men have made this their turf, inspiring the media to dub it Bad Boy Hill. Hard not to wonder what's going on down all those exclusive driveways. You don't actually have to see the girls to know there has got to be numerous A-one beauties coming and going, rocking around the clock. You see, the truly brilliant bad boys make the action come to them.

Frankie wasn't one of those boys. If he had been, I would have heard of him. I assumed he was one of those guys who enjoyed being on the same hill as his notorious neighbors, if not the same playground. And Frankie was obviously willing to pay big for the privilege of sharing a property line. Hard to say exactly how much of a bankroll he had. A prime location like this one, midway between Coldwater and Benedict Canyon, was probably worth, at least, five million. Question is, Was Frankie an owner or a renter? And if a renter, how long could he handle the five-figure monthly payment?

The whole setup was a case of mixed messages. Normally a party like this, in a place like this, would call for valet parking. But to my surprise, when I drove up there was nothing. No problem since there was plenty of parking all along Mulholland. But for those who showed up late it would mean a quarter-mile walk from car to door, unless, of course, they arrived by limo.

The driveway was steep and I was wearing very thin Jimmy Choo heels. I had no choice but to inch my way down toward the house as if I were negotiating a steep slope on Ajax Mountain. I'm sure I looked ridiculous but what did I care? I wasn't trying to impress the big burly guy who stood guard at the front door with his clipboard and list.

"Who are you?" he asked.

It's a question I despise because what it really says is if you were *somebody* I wouldn't have to ask.

"Christine Chase."

He scanned the list. "Okay." He stepped out of the way, unblocking my entrance to fantasyland. "Have a good night."

★

THERE WERE about forty or fifty people already there, scattered around the living room and dining area where a bar had been set up. As I looked through a sliding glass door out to the garden, I saw another two dozen guests and a second bar. I wandered around, searching for a familiar face as I took in the whole scene. The house, decorated in what I call generic expensive, looked as if it had been furnished suddenly. As if a van had recently unloaded a shipment of rented furniture and it would all be returned bright and early Monday morning. There wasn't a personal touch anywhere unless you gave Frankie the benefit of the doubt and assumed he'd at least personally ordered the floral arrangements.

There was no sign of Jennifer but I did see a couple of girls I vaguely knew, but knew enough to know they were party addicts. They were the kind of girls who don't go to parties to work their career, they work their careers in order to get invited to parties. They're the girls who are inevitably the most celebrity-obsessed. Even beyond Jennifer's level of obsession, which was at least a little discriminating. Not these girls. They'd go after anyone who had enough money or fame to make their material life easier. And if the guy owned or had access to a private jet, he should know he's in their cross-hairs. Big-game hunters, I call them. It's all a little too *Wild Kingdom* for me.

I found my way out to the garden and then over to the pool, where there was a third bar set up. Three full bars and only three trays of appetizers. So what does that add up to? Four thousand for booze and forty dollars for vegetables and dip? But Frankie had shelled out the bucks for a professional deejay who was spinning everything from techno to reggae.

I finally spotted Jennifer grooving on the makeshift dance floor. She had a couple of girls with her and a cosmopolitan in her hand. For a few moments I just watched as she moved, undulating for an audience of mostly appreciative men, including William. He, too, had a cosmopolitan in his hand and was surrounded by a couple of girls but his attention kept drifting back to Jennifer, who had more moves than a stripper. But she also knew how to keep it interesting. In a flash, she would go from grinding her hips to keeping the beat with the subtlest swaying and an occasional snap of her fingers. From sleazester to hipster in the blink of an eye. When she looked my way and saw me standing there, she waved me over. Judging by her hug, I'd say that was her second drink.

"Dance with us," she said. And then she leaned close and shouted in my ear, "Leo's coming. And so is Kevin," meaning DiCaprio and Costner. She then offered me her cosmopolitan. "Have some," she said. And I did, taking a big sip so I could get a little lost in the music and the night. I wasn't there to hunt big game. And I wasn't there looking for a job, not that I couldn't use one. I was there for one reason only—to get lost temporarily in the music and the night. I was there to turn off my brain. To forget about my life and especially my work. To forget that I was no closer to finding Richard Gault and may never find him. Maybe being at a big, loud, three-bar party would at least for a few hours knock this nagging thought out of my brain. Was I just another Hollywood dreamer hustling another bad idea?

★

THERE IS, HOWEVER, an all-important aesthetic to getting lost. What you want to do is be carefree enough to have a good time but not so carefree you end up, like one girl, falling on the floor from mixing a quaalude and a martini. I have to say the girl's date nonchalantly picked her up and kept her standing up by holding on to the collar of her sweater. I guess chivalry comes in many forms.

I flirted with the line between enough and too much, which is why much of the evening can only be recalled in fragments. I know at one point I ran into Waz, who was leaning against a hallway wall talking to a statuesque Danish blonde. Turns out she was the actress in the commercial he had just finished shooting. On the set, they claimed it was all business. Now, with a drink in hand and the deejay playing Moby, they appeared to be having a serious conversation.

"I hope you guys aren't talking about business," I joked.

"We're talking about Akhenaten," Waz replied.

"Who?"

"Pharaohs of the Sun. The exhibit that'll be at LACMA in March."

"You're talking about pharaohs?"

"And queens. Nefertiti."

"You're in L.A. You're at a Mulholland party. It's a Saturday night, and you two are talking about ancient Egyptian art?"

"Well, that and blow jobs," the Danish model laughed.

★

I MOVED ON, content to just drift from room to room, stopping every so often for a little party chatter. Turned out there were enough people there that I knew so drifting was an option, not a necessity. I was feeling good, having finished off one cosmopolitan with no plans for a second. Didn't need it. I was fine, flying high until my cruising altitude took a dive when I found myself locking eyes with a face that disturbingly held my attention but didn't compute. Though oddly familiar, no name came to mind. And then, a few seconds later I got it. It was Psycho Girl but she'd dyed her hair red. She saw me but then quickly turned away and went back to talking to the same "joined at the hip" entourage that had enveloped her backstage at the theater. Undeterred, I tapped her on the shoulder. "Is James here?"

"Not to my knowledge." She was doing her ice-princess routine, which might have had some effect if my ex-husband hadn't clued me in to how insecure she was—which, of course, he found endearing.

"I'm Christine. We've met before."

"I know who you are."

I wanted to say, Relax. I'm not trying to get him back. He's all yours, honey. But, unpredictably, she thawed slightly. Referring to her two sidekicks, she said, very properly, "Have you met Antonia and Christmas?"

"Uh, no. I haven't met Antonia and *Christmas*."

Christmas didn't look old enough to have a name that sounded like the result of being born on a commune in the seventies.

"Are people constantly asking you if you were born on December twenty-fifth?" I asked her.

"Constantly? No." She acted as if answering my question was being disloyal to Psycho Girl. Antonia was older and, though the kind of masochistic sycophant who would probably take a bullet for her friend, she obviously didn't think talking was a form of treason.

"We all have holiday birthdays," she said. "I'm Fourth of July." She smiled at Psycho Girl. "And she's Halloween."

"Halloween. Really? What's it like having a birthday on Halloween?"

Instead of answering, Psycho Girl tugged on Antonia's sleeve. "That bartender is still staring."

I looked over to the bar, where there were two bartenders, both busy at work, neither one even looking in our direction. However there was an older man, early fifties, standing to the side of the bar with Harry Dean Stanton. He was staring, though not at Psycho but, surprisingly, at *me*.

"Who's staring at you?" I asked, confused.

Psycho Girl sighed as if exhausted by my obtuseness. "I'll deal with it."

"The bartender, the one with the goatee. He keeps looking over here," Antonia explained.

"I don't know how you do it," Christmas said, coddling Psycho Girl as if she were some heroic martyr.

I glanced back at the bar. Neither bartender seemed to be even remotely aware of our presence, which was obviously beside the point to Psycho.

"I just can't go out anymore without someone trying to come on to me."

I wanted to say, Whoa, honey, hold on to your delusion. I wanted to tell her no one was looking at her. I wanted to tell her that in fact the only person paying attention to us was the older man leaning against the wall, and as shocking as this may be to her, and to me, he was looking in my direction. I knew that would be a blasphemous thing to say in this little group. After all, she was the twenty-two-year-old actress with legs that stopped traffic. So, instead I smiled and said, "All you get is a very small violin for that sad story. A very, very tiny violin."

She looked at me. Her eyes piercing. Was I criticizing her for being melodramatic or complimenting her privileged life? After a moment, her stare softened and a glimpse of some pervasive sadness surfaced. She gripped my arm affectionately. "I like you," she said. And I have to say as crazy as she was, at that moment, I could see why James got hooked.

★

I SHOULD HAVE left at midnight when William did. I spotted him as he was heading out the door. "I know, I'm great, she's great, we're all great but you have to leave."

He got right away that I was teasing him about his quick exit on ecstasy night.

"Thought I'd cut out before the second wave hits."

"I should, too," I said. "Or else it could end up being one of those nights that goes from midnight to four A.M. in about five minutes. Although, every so often I do get nostalgic for those days."

"Yeah, those days when you could party all night and get up at seven A.M. and go to work and actually function. It's called being twenty."

"I wouldn't want to be twenty again, but it was kind of nice to be so optimistic I'd jump into things thinking they were great adventures and when they turned out not to be, I'd be miserable until the next guy came along, which was usually the next day."

"And now it takes you, what? A week?"

"Now it takes me forever because I actually think before I act."

"That could be a problem. You can probably think yourself right out of a lot of fun."

"I'm all for being a free spirit but the trick is to make sure that each fuck doesn't leave you with a little less spirit."

He laughed. "That's a pretty easy trick," he said. "Once you know the system."

I couldn't tell if this was the beginning of a much longer conversation or it was another tag line. We were standing in the doorway, neither in nor out, until a few of the departing first-wavers bumped into me. As they tumbled outside they shouted their apologies amid giddy laughter. I was speechless. I can handle the accidental shove, but not one that lands me against William and his very hard dick. I'm not taking credit for it. I don't think I was the inspiration. He could have been fantasizing about Jennifer or any of the many other hot girls floating around flaunting flesh. Or maybe he'd just had some moment with some girl and was walking out of there with something to remember her by besides her phone number in his back pocket.

"Sorry," I said as I stepped back into the doorway.

He laughed. "Don't be."

"It's great," I said. "I mean you're great." I should have remained speechless. It's great. *It's?* Now he knew for sure I had his dick on my brain. The etherized patient definitely had a pulse.

He didn't apologize or explain. He wasn't at all un-

comfortable with his PDT—Public Display of Testosterone. He took a step away from the door, checked out
the sky as if looking for a sign. Finding none, he turned
back to me with a sly smile.

"Don't feel guilty if you end up dancing till dawn,"
he said.

"Can't," I said, "I've got work to do."

It was a lie. I had nothing to do but wait for a phone
call that might never come but I didn't want William to
know that. Self-doubt I could live with. William's doubts
might trigger a public display of insecurity, which is the
ultimate taboo at a Hollywood list party.

He lingered for a moment more as if trying to decide
his next move. And when it came to him, he chuckled.
"You ever think," he asked, "that Richard Gault might
have turned into some tequila-chugging loser? Or maybe
he's settled for a compromised life and now gets his thrills
by hanging out in Internet chat rooms."

"I just hope I get close enough to find out."

"Got it," he said.

I was about to say, "Got what?" when he grabbed
me, kissed me good night, and without another word
walked away.

I have to admit I was confused. The kiss was more intimate than appropriate, but then what's appropriate
when you've had a few drinks and the guy's already ex-
perienced me slobbering all over him the night I was on
X. I couldn't figure out what William wanted, what he
was thinking, or what any of this meant. In fact, there
was really very little I knew about William, which made
it even odder that I now knew he had a very big dick.

★

ONCE YOU'RE PART of the second wave, chances are even if you promised yourself one, two drinks no more, you'll find yourself refilling your glass. Or worse, someone else keeps refilling it without your even noticing. My refiller was an aspiring director whose ten-minute short at film school got him an agent, and he was now trying to raise money for his first low-budget feature. We had a lot in common if this guy wanted to talk about his career. He didn't.

"Spend the night with me. It'll change your life."

I laughed. There was something about the way he delivered this line that was amusing. A cross between a naughty schoolboy and a scholarly hedonist.

"I'm serious," he said.

"I'm not looking for a life change." Well, I was, but one that was much bigger than what could be brought about by his tongue. The guy had a reputation that backed up his arrogance.

"Wrong attitude. Come on. Right now. Come home with me."

He was smashed but not in a sloppy way. Chivalry was fast becoming one of my big issues and he was passing the test. He lit my cigarette. He was unfailingly polite to anyone who came over to say hi and respectfully refrained from touching or crowding me.

"Uh . . . no. I'm not going home with you," I said.

Looking around the room, I could point out a dozen girls who had slept with a staggering number of guys and were always open to an invitation from a cute aspiring director. "What about her?" I asked, as one of these girls drifted by, wearing a gold necklace that spelled out MINE.

"Sheila," he said without much enthusiasm.

"Oh, so you already know her?"

"She did a job for a friend."

"What does Sheila do?"

"Feng Shui."

"You're kidding?"

"Nope. That's what she does. Why does that surprise you?"

I looked over to where Sheila was sitting on the arm of a chair, flirting with two men. I noticed she was wearing a Victoria's Secret bra. Hard to miss because she'd just flashed her little audience. She did not appear to be the kind of girl who understood the concept of balancing energy in one's environment.

"I'm iffy on the whole Feng Shui thing to start with, but with a girl like this, I really don't get it. She doesn't want negative vibes in her house but she'll let sleazy guys in her body."

"It's a job," he said. "She's paying her rent."

He had a point. A depressing one, but a point.

Sensing a small victory, he gently gripped my wrist. "I live ten minutes away."

"Not going to happen," I replied. "I'm just not very adventurous these days. Why would I be? I live in Hollywood, where the chances of having a healthy relationship are so slight, you'd think there was some anti-love airborne virus floating around."

"I'm not talking about love," he said. "I'm talking about eating your pussy."

★

AN HOUR LATER, I was still there, waiting to use the bathroom. Five people in front of me, six behind.

Hundreds of guests and only two bathrooms. Bad math. The girl next to me was annoyed by the wait. I took note of her because she kept grinding her jaw the way you do when you've done one line too many. Abruptly she turned to me. "I just ran into the one person I despise," she said as if she and I knew each other.

"Happens at these parties," I said.

"Alexandra Lawton. Do you know her?"

"No."

The door to the bathroom swung open and two girls came out giggling. Sex. Drugs. Or redoing their makeup. All possibilities.

"Why do you hate her?"

"Because she's evil. You know what she did?"

She didn't need a response from me to launch her attack. "Three months ago my boyfriend Doug and I were going to Cabo for five days. Two days before we're going to leave, Alexandra and her boyfriend break up and she's depressed so I invite her to come with us. I tell her she'll feel better soaking up some sun, having some margaritas. So she comes with us. First night fine. Second night fine. Third night I get a little wasted and crash early. The next morning Doug tells me he and Alexandra slept together. I couldn't believe it. When I confronted her, you know what she said? 'Well, you left the room.' YOU LEFT THE ROOM. Do you believe that bitch said that to me?"

"That's pretty evil. Thing is, I think there are a lot of

women at this party who would fuck your boyfriend. Only difference is most of them would do their best to make sure you never found out."

"That," she replied, "*that,* I could understand."

★

AT AROUND 3 A.M., I went looking for Jennifer to say goodbye but couldn't find her. When I got outside the big burly guy was still there, and people were still arriving. He was drinking a beer and in a better mood. He nodded. "Be careful walking up that driveway."

And then a voice came out of the shadows, "I think she can handle it."

I turned around to see the older guy, the one who had been watching me earlier from the bar. "Hi," he said. He had a slight Texas accent.

"Hi."

We walked toward the street together, his pace slowed considerably by my efforts to walk uphill in slingback stilettos. The oppressive day had turned into a beautiful night, one that unexpectedly contained a hint of the cooler temperatures to come. It was invigorating. Even if it was 3 A.M. and I'd had more than I planned on drinking.

"Are you a friend of Frankie's?" I asked.

"Known him for years."

"Who is he?"

"There's no simple answer to that."

"Is he a good guy?" I don't know why I asked that. Some concern for Jennifer? Even so, it wasn't likely that this stranger who'd known Frankie for years and had just enjoyed his hospitality would give me anything but the positive spin.

"He's Frankie. That's good or bad depending on your taste. He's had an interesting life. Made some money in the clothing business and now wants to be in the movies. It's a bad idea but I guess he can always go back to selling blue jeans."

★

WHEN WE GOT to the top of the driveway, he stopped and lit up a cigarette as if we were sitting at a bar and he was settling in for a few beers. "What about you? How'd you meet Frankie?"

"Didn't. Jennifer invited me. You know Jennifer?"

"Just met her tonight. She's the one who told me I should talk to you."

"She did?"

"Yeah, she said you've been looking for me. I guess I should check my messages more often."

It took a second before I realized what he meant. "Oh my God." I took a step back, overcome by the serendipity of it all. "Are you R.D. Swanson?"

He smiled broadly. "Yep. Beautiful, the way it all works sometimes, isn't it?" His eyes sparkled and it wasn't from too much alcohol. He simply had a spirit about him and it was very appealing. Men in their fifties with a lively spirit were a taste I was just beginning to acquire.

"There are about a thousand things I want to ask

you. Did Jennifer tell you I'm trying to do a documentary on your pal Richard Gault?"

"She mentioned something about that. You know others have tried."

"Can we get together sometime so I can ask you some questions? I'll take you to lunch. Dinner? Wherever you want."

"I'm only around for another week and then I'm going back to Colorado."

"What about Thursday night?"

He thought for a second. "I think I can do that."

I pulled a card out of my purse. "Here, I hate cards but sometimes they're useful. Call me tomorrow and we'll figure out time and place."

He put the card in his pocket. "You going to be okay walking to your car?" His accent got a little thicker but there was nothing suggestive in his question. He reminded me of those good-guy cowboys who always tipped their hat to the ladies. R.D. was an easy guy to like. It took all of a walk up the driveway for me to feel comfortable with him.

"Uh . . . I think I can handle it." I smiled.

"I know you can, but if you need backup, I'll be right here." And he was, watching from the top of the driveway until I was safely in my car and on my way.

★

AS I DROVE HOME, I realized Leo and Kevin never showed up. Not that it mattered to me. I got to meet the only person in L.A. I wanted to meet that night.

Whoever helps you move forward is always the most important person in the room—unless there's someone there who can really make you laugh or someone you can fall in love with. I'm a typical girl. Falling in love is always going to be my favorite forward motion, but since that wasn't happening, a step toward a work agenda would have to do. Besides, rarely do my career and romantic life ever flourish at the same time. In fact, never.

I also thought about William. What if he was interested in me and I went on a date with him? Could a normal guy—well, normal for L.A.—help me out of the lull or plunge me even further into the big nothing?

But mostly I thought about Jennifer. And how this twenty-three-year-old celebrity-obsessed poacher actually delivered a very important connection. This is what makes L.A. so tricky. You never know who's going to prove helpful. Someday maybe the evil Alexandra Lawton would deliver a connection to the girl in line for the bathroom and all would be forgiven. L.A. may not be the most moral place on the map, but it does occasionally offer its own version of absolution.

chapter fourteen

An Italian restaurant is always a boost to a girl's self-esteem. The Italians know how to do it. Specifically the ones at Ago. When Stefano takes your reservation, he tells you, "Of course you can have a table for two on the patio at nine. Anything for you, darling." When you show up, he gives you a kiss and tells you how beautiful you look even when you don't. Paulie, who oversees the action, gives you a hug and tells you which of your friends are there that night. As for Ago, the chef (hence the restaurant's name), he'll whip you up a special order of sausage risotto that'll make you forget you ever considered going vegan.

But the thing that makes Ago so special is that unlike Mr. Chow's, where you get the feeling that they would boot you out of your table, without an apology, to make way for an A-list name, this place relishes its family feel. Once they know you, they take good care of you whether you're an A-list actor or a struggling anything else.

R.D. was there when I arrived, sitting at a table on the patio, drinking a three-olive martini and smoking a cigarette.

"Nice shirt," I said. He was wearing a deep-blue cotton shirt that looked soft enough to wrap a baby in.

"My stepping-out clothes," he said.

I'm sure this guy stepped out plenty but the down-home lingo suited him.

Nino, one of my favorite waiters, was at the table a second after I sat down. "Can I get you a limoncello tonight?" he joked.

"Limoncello," I explained to R.D., "is a killer drink. Don't even ask me what's in it. Tastes like some kind of lemon vodka. All I know is if you're not careful you can end up with your lips locked on whoever's sitting next to you. And that's after just one glass."

Nino laughed. "She's exaggerating."

"Just a glass of Chardonnay tonight, thank you. I'm working."

Nino looked over to R.D., who held up his half-filled martini glass. "I'm good."

With drink orders out of the way, I pulled out a notebook and a pen and put both on the table without opening either one. "So what does R.D. stand for?"

"Robert Dixon."

The name suited his craggy, likeable face. "So, how did Robert Dixon Swanson end up in Hollywood in the seventies?"

★

WE WERE already into our entrées before R.D. finished with his bio. My fault. I wanted more and more. I guessed correctly that he was one of those guys who'd hung out at the Troubadour back when Don Henley, J.D. Souther, and Linda Ronstadt were all getting started. I got him to talk about the tunes he had on a couple of big albums in the late seventies. He still wrote songs. Lived modestly in Aspen. Owned a bar. "A locals bar," he emphasized, "not a tourist hangout." He had "a terrific wife and two kids, one a stepson."

Gradually we got around to what we were there for. I asked where Richard Gault lived back in his Hollywood days. I'd heard it was an apartment on Sweetzer Ave. What was his bedroom like? What books was he reading back then? R.D. remembered he was into history and thrillers. And occasionally psychology. "I definitely remember him reading something by Otto Rank, who wrote about creativity and sex. One of those heavy books that also attempts to explain existence. And a lot of erotic literature. And *Racing Form*. He loved betting horses."

"And was there a particular girl he shared all this with?"

"From time to time."

I had a feeling that R.D. wouldn't offer up much in this area and I respected him for that. Of course, I still persisted. "Or were there just lots of different girls coming in and out?"

No answer. R.D. just kept eating.

"I'm sorry. I can't tell what's an appropriate question anymore. Where's the line between information and titillation? Hard one to call in the infotainment decade."

He put his fork down. "I've got a story for you. This is my only story on this topic. Once, he and I were at the airport in New York, on our way to L.A. The flight was delayed an hour. Ten minutes into waiting around, Gault goes up to this beautiful woman—a complete stranger— who was on her way to Miami for her brother's wedding the next day. Gault gets into a conversation with her, and right off she's laughing her head off. By the time we boarded, she'd switched her ticket and joined us. She spent the night with him in L.A. and got the first flight out the next morning."

I laughed, maybe a little too heartily, but the etherized patient had just been jolted upright. "Wit and confidence in a man always gets me," I confessed.

"Then what are you doing living in L.A.?" he asked.

★

A DISTRACTION at the entrance to the patio caught my attention. Jennifer and Psycho Girl were being shown to a corner table. It was just the two of them. No entourage. No Antonia or Christmas. And definitely no James.

Jennifer spotted us right off and ran over. She kissed R.D. like they were old friends and kissed me like we were lovers. "I can't stay and talk, because you know who I'm with." She glanced back to see how Psycho Girl was coping. "She's had a rough day and she needs to talk about it. Figure some shit out."

"Well, that should take her a while. You know what they say about psychotics? The shortest distance between two points is a maze."

R.D. gave me a slightly reprimanding look as if I'd just blasted a Coke can from a few yards using a twelve-gauge shotgun. Too much firepower for the job. Very amateur.

Jennifer protested. "It's a serious problem."

I shrugged. "Ignore me. I'm just being a bitch for no reason."

Jennifer giggled and grabbed a cigarette out of R.D.'s pack. "This is all going to work out."

As she raced back to her seat, R.D. asked, "Is she always so happy?"

"Happier than most. And I don't think she's faking. And just for the record, I was being a bitch for a reason. That girl gets to me. Okay, she is dating my ex-husband but that's not why I don't like her. It's her type I don't like. Talks tough. She's very 'fuck you' about everything. But if someone gets tough with her, she crumbles and plays victim. In my old neighborhood, you don't throw a punch unless you can take a punch. I can't stand people who want it both ways."

R.D. laughed. "Righteous indignation. Doesn't mean

you're right, of course, but Gault would love you for it. It's old-fashioned. Being indignant. Wanting things to be fair. Very sixties."

"Are you an old-fashioned guy?"

"Can't afford to be." He grinned. "Or maybe I'm just getting lazy."

His honesty made me comfortable. I felt free to say it like I saw it. Not that he didn't bust me on my contradictions. Gently. What we had, right from the start, was my favorite form of bonding—unconditional like. What a great guy, I thought. It's always affirming to know there are great guys out there. I just hoped he wasn't another great guy skulking around L.A., cheating on his terrific wife.

★

IT WAS R.D. who finally got to the point. "You want to know how to find Richard Gault?"

"That would be big."

"Colorado."

"Aspen?"

"No. Never. An hour and a half away. A town called Silt. Spring Creek Ranch."

"Is he a rancher? Is that what he does?" I couldn't picture it.

"He does a few things. He gets by nicely." He paused for a second. "You're not going to show up on his doorstep, are you?"

"No. No. Are you kidding? I am not an intrusive person. I think it's rude to have Caller ID."

"Probably the best thing would be to write him a letter. But don't expect much. He doesn't do interviews. He gets calls for that kind of thing occasionally but I've never heard of him doing any."

"That's okay. I'm good at having low expectations."

★

TOWARD THE END of the dinner, I glanced over to Jennifer's table. A gray-haired lanky guy wearing an ill-fitting expensive leather jacket had joined them and was talking effusively.

I turned back to R.D. "See that man over there. He made a fortune, something to do with computers, and now spends his time trying to pick up young actresses. Often while his girlfriend is sitting right there at the table. I don't know why these things fascinate me. Fascinate me in the way a Diane Arbus photograph might. It's a fucking freak show."

"You want a Gault-ism on the subject? Rock-paper-scissors. You remember that game kids play?"

I nodded.

He clenched his fist. "Rock is fame." He spread his hand flat. He had beautiful fingers. Piano-playing fingers. "Paper is cash." He split apart the middle and index fingers of his right hand. "Scissors is sex. Scissors cuts paper, right? Sex has more power than cash."

I nodded, going along with it, even though I was thinking, Who are we talking about here? A sexy woman has more power that a rich woman. But a rich man has more power than a sexy guy.

"However," he continued, "rock breaks scissors. Fame beats sex."

Okay, he got that right. Famous people do get more sex than sexy people. Famous men definitely do. And famous women, too. Madonna, in her forties, is still very much on the playing field.

"But," he added with a flourish, "paper covers rock. Real money, big money, Onassis money beats fame."

In spite of my questions, I liked the sound of it. I liked how it all fit into a system, so of course I immediately tried even harder to disprove it.

"But in Hollywood, there are a lot of people who are rich, famous, and sexy."

"Rich maybe, but not big-money rich."

"But rich enough so that an argument could be made that they have it all. And if they have it all . . . then what?"

He put his hands behind his head, open and sure of himself on this one. "Then you become addicted to having whatever you want when you want it. And honey, I've been around awhile and let me tell you, there's no rehab for that disease, though there should be."

★

WAZ APPEARED as R.D. and I were wrapping it up. Perfect timing though it was a bit of an ambush. Waz introduced himself and shook R.D.'s hand.

"Waz?" R.D. said. "Nice name."

"He's my cameraman," I explained. "His stuff is in the car."

R.D. did a slow turn toward me. He knew what was coming.

Waz flipped open my notebook. All blank pages. "Nice notes," he said.

R.D. sat there, calmly; he wasn't going to do the work for me.

"I wondered if we could get you on camera—just saying one or two things about Richard even if all you say is you don't want to say anything." I realized I was now referring to Richard Gault as Richard. What did that mean? What corner had been turned here?

Waz jumped in. "I know this sounds like bullshit but I'm a big fan of yours. 'Texas Time' and 'Love Lies.' Great songs."

"Thanks," R.D. replied as he sized Waz up. "So you're doing one of *those* documentaries."

"Yes," I answered quickly before Waz mentioned anything about it being a ten-minute demo tape. No one wants to put time in on a long shot unless it's their long shot.

"It's as much about trying to get to Richard as it is about actually getting to him," I explained. "So anything at all that happens while we're looking for him is part of the story."

Waz took a different approach. "Look, if you just want to let us shoot you talking about your songs, that would be cool too? Right?" Waz looked to me for confirmation.

Every so often I forgot I was the director. "Yeah, yeah. That'd be great."

"How long would it take?"

"Ten, fifteen minutes."

"Right here?"

"Outside."

Nino dropped the check on the table and I grabbed it.

"No, no, no, little lady. I can't let you do that." R.D. was adamant. But I had the two words to dissuade him.

"Expense account," I lied.

★

WE SHOT RIGHT there on the sidewalk in front of the restaurant. It was nothing that was going to attract attention. L.A. is filled with people and their digital cameras shooting whatever all the time.

R.D. was perfect. A natural. He had a little Kris Kristofferson in him. He didn't say too much, but one colorful anecdote about his adventures with Richard Gault in Mexico goes a long way.

When we finished I asked earnestly, "What are the chances that I'll hear from Richard?"

"Hard to say," he replied. But then he did something that told me he thought they were slim to none. He took a hundred-dollar bill out of his wallet. "Here, I feel bad about you paying for dinner."

I think he probably felt bad that I was chasing after something so seemingly out of reach. I guess he'd been out of L.A. a long time. Didn't he know that chasing after the elusive is what girls come to Hollywood to do? "I'm not taking your money." I smiled, gently pushing him away.

Reluctantly he re-pocketed his C-note and then gave

me a hug. "If you do get to see him, ask him about the Lucifer thing."

"What's that?"

"If you find out, you can explain it to me."

As I walked to my car, which was parked right near the entrance to the restaurant, I looked inside the patio. Psycho Girl and Jennifer had lost the loser rich guy and were back to being an intense twosome. Psycho Girl was doing the talking as Jennifer reached over and played with her hair. Two glasses of limoncello were on the table.

chapter fifteen

Later, a number of people told me they knew it was going to be a weird night and it wasn't just because the Santa Ana winds had blown in. One girl said she was afraid to leave the house. Couldn't figure out why. Others mentioned random disorienting incidents that ranged from losing keys to losing nerve. The night before I had had a flash of something. A snippet of a dream. A guy in a *blue plaid shirt* told me something upsetting, but upon waking I couldn't remember a word. It was also early October, the month the clocks get pushed back and people begin to gear up for shorter days and light deprivation. No one seemed happy.

It didn't help that the holiday season was rapidly approaching. Halloween stuff had been in stores for weeks—since the Tuesday after Labor Day. It was over-kill. But nothing compared to the countdown to the millennium. Every other story on the news was about the impending turning point. In fact, it had gotten such extensive coverage it had already become old news. Maybe that was the message for the new century. Things becoming old and boring before they even happen. The media had already sucked all the life out of New Year's 2000. No wonder battling the big lull had proven so challenging.

★

AS SEVEN O'CLOCK approached, I forced myself out of the apartment and made my way down Sunset Boulevard. The light at the corner of Fairfax was out and the cop directing traffic was taking out his frustrations on all motorists. It took me five minutes to get across the intersection. Fortunately I hit a good run on the radio—old INXS and some new Lenny Kravitz to keep me company.

West of Crescent Heights, the street turned into the land of theme restaurants. Miyaki, the front of which was designed to look like a Japanese temple, if your idea of a temple is something you'd find at Disneyland—but not as authentic. Across the street was Dublins, an Irish pub. Want fifties? There was Mels's Drive-In. What about a little soul food? How about the House of Blues with its eye-catching tin-shack motif? And on and on. Can people have a meal without being in a theme environment? The idea of a generic restaurant was starting to feel exotic.

Traffic crawled in front of a large video screen opposite the Hyatt House Hotel. Forget worrying about
cell phones causing accidents. Two young guys in a VW
convertible slowed to watch some blonde cavort in a
pink bathing suit. I couldn't tell if she was part of a
commercial or a movie promo. I'm sure it didn't matter
to the young guys. It was automatic. They're guys and
she's flashing her tits. They've got to look. And so did
I. What else was there to do? With traffic jammed up
ahead, my only option was to enjoy the scenery. I would
have liked to have taken a quick left down La Cienega
and be on my way back home. Guilt kept me on Sunset.

I was headed to an event that required my presence.
In the name of friendship, you go to these things. You
support your friends in their triumphs even if it's one of
those days when leaving your apartment feels as scary as
if there actually were ghosts and goblins hovering in
every corner.

★

ELIZABETH WEST had assembled her usual eclectic
bunch of friends to help her celebrate the publication of
her first book, *Dining, Dating and Dodging Bullets in
L.A.*—a collection of nonfiction essays about a single girl
surviving in the traditionally boys-only club of action
screenwriters. The event took place in the Book Soup Annex, an adjoining space to the popular Book Soup store.
The room was crowded, especially in front of the podium
where Elizabeth was to stand and read a chapter or two.
Already, it was chaos. More than fifty people had shown

up and the little standing room there was, was made even smaller by a dozen stacked boxes that served as a bar. The guy tending it was one of the bartenders from El Carmen and for a second I worried that he might recognize me as that crazy girl on X. But I was able to muster up the kind of fuck-it attitude that I can only access when I'm feeling very very good or very very bad.

"I'm having a collapse," Elizabeth said calmly when I finally got her attention.

"It doesn't show," I reassured her, which was mostly true. She looked the epitome of confident West Hollywood chic, dressed in black and wearing matching leather and silver wrist bracelets. But certain gestures gave her away. Occasionally, she'd gently tug at her bottom lip or fidget with one of her twin cuffs. But mostly, it was the way she managed to turn her head so her hair fell into her face. It was her way of hiding without wearing the tinted lenses that half of her audience was sporting.

"I think everyone's having a collapse today," I said. "What's your deal? A guy thing?"

"What else?"

I knew that meant Jake was a no-show. Jake was the guy she was in love with. A director known for his hedonistic lifestyle and his brilliant mind, which wasn't reflected in his blockbuster action movies. But no one gave better conversation. They had an unconventional off-the-radar relationship that flourished in spite of his bimbos, his on-location romances, a high-maintenance ex-wife, and eighteen-month-old twin daughters. Theirs was a very private thing, but had it been public Elizabeth would have been hit with a barrage of criticism, the worst coming from her girlfriends. She'd have to hear the usual stuff. What's in it for you? How can you deal with all these other women in his life? One day I was at Elizabeth's house when her friend Mimi stopped by.

"He's using you," Mimi said.

"Mimi," Elizabeth said laughing. "That is so old-school."

"Since when do guys play by new rules?" Mimi replied, concerned.

"Do I look worried?" Elizabeth asked playfully. "Think of it this way: Jake is my reward for not having sold my soul."

Mimi thought about that. Though a big believer in holding on to one's soul, she is an even bigger believer in tangible proof. "I love you" is never going to do it for her unless it comes with a De Beers diamond. "That's not much of a reward," she sighed.

Elizabeth just smiled. "You wouldn't say that if you'd ever fucked him."

★

ELIZABETH HAD my vote but that doesn't mean I didn't see how hard it could be on her sometimes. Still, a public display of despair was not her style so she cheerfully signed a book for a fan while turning the Q&A on me.

"Are you alone?"

"William is meeting me here."

"Who's William?"

"The guy who's helping me with the research on my documentary."

"Research is a great thing, isn't it?" She grinned mischievously. "It's a good excuse for so many different things."

★

I BOUGHT two copies of the book and took a seat in the back of the room, saving a place for William. He was over at the bar getting a vodka tonic, which turns out was the only drink offered. In no way did it thematically connect to the book and it was completely out of the ordinary to have anything like this at a book reading. At most you might get a glass of bad wine. And even that might not be legal. But Elizabeth had decided that since everyone she knew had had such a stressed-out week, we all needed something a little more potent. I hadn't had a drop of alcohol for two weeks. I'd been on a health kick. Therapy. Acupuncture. Yoga. Vitamins. So how come I felt so fucking bad? But vodka tonics weren't my thing. Damn.

★

"HEY, BABY." Suddenly James was there, taking the seat I'd saved for William.

"Hi, honey." We kissed hello. Public display of disarmament. "Are we divorced yet?" I asked.

"I don't know. Has it been six months since we signed the papers?"

We both knew it hadn't but this silly chatter gave me a chance to regroup. On first sight of him, I almost gasped. He looked trashed. Normally, James shows almost no wear or tear no matter what late hours he's been keeping. I'd seen him wake up on a Monday morning after a weekend of debauchery and still look like an advertisement for *Men's Health*. He credited good genes and cold showers as the source of his recuperative powers. Judging by the circles under his eyes and his sallow complexion, he had either pushed his genetic luck too far, succumbed to more normal bathing temperatures, or had, like the rest of us, found that when the going gets tough, the tough look like shit.

He reached into his pocket and pulled out a new pair of glasses, amber lenses.

"It's really nice of you to show up," I said.

"Yeah, well, I've always liked Elizabeth. She's the only friend of yours I do like. The only one who didn't think you screwed up your life by marrying me."

"That's because she thought it would only last three months. I was young, and she thought I could afford a three-month mistake. No one expected it to last six years."

"I want you to know something," he said.

"And what might that be?" I thought we were still in the kidding mode, so I was expecting some lightweight slam. I didn't expect him to look me right in the eye, granted through tinted lenses, and say with great seriousness, "It was always good with us."

He waited, anticipating something equally significant from me.

"It was, wasn't it?" I smiled warmly. I wasn't sure that my "it" was the same as his "it" but it didn't matter. James seemed relieved that we were both in agreement.

★

ELIZABETH HAD pushed the podium aside, dragged a small wooden table out of a corner and sat cross-legged on top of it. She had everyone's attention as she began her reading. And she kept it as she continued. No easy thing. At most readings you're sitting there thinking, Okay I'd rather be watching some bad L.A. theater production than sitting here under unflattering lighting listening to an author try to inject life, or worse, some nonexisting acting talent, into their words, which Elizabeth wisely refrained from doing. William had claimed his seat next to me now that James was off on the sidelines, hanging out near the bar exchanging whispers with the El Carmen bartender, whom of course he knew. Whenever anyone walked into the annex, James looked up expectantly. My only thought was he was hoping Psycho Girl would walk in. Doesn't he know girls like that don't come to things like this unless they're the ones doing the reading?

William draped an arm over the back of my chair as he listened to Elizabeth with great interest. He nuzzled close and whispered, "I can see why you two are friends."

"You'll love her," I said, as if we were all going to be hanging out together.

"We should sell her book at the Centerfold."

"Don't you just sell magazines and newspapers?"

"We sell cigarettes. We sell Altoids. We sell fucking lottery tickets. Why can't we also sell books?"

I smiled. He squeezed my shoulder. Suddenly I felt like I was on a date. But this wasn't a date. We were just buddies, going to a reading together, weren't we? A date implies the possibility of sex at the end of the road or, hopefully, the night. Without that it's not a date, regardless of any erotic dreams that resulted in me waking up naked and sweating. Sex fantasies aside, I wasn't ready to date William even if he'd consider it. I wasn't ready to worry about who I was to him, who he was to me, and who we were to each other. Divorce was giving me a moratorium from second-guessing everything I did and I was enjoying it. The upside of the lull was I knew what to expect every day. More of the same. It was oddly comforting. Life was simple. I had no attachments except to the phantom Richard Gault and I could handle an attachment to a phantom. Besides, if this were a date, I was wearing the wrong underwear.

The reading lasted only fifteen minutes. The vodka tonics had loosened up the audience and they were more than politely responsive. They got the humor. Appreciated it. Celebrated it. I watched Elizabeth closely throughout her reading and was aware of the moment when everything shifted, though I may have been the only one who caught it. A few minutes in, something or someone caught her eye in the back of the room. For the briefest second her gaze lingered there, her face softening at the same time her adrenaline kicked in. Prior to that moment, she was very professional, giving an acceptable eighty percent to her recitation. From that glance on, she upped it to a hundred and ten and it flowed effortlessly.

I swiveled around to see what or who could inspire such a shift. I should have known it'd be a guy. Jake was standing just inside the doorway, by himself, her book reverently clutched in his hands. He didn't do the usual Hollywood scan—a quick look around to see if anyone important was there. Though there were plenty of people there who made note of his presence. His eyes stayed on Elizabeth the whole time. I found it wildly romantic. It was subtle. It was discreet. It was simple. And most important of all, it was intimate. More and more I find myself being enchanted by the small, private gesture. You can keep the big proclamations of love, the announcements made to and for the public. Give me a guy who stands silently back but never loses track of me in a crowded room. He's the one for me.

★

LATER, the next day and the day after that, I heard all kinds of stories about the crazy things that happened at the book party. By that time, none of it came as a surprise. After the reading, a group of us went to the restaurant next door, a themeless one, thank God. Jake didn't join us, but judging by the smile Elizabeth wore for the rest of the night, I assumed she'd be heading over to Benedict Canyon by midnight.

For a while, I believed the ominous omens from earlier in the day had blown over. The winds had died down and people seemed ready for a break in their bad moods. There was more table hopping than usual and William had no trouble mingling on his own. Though some of the people present were pretty formidable—at least when it came to their résumés—William didn't hesitate to strike up a conversation and had no trouble admitting he worked at a newsstand. I loved him for that. Here's a guy who read the trades, read about all these people making the big money and the big deals, and it didn't make him feel like an outsider. So what if his weekly paycheck was equal to what they dropped at a typical dinner out. That didn't intimidate him. William believed he knew what was really going on out there on the street and that the people running the business only caught on after the fact. He had the cockiness of a participant, not a spectator. No wonder he loved Richard Gault.

I breezed by him as he was talking to a white guy who had shoulder-length rasta hair and a Bob Marley tattoo on his arm. Rasta Guy was making a case for why breaking up is the best thing for a songwriter's career. William was shaking his head in agreement. "Yeah, Al Green aside, happy-in-love songs make me want to puke."

I had to laugh at that one. He responded by lightly touching my lower back and smiling the way you smile at someone you've just recently fucked and know you'll be fucking again very soon. What is going on here? I wondered. It's not as if we even showed up at the reading together. Separate cars. How can that be a date? And yet more and more that's the way it felt. I'd had a couple of surprise birthday parties in my life, but this was definitely my first surprise date.

I walked around looking for Elizabeth but instead

was pulled over to a quiet corner table by James, who was sitting alone. Something was definitely wrong. James was never alone. He wasn't the type to be at a gathering and not be the center of a lot of female attention. I used to kid him all the time and tell him he had the most successful personality of anyone I'd ever met. People loved being around him and he loved being loved. That was the newlywed in me talking. After living with him for a while I discovered there was a dark side to his personable nature. He needed constant distractions. Silence was the enemy. And if there weren't any people around, he'd settle for noise. From the second he awoke, the TV was turned on. Alone was not an option.

"Sit with me," he said.

"Are you solo tonight?"

"So it seems." He tried to sound cavalier but unlike his shaded eyes there was no way to disguise the pain in his voice.

I pulled up a chair. "Late night?" I asked him.

He touched his unshaven face. "It's my new look. Don't you like it?"

"It's a look."

He took a sip of his drink. "Want some?"

"Uh . . . no. I'm saving my liver for special occasions."

He smiled sadly. "I guess you could say this is a special occasion."

I knew he wasn't talking about the debut of Elizabeth's book.

"I'm a free man again," he added quickly.

It was the opening line to the story he needed to tell and he knew he could count on me for support. I may be his ex-wife but my loyalty ran deep. When it comes to someone I love or once loved I'm like a cop—there to serve and protect.

The details don't matter. Psycho Girl had a psycho episode. Something was said. Something misunderstood. An argument. An explosion. A window smashed. A match lit. A fire extinguished. Threats made. A door slammed. And reopened. And slammed again. And reopened. And then left open because it had been knocked off its frame.

"You've got to get stronger doors," I said, going for a touch of levity.

"That's what I told myself when she was driving away."

James didn't offer up a lot of specific details. He's a guy. He probably didn't remember half of them. So after he rendered a two-minute version of what had happened, we talked generally about life, love, and how you've always got to think twice about getting involved with someone whose deepest commitment is to her mirror.

I listened. I gave my best advice. Occasionally I made James laugh. And I kept silent about my blue-collar, factory-town, street-fighting urge to (at the very least) annihilate Psycho Girl with a sentence the next time we crossed paths. Not that I would. I was working hard to be less Sicilian these days. I also knew that I could share James's pain, get all riled up on his behalf, and tomorrow they'd be back together.

★

AFTER AN HOUR, I walked James out to the street where his car was parked in a red zone with a hundred-dollar ticket on the windshield. As we said good night, he pulled me close. We hugged like two people who had been through a lot together and were grateful to still be standing. As I comforted him, I thought about what he'd said earlier—that "it" was always good with us. I thought that his "it" was probably sex and guessed he would love a little of that tonight provided it came with a disclaimer: This doesn't mean we're reconciling. All it would take on my part to make that happen was one small gesture or sound. A hand on the back of his neck. My lips on his ear. A moan. A sigh. None of which I did because, with or without a disclaimer, I wasn't about to revisit that chapter. I stood there thinking I genuinely want him to be happy and in love—with someone else. And with that thought, I realized that our romance was truly over.

★

WE DETANGLED and stood there on the street trying to find a way to say goodbye. "Was it love or distraction? That's a line from a Richard Gault song," I said.

James nodded but I knew he wasn't thinking about any Gaultian philosophy. He was probably thinking, Fuck, she's *not* going to fuck me.

"How's that going? The Richard Gault thing?" James asked.

"Fine. It's fine." I couldn't admit that Richard had never replied to my letters. I'd sent two, by FedEx, and he'd signed for both. I'd checked.

Someone shouted out my name. It was William beckoning me back inside and I was more than ready to rejoin him. I did not want to stand there with my ex-husband, lying about my nonexistent career or thinking about the ultimate ending to my marriage, which just took place on the sidewalk in front of Book Soup.

James got in his car. Music blasted on as he started the engine: "Walking Wounded," the title cut from an Everything But the Girl album. If this was off the radio, then it was yet another case of life's soundtrack being almost too appropriate. But James could have programmed his CD for some long, dark solo ride. He waved goodbye before picking up his phone and merging into the traffic. I watched him till he disappeared and then headed back into the party. I needed a drink.

★

I GOT SMASHED. And since I was smashed, I started acting like William and I really were on a date. Beyond that, that we were already lovers. What else explains the fact that at one point I had my head in his lap. He handled it well but it did put the brakes on his own drinking. I guess he figured both of us smashed would not be pretty. Or maybe he was saving his liver for someone else. Or, it's possible he really was a chivalrous guy. I hate to admit this, but I have no idea what I babbled about for hours but I know I said it all very earnestly. I think I may have offered to fuck him while wearing nothing but my Gucci stilettos. If I did I can't remember if he agreed to the plan or not. The fact that I ended up in his car at the end of the night could simply be a testament to his self-appointed role as my designated driver.

He took Melrose Ave. east, which meant we were headed to my apartment, not his. I remember thinking he'll never find a parking spot on my street. It was at this point that I decided everything would turn out okay as long as I hadn't misplaced my keys. If I found them it would be a sign that I should sleep with William. After much searching around, I located my bag on the floor of the car. As I grabbed it and pulled it up onto the seat, the light ahead of us turned green. At that moment a guy in a Chevy Blazer heading south on Citrus jammed on his brakes. For a second the Blazer's headlights lit up William's face, his features scrunched, teeth clenched as he yanked the steering wheel hard. Strangely enough at that moment, his expression resembled the look I'd seen on the faces of rock musicians when they're getting down to some serious guitar riffs. And then in an explosion of glass and metal, with tires screeching on asphalt, we crashed into a parked van. For one very long second, nothing and no one moved.

A door opened in the house across the street. Voices and footsteps approached. William's arm was still stretched protectively across my chest. Someone pulled open the driver's-side door.

"Are you okay?" It was a bystander with a cell phone, already on the line with 911.

"I think so." William looked over at me. "Are you all right?"

"So far." I wasn't sure what it was going to feel like

to actually move but I was instantly alert to the fact that I'd gone from drunk to almost sober.

"I'm so sorry," William said even though we both knew it wasn't his fault.

★

THE POLICE were there within minutes. They'd been cruising a couple of blocks away when they'd gotten the call. Lucky us. Or so I thought.

"Step away from the car." There were two officers, one male, one female, and the man in charge was talking to William. His manner was gruff and official.

"What?" Almost sober meant I was aware of everything going on but not so sober that I had the wherewithal to keep my mouth shut. "Step away from the car? What does that mean? This isn't a crime scene."

"We're not talking to you," the cop replied. The female cop shined her flashlight at me and then around the interior of the car.

"Is the driver of the other car okay?" William asked as he stepped out onto the street.

I looked out the back window. Though the jeep appeared totaled, the driver was at least upright and in conversation with two other officers who had just shown up in a second squad car.

"Move to the other side of the street," the cop in charge ordered William.

I glared at him, indignant. "Why are you treating him like a fucking felon?" I made a move to open my door and join him when the female cop turned back in my direction. "You stay where you are." She then stood guard as if ready to tackle me if I tried anything.

What was going on? "This is an accident," I said. "Aren't you supposed to be helping the victims? I could have internal bleeding. I could have a bleeding aorta like Princess Di."

She shined her flashlight on me again and demanded my name, address, and driver's license. Okay, I'd heard horror stories about the LAPD but they hadn't prepared me for this. Where was this instant hostility coming from? Was it the Mustang convertible? The fact that William looked like a rock and roller and that I looked like the kind of girl who likes rock and rollers? Was it the fact that these cops had been fucked over by so many people that they lived in a natural state of paranoia? In their eyes, was every citizen a potential ax murderer? If so, their paranoia was now getting introduced to my paranoia. A head-on collision of a different sort.

"I don't have my driver's license." Truth is I'd lost it months ago and couldn't bring myself to stand in line for two hours at the DMV to replace it.

She looked at me like I was a freak. "Name and address then," she said coldly.

Blame it on the cosmopolitans I'd been drinking but I let it fly. "I get that you're doing a tough job and they make you wear a uniform that would be unflattering on Pamela Anderson but is there a female hormone left in your body?"

She officiously took a notebook out of her pocket and

wrote down exactly what I said. However, what she didn't write down was what *she* said. "That'll sound good on the record when your boyfriend's charged with a DUI."

"He's not drunk," I said, not bothering to correct her on the boyfriend stuff.

"We'll determine that."

"Will you?" I was moving into hostile territory myself. Authority figures do that to me. "Well, don't let the facts slow you down," I screamed.

"That would be a four-fifteen," she warned. It was cop code for disturbing the peace. I'd learned that from one of Elizabeth's action flicks.

"Three thirty-two," I replied. She looked confused. Of course she would. I'd made up those numbers.

★

ACCIDENT KARMA is something you can find yourself thinking about even if you don't believe in it. If you saw the Mustang's crumpled left front end, you might comment that I was lucky to get away without a scratch and William was lucky to get away at all. Jennifer made the point that William and I must have some intense karma together. Why else would we find ourselves in a smashup? Some suggested it was destiny and I should marry him. Others concluded it was a sign of our combustible energies and I should run for my life. It's part of the charm and the kookiness of L.A. that people see signs and lessons everywhere. Everything is subject to a quasi-biblical interpretation, even if sometimes the lessons are from a twelve-step bible.

What wasn't up for interpretation was that the accident had instantly changed my feelings about William. As I watched the cops handcuff him, I was overcome by a desire to protect him, no matter what. It was the same wiring that got charged whenever a *boyfriend* of mine was under any kind of attack. Was my wiring telling me something my brain had neglected to compute? Had the accident knocked some senselessness out of me? What if William and I. . . . ? A scary thought.

★

I BOLTED OUT of the car, ready to protest to every cop there—and to the whole fucking police force—that they had no right to lay a finger on William. I made it halfway across the street before cop lady and one of her reinforcements—a kid who looked like he was in his rookie season—blocked my way.

"We called a taxi for you," the lady cop said. "It'll be here any minute to take you home."

"Take me home? Are you insane? You're hauling my *boyfriend* off to jail and you think I'm going to go home? No. No. No. No. No. I'm going wherever he's going and I'm going to bail him out."

"He might be there for a while," the rookie said, trying to be nice.

"Then I'm there for a while." I watched as they pushed William into the backseat of the patrol car. "So where exactly are you taking him?"

chapter sixteen

Parker Center is the hub of the LAPD. It's where they took O.J. for questioning. Located downtown, it's just a bigger version of a typical metropolitan police station. Fluorescent lighting and the standard coin-operated candy and soda machines in the lobby.

At 1 A.M. it was pretty quiet. The officer doing desk duty barely looked up when I walked in. I guess doing that job you've seen it all. Unless you're a member of the Lakers' starting lineup you're probably not going to elicit a reaction.

"A friend of mine was brought in on a DUI and I want to bail him out."

"What's his name?"

"William Finch."

He checked names on a list. "They haven't processed the paperwork yet."

"Can I see him?"

"Are you his lawyer?"

"No."

"Are you his priest?" He asked these questions in the same monotone cops use to read the Miranda rights.

"No."

"Then you can't see him."

"I can't see him? Not even for a minute?"

"That's right."

I should have lied and said I was his lawyer. Not that I looked like one in my Earl Jeans and leather jacket. An entertainment lawyer, maybe. I should have asked if I could at least get a note to him. I should not have burst into tears because nowhere on the planet are tears as commonplace and as ignored as in a police station. But I couldn't help it. Being up against a logjam of paperwork that had to be moved (slowly, no doubt) through the system pushed me over the edge. I could handle a car accident, a failed marriage, and a stalled career but not the frustrations and delays that come with the LAPD's rules and regulations.

The desk cop was unmoved by my outburst. Maybe a girl is entitled to only so much chivalry in one evening and I'd exceeded my limit. Okay. Fine. I wiped away my tears and, like an earnest character in a Lifetime movie, took matters into my own hands.

"Where are the yellow pages?"

He pointed toward a row of pay phones in an alcove. I marched over there and flipped through pages of ads for bail bondsmen, many who could *habla español*. But did they speak English? Not the first one I called. The second one sounded like Sidney Omar on the *L.A. Times* call-in horoscope line. Like a voice from beyond Pluto. A woman named Dorothy sounded promising, if I wanted to wait around till 6 A.M. She had a busy night. She was a single mom, two kids, working the late shift. Now there's a TV series. Finally I found Sammy Potts, who said he could help me out as long as I had an AmEx Gold card. He told me he'd get there in an hour. "I'll be the woman sitting on the floor crying," I joked.

"Could you be more specific?" he asked.

"I'm wearing a black leather jacket, jeans, and hoop earrings. What about you? What do you look like?"

"I'm six feet, glasses, and I'll be wearing a blue plaid shirt."

A BLUE PLAID SHIRT. The guy in the dream I'd had the night before was wearing a blue plaid shirt. See what I mean? It was one of those nights.

★

SAMMY POTTS showed up at 4 a.m. and offered no apologies or explanations as to why it took him so long.

"You're lucky you got me," he said. "I was on my way out when you called." He immediately got down to business, pulling over an extra chair and using it as his desk.

"William wasn't drunk," I said as I filled out the first form he handed me.

Not that it mattered to Sammy. "They've been getting a lot of false positives on their alcohol tests. Your friend could hire a lawyer and spend forty thousand dollars fighting it in a jury trial but I wouldn't recommend it."

"Don't you just hate a rigged game?" I asked.

Sammy just shrugged. "I make a living off of it."

★

WILLIAM WASN'T RELEASED until 5:30 A.M. While I waited I watched the traffic coming in and out of the station. Nothing like a night downtown to give a Hollywood girl a little perspective. I struck up a conversation with a guy in his twenties who was waiting for a friend who had been busted for drugs. He had the number of his own bail bondsman tattooed on his ankle. Or so he said. He was either flirting or psychotic. It's a different world down at Parker Center. It was so disorienting that I forgot to check my messages. I couldn't remember the last time I let eight waking hours go by without checking my voice mail. I always checked it. In fact, it occurred to me that it was very possible that since getting a cell phone and voice mail, I may have never let eight hours go by without checking for messages. EVER. But there it was, almost dawn, and the last time I'd checked in was right after Elizabeth's reading. Not that I expected a lot of action between 9 P.M. and 5 A.M.

And never did I expect this. "Hello." It was a man's voice. Unfamiliar but immediately appealing. "It's Richard Gault, calling at nine-thirty Monday night." That was it. That and his number in Colorado was the entire message.

And that was all it took to put the brakes on my

"destiny" with William. Talk about what-ifs. What if I actually got to meet Richard Gault? What if he wiped every other guy off the playing field? What if even thinking about this was the equivalent of having no moral compass? What if this was the problem with trying to have even a quasi-normal life in Hollywood? Just when you were thinking about doing the reasonable thing, the possibility of a bigger-than-life experience seduces you into the same fast lane that Richard Gault had warned TV viewers about almost thirty years before.

Nothing like a little confusion to get me off the floor and back into fighting form. The spirit was once again willing and now all I needed was a little sustenance. I walked over to the candy machine and bought a Kit Kat. I bought another two. I gave one to the desk sergeant and one to the guy with the bail bondsman tattoo. I had a big smile on my face. They probably thought I was a little schizo. Or maybe just another woman with mood swings and a weakness for chocolate.

I got to see this. No really. This is one road trip I've got to witness. Silt, Colorado. Who lives in a place called Silt? Richard Gault, that's who. I got hit with this travel plan the second I'm out of the lockup. Christine was there waiting for me. She's the one who got Sammy Potts on the case. That guy knows his stuff. I'm going to pass his cards around. Everyone should have the number of a good bail bondsman.

"We're going to Colorado," she said.

"Can I go to sleep first?" I asked. All I wanted was about ten hours of shut-eye in my own bed and then I'd consider all offers.

Then she tells me that she got this message and though she hasn't called back yet she's decided the next step is to go to Colorado and see what happens. She was all excited about her plan, which from the start struck me as something I could see myself doing but I was too trashed to show much enthusiasm. That's when she said, "And of course Jennifer will come with us."

"Oh yeah," is all I could come up with but I was thinking, What's the deal with Christine? Half the time she's trying to get me and Jennifer together and then she gets drunk and puts her head in my lap. And it's not like she was taking a nap down there.

And last month at that Mulholland party, Jennifer gives me this big hug with a lot of grind in it. Then she giggles and says, "Wait, what are we doing? I can't do this." She's asking me, "What are we doing?" I should of said, I'm just standing here watching you introduce yourself to my dick. But she was already onto someone else, giggling with some girl she hasn't seen since St. Barts. So I figure, I'm out of here, but then Christine stops me at the door. I didn't intend it but she got the same introduction. But she acted like it never happened. Okay. Got it.

You just never know with women these days. I don't think they know. And a lot of them see shrinks, which leads me to believe there are a lot of bad fucking shrinks in this town. If you ask me the fucking quality of shrinking has shrunk. But every time I think fuck all that. I got the NBA. I got my music. I got Sarah's great blow jobs. That's all I need. But then Jennifer will show up at the newsstand and what can I say, "there's something in the way she moves."

When I told my boss I needed a couple of days off, he said, "Take them." Flexibility is the new Centerfold policy. I started to explain about Christine and the documentary but my boss couldn't care less about this stuff. "I don't get it," he said, "but do what you have to do." Which made me think. What exactly was I doing? I'd started researching on the Net for Christine and now I was part of this traveling circus. Okay by me. But it's not a situation that lends itself to easy description.

I got to be honest though. I wouldn't go off to Colorado for just anyone. Richard Gault used to be a fucking great songwriter, and I wouldn't mind talking music with the man.

chapter eighteen

I hate flying. Who doesn't? There's nothing about the experience that is anything but aggravating. Even if you've used up all your AmEx Membership Reward points to upgrade to first class, you still have to deal with the airport. Lines. Delays. Bad food. Strangers sitting next to you. Small talk from tired salesmen who have ordered a cocktail before the cabin doors are even closed. No wonder men who own their own planes get so much action. Forget the casting couch. That's for amateurs. More and more Hollywood girls are likely to give it up for privacy and a cushy leather seat on a Gulfstream Five.

Though traveling with my "team" did spare me the small talk from strangers, it did not mitigate the anxiety that always comes when I put my life into the hands of the FAA and their version of security. If I thought about it for too long, I'd have to double up on the Xanax.

Waz sat next to me, calmly reading a book, unfazed by any personal or aerodynamic turbulence.

"I have a question for you," I said. Waz was one of those guys you could throw anything at. You could talk shoes or "string theory" physics with him and he'd give you his complete attention.

He looked up from the page. "That was normal turbulence."

"No, not that. My new rule is unless *you* start to panic, there's nothing to worry about. No. It's something else. You know how some people are attracted to a high-stakes game?"

"Like everyone who comes to Hollywood?"

"Question is, Have you ever known someone who happily walked away from the table? No regrets. No turning back?"

"That's not a question, that's a thesis."

"You know what I mean."

He closed his book, marking his place with a cocktail napkin. "I personally don't know anyone who happily walked away from a high-stakes game while there was still a chance for a win. I do know some who've walked away 'cause they didn't have the nerve to stick it out. And some of them ended up happy." He smiled. "But you're not one of them."

"I could be."

"Retrace your steps. Follow the trail of crumbs out of the forest, Gretel. You haven't made a safe choice in your life. Home is the gambling table."

"That is so not true."

"You like the rush of laying down the bet and wait-ing for the dice to roll. You're hooked on that moment. But the game takes its toll."

He said this lightly, an interesting contrast to the ef-fect it had. I felt like he'd sliced me open and correctly identified the only two modes my system operated on: the "moment" or the "lull."

"Do you think Richard Gault happily walked away from Hollywood? Or did he just disappear? Drop out. Hide out. Get out fast."

"If he's the kind of guy I hope he is, I think he sailed away laughing."

★

SO EVEN WAZ had hope. Waz, who usually came at things from an informed but modulated perspective, had elevated Richard Gault to one of the few who exited laughing. Is this why Waz agreed to do this project? To meet someone who might be able to relate to his own weird personal odyssey. To meet someone who would understand the struggle that comes with spending your nights working on hauntingly beautiful paintings of vacant staircases and spending your days working on big-budget celebrity-driven commercials for Nike and Revlon.

I'd often wondered what it was that Waz was hoping to get out of this excursion. I knew William was look-ing for inspiration. Jennifer was along because she wanted a job title. "I'm associate-producing a documentary" is the line I'd heard her drop a dozen times. I didn't bother to correct her. Truth is, I know producers who've walked away with an Academy Award for contributing less than Jennifer already had. But what did Waz want? Was he on his own private quest for guidance? Early on, for about a second, I wondered if he had a crush on me. But I wasn't really his type. He liked those six-feet-tall Danish models. Only a girl like Jennifer could make a guy forget his type was a six-feet-tall Danish model. And though Waz and Jennifer got along just fine, I don't think she was the reason he was sitting in coach, eating bad food on his way to a town called Silt.

I looked over, across the aisle to where Jennifer was sitting next to William. He had earphones on and was lost in the music. Jennifer was working her way through a stack of newspapers and magazines she'd bought at the airport gift shop.

"It's like this book I'm reading," Waz said. He held it out to me but I didn't take it because at that moment while my focus was still on Jennifer, she began to shake. Nothing epileptic but definitely outside the range of normal even for someone who had recently downed two iced mochas. Her eyes were locked on something she was reading in the *Enquirer*.

"Are you all right?" I asked. She closed the tabloid quickly.

"I can't believe it. I cannot believe it. That fucker."

"What? Who?"

Jennifer buried her head in her hands.

William glanced over with a smile until he realized something was wrong. He yanked off his earphones. "What's the matter?"

Jennifer continued to shake silently. William looked to me for an explanation.

"I don't know. I think it might have something to do with her celebrity boyfriend and that paper."

William picked up the tabloid but Jennifer grabbed it out of his hands. She sat up and I noticed her right eye was slightly twitching.

"I can't believe he would do this and not tell me."

"Do what?" I asked.

"He was seen out with that stupid talentless bitch."

"Which one might that be?"

She hesitated. She might be agitated but she wasn't about to reveal all her secrets. "I just spoke to him last night," she continued. "I can't believe he didn't mention it. DID NOT MENTION IT. He acted like everything with us is great."

"It probably is great," Waz jumped in. "Great for him."

William gently touched Jennifer's face, the spot right alongside the twitching. And amazingly enough, it stopped. Though Jennifer's hands were still far from steady.

I felt bad for her but this was an old song. I've known plenty of girls who've been ambushed by a tabloid story. And yet when you ask them, after their initial outrage, what they're really upset about, they can't really say. It's not as if they were the famous guy's girlfriend. It's not as if they didn't know he had other women in his life and was always on the prowl for a new recruit. What none of them ever said, but I surmised, was that beyond the hurt and the anger was a more debilitating confusion. Did the guy owe them an explanation? In this high-stakes game where everyone knew what they were getting into, where was the line between the right to privacy and manipulation? Like the line between intuition and paranoia, it was getting tougher to find.

"How do you know it's true?" William asked. "You're always saying the tabloids get it all wrong."

"They do get it all wrong but that doesn't mean that even if it isn't true, it couldn't be true."

This was the moment when I was supposed to make Jennifer feel better by reminding her that even if it was true, it might only be true for one dinner. For one night. Just because some tabloid reported it didn't mean it was a "to be continued." The supportive girly thing to say was that the reason he didn't mention it to her was because in his mind it was no big thing. Nothing that changed *his* landscape. But instead, I asked her the question I've always wanted to ask girls like Jennifer who find themselves in these situations:

"This guy, whoever he is, he's a Hollywood bad boy, right?"

"Right."

"And you like that bad-boy thing about him, right?"

"Love it."

"Okay, well, let me remind you, bad boys fuck other women. That's why they're called bad boys. They fuck women they've just met in an elevator. They fuck in elevators. They have affairs with their costars. They go out with several women at the same time. You can't go out with a

Hollywood bad boy and expect him to act like a dentist who lives in the Valley. Because if he ever fulfills your expectations then he wasn't really a bad boy to begin with."

She looked at me, guileless. "Maybe I want to be the one he gives up his bad-boy ways for."

Waz chuckled. I knew what he was thinking. Dream on.

I understood Jennifer's fantasy but I didn't have a lot of patience for it. "I don't think these guys really change—and depending on your point of view, that's the good news."

William was fidgeting with his earphones. A conversation about Jennifer's obsession with taming Mr. Celebrity was not worth missing out on some decent tunes. I could see he was looking for the right moment to exit the discussion.

"Look," I said, "we all know those girls who hook up with a bad boy who's not really a bad boy so they can perpetuate their reputation as the kind of girl who could tame the wild one. But it's all a lie. The guy was never a lion and the girls are no lion tamers. But that's not you. You can handle the real kings of the jungle. You're not out there looking for a fake." I wasn't sure she wasn't and I couldn't believe I had succumbed to animal metaphors, but I knew that saying this would be more effective than a recitation of all the reasons why Mr. Celebrity's latest dalliance was probably doomed.

Jennifer sat up tall, as if in preparation for landing. "You're right," she said. "I'm not one of those girls." She pulled her hair back into a ponytail and took a deep breath. "But he's still an asshole."

★

GRAND JUNCTION has the kind of airport you'd expect from a town that is best known for being the place you fly to when the weather's too bad to land in Aspen. It's passenger-friendly if your idea of friendly is nothing too big, nothing too flashy.

While the guys went off to see about the rent-a-car and Jennifer was off redoing her makeup in the ladies' room, I plopped down on a seat in the lounge, surrounded by everyone's carry-on luggage. Waz's book was on top of his zipped duffel bag. I picked it up, always curious about what he was reading. It was a novel by an author named John Simmons. Set in Boulder, the book opened with a police detective being sent to an upscale neighborhood to investigate a robbery. From the first page, I could tell that the plot of the book was simply a jumping-off point for the detective's investigation into his own life and times. I'm always a sucker for a good opening line and his made me laugh. "I've never considered myself the kind of man who'd be attracted to crazy but there I was engaged to Allyson, a woman I've since come to describe as Sean Young, minus the beauty and talent."

Before I could get any further, Jennifer showed up, considerably calmer now with her makeup perfectly restored. "I think I'm going to call him," she said. "I think I'm going to leave a message on his voice mail."

"No, you're not."

Jennifer was surprised by my emphatic response so I explained. "The Xanax I took is still very much in effect and since Xanax is the perfect pill to take when you want to prevent yourself from making the call you'll later regret, I think we should use my tranquilized state to make the judgment call on your crisis."

"It's not a crisis. That's why I can call him. It's fine. I get it. I figured it out."

She sat down next to me and pulled a tiny tin of ginger and honey gloss out of her pocket and gave her lips a double coat. "The stupid talentless bitch leaked it to the tabloids."

"Don't call," I said.

"Why?"

"Just don't. Wait a day, at least."

"I don't play those games," she replied.

She seemed too calm for a girl who was still in the planning stages of her retaliation.

"You already left the message, didn't you?"

She bit her double-coated glossed lip and then smiled coyly. "I had to."

"What'd you say?"

Jennifer giggled. "I kept it simple. I said, 'I'm mad at you but I miss fucking you. Come home soon, darling.'"

"That's the message you left?"

She giggled again. "He'll love it."

As much as I didn't want to agree, I knew she was probably right. It was the perfect blend of defiant and provocative. A lot of guys loved that stuff, or at least they loved it as long as the sex was hot. And going by Jennifer's renewed levity, she realized she still had the sex card in her deck.

The sound of a pool cue breaking open a new game is one of my favorite sounds and I don't know why. I don't even play pool. Or if I do, I play it badly. That night I spent a lot of time watching Jennifer and Waz duel it out, and when one of them got tired or bored, William filled in. All three knew how to handle a cue and Jennifer knew how to hold a pose while setting up her shot. I think she especially enjoyed flaunting her perfect butt in front of William. Not that every other guy in the place wasn't also checking her out—including R.D.

He was surprised to get the call saying we were in Colorado but immediately encouraged us to make the hour-and-a-half drive to his bar. I was thrilled to have an alternative to my first plan, which was to stick my head in an oven. Nothing like arriving at your road-side motel to a message from Richard Gault saying something came up and he had to leave town. Crushed doesn't begin to describe it.

Waz was practical about it. He turned the camera on and got me looking devastated as I read the message. William thought it funny in a life-sucks kind of way. Jennifer just said, "Fuck him" and "How far are we from Aspen?"

In addition to the lovely sound of the pool balls being knocked around, there were also some pleasingly familiar country-rock tunes coming from the jukebox, which along with R.D.'s reassurances were helping me make it through the night.

"Something did come up with Gault," he said. "He wouldn't just cut out on you that way. Not when you're showing up with your crew."

"Uh . . . well, I didn't mention that part. I just said I wanted to talk to him about my project."

R.D. stepped back and squinted as if trying to refocus on the whole picture. Then after a minute of scrutiny, he smiled. "I like your style."

"It's not confidence, it's fear," I said. "I hate traveling alone."

"With or without your crew, Gault wouldn't cut out. Like I said, something came up."

"What?"

"It was personal."

"And he had to leave town immediately?"

"That's right."

"The 'something's come up' line is shorthand for 'I'm

blowing you off and I don't owe you an explanation.' It's either that or—right now you're looking at the girl with the worst timing in the world."

"You're an either-or kind of person, aren't you?"

He was teasing me and it was working. I was feeling better. I was up to miserable.

"Am I?" I have to admit I was liking the attention, so of course just as I was warming up, the attention strayed.

"But she's not," R.D. added as he watched Jennifer strut around the pool table as she contemplated her next move. "That girl has a lot of colors in her crayon box."

Colors? Is that what the deal was? "What am I? Beige?"

"What you are is honest."

I liked the sound of that until it occurred to me that maybe being honest wasn't all that sexy. In a guy it can be. But in a girl? Seems to me guys are always obsessing over the girls who confuse them and give them a hard time. And if a girl can do all that and provocatively pose while shooting pool then she's going to be a magnet for obsession. Doesn't mean she wasn't also accumulating a little scar tissue as well. Every so often when Jennifer didn't think anyone was watching, she turned off the bubbly personality and that's when you noticed her sad eyes. I guess no girl escapes the wear and tear that comes with falling for Mr. Celebrity.

★

JENNIFER EVENTUALLY enticed R.D. into teaming up with her in a game. They took on Waz and some girl in tight jeans, an even tighter T-shirt, and a cowboy hat. R.D. displayed skills worthy of a professional, though he wasn't showing off. Another point in his favor. Here was a guy who, though clearly the best player, sacrificed his game so everyone could have a good time. Impressive. Is there something about the Rocky Mountain air that breeds kinder men? After I got over my initial devastation I had to admit that the message Richard Gault had left was thoughtful. To begin with it was handwritten. And though not something you'd put under your pillow, it did inspire me to memorize every word.

> *Dear Christine,*
> *Sorry to tell you that something's come up and I have to leave town. It's not my style to cancel at the last minute so I do feel sufficiently guilty about you coming all the way to Silt for nothing. But even if I was here, there's a good chance all you'd get is a meal and a talk with a guy who'd rather just listen. Maybe it'll work out another time.*
>
> > *Best regards,*
> > *Richard Gault*

A polite, to-the-point note but a *handwritten* polite, to-the-point note. Not a typed note. Not a faxed note. Not an e-mail. It was personal. And because I now possessed a signed note from him, I felt like a connection had been established even though there was no guarantee that the proposed talk in the future was anything more than a way to sign off. Forget what the facts added up to, the reality was that my feelings for this stranger were growing along with my fear that I was insane. I was too old to be a groupie and besides, this man wasn't even a star. Plus groupies at least know what their idol looks like. I was infatuated with a phantom. William came up with a photo taken in 1989 but it was a group shot and all I could really tell was that Richard Gault still had his hair and still had a fondness for black T-shirts.

★

AS JENNIFER WALKED around the pool table to set up her next shot, she did a quick detour over to where William and I were standing. She squeezed his arm suggestively and whispered something in his ear. He was still smiling, long after she sashayed away and failed to land the eight ball in the side pocket.

I gave him a light jab. "You can thank me later," I said.

"For what?

"You and Jennifer."

"That's not happening."

"It looks like it could be moving in that direction."

"That's Jennifer. She always makes it look like it could be moving in that direction."

He ordered another beer and glanced over at the couple sitting nearby at a cozy table for two. The guy looked as if he could handle life on the range and the girl looked like she knew how to handle her cowboy. She kept one hand underneath the table and it wasn't because she was trying to sneak a smoke. Every couple of minutes, he'd give her a big deep kiss that made me wet just watching them.

"They make it look simple, don't they?" I said. "It's like watching animals."

"I'm sure it looks simpler than it is," William said.

"Later maybe, they'll be throwing lamps at each other but right now it's pretty basic."

The bartender overheard me and refilled our glasses. "Here's to the basics," he said.

"Go easy here," William said, playfully indicating I could get a little wild. He touched the back of my neck affectionately.

"I can handle a glass of wine," I said. "Just don't let me drink three cosmopolitans. I tend to get friendly and forgetful."

"The perfect date," he joked.

It was the first time that either of us had referred to the night of the accident. I had refrained from bringing it up because an accident isn't the kind of memory you cherish. Besides, it was a little awkward since I couldn't remember whether or not I blew him.

★

WE STAYED at a place outside Aspen. As I slapped down my credit card I decided I didn't even want to begin to add up what this adventure/project was costing me. The plan was to drive back to Silt the next day and do some interviews with locals: a clerk at 7-Eleven, a gas station attendant, anyone who knew and would talk about Richard Gault. I had to get something out of this expensive excursion even if it was footage that would end up on the cutting-room floor.

Jennifer and I shared a room with double beds covered in plaid bedspreads and paintings of horses on the walls. While we both crowded into the bathroom to take off our makeup and moisturize, we fell into the kind of girl talk that is particular to late-night gab sessions. We got close and personal without sharing anything that could be used against us in the morning.

"Is Richard Gault married?" Jennifer asked.

"Was. Once."

"And now?

"I don't know."

"How could you not know? It'd be the first question I would have asked R.D."

"I don't want to know."

"Why?"

"Because I . . ." There was no good answer to that question. Certainly not the truth, which was I was enjoying the reprieve that came from not knowing whether or not he was attached. I liked the fantasy world I'd created and I wasn't ready to give it up for some hard, and probably cold, facts.

"Because Waz and I made a bet," I said, knowing this made no sense.

Jennifer wiped off her mascara. My inept attempt at a response had told Jennifer everything she needed to know. "Oh, okay," she replied, letting me off the hook. She was savvy about these kinds of things. She knew there was no upside in pursuing this unless she had any interest in Richard Gault's availability. And at that moment, she was too obsessed with her rock-star lover to be anything more than curious about a fifty-year-old recluse. So she quickly and effortlessly moved on.

She pulled a tiny jar of very expensive moisturizer out of her makeup bag. "Would you fuck William?" she asked. "I think the two of you have something for each other."

"Would I? I think the question is would you. You're the one he's crazy about."

"Would I fuck William?" She said this as if the idea had never occurred to her. "William's adorable but he's not for me." She turned from the mirror to look at me face-to-face. "I'm going to confess something to you," she said, "even though it makes me sound hideous." She sighed, then grinned, a mixed message that suggested she may be hideous but she was having a good time. "I don't know if I can fuck guys like William anymore. Once you've fucked rock royalty, how do you follow that up? It changes everything." She stated this in a matter-of-fact way as if she were saying that after you've used the two-hundred-dollar-a-jar moisturizing cream you can't go back to Clinique.

I applied a dollop of my sixty-dollar-a-jar cream to my forehead, which was badly in need of Botox injections. "What if he got a record deal?" I said facetiously.

"On a major label?" She considered that for a second before letting out a scream. A terrifying scream that had me looking for a potential rapist outside the window or, at the very least, some scurrying feral critter looking for a way out of this pajama party. But there was nothing of the sort in the room. Nothing at all out of the ordinary except for the look on Jennifer's face as she stared at herself in the full-length mirror that hung lopsided off the back of the door.

"Oh my God, what is that?" She pointed to the inside of her right leg.

"What's what?"

She moved so the light illuminated the spot. "That. That ugly blue thing sticking out of my leg."

"Oh, that." I tried to sound low-key, knowing the same discovery would have me shrieking and in need of all the reassurance I could get. "I think it's a vein. One of those varicose veins."

"How could I have one of those? I'm only twenty-three."

"It could be hereditary. Does your mother have them?" Wrong question. Jennifer slumped on the floor and put her head in her hands. The answer was obviously yes. She just sat there like that, not moving, not speaking.

"You can get it fixed," I said. "They can inject it with something and it goes away."

Slowly she lifted her head. "Permanently?"

"No, but it lasts for a while. Four months. Six months."

She started to shiver as if the temperature in the room had suddenly and severely dropped.

"It's not a big thing," I said. "I know a lot of girls who have this problem."

She took her time responding and when she did her voice quivered. "Doesn't matter," she said. "What matters is that this is the end of something. The end of *not* having to think about stuff like that."

Her simple statement moved me. She was right. This was a turning point. In Hollywood, this is what passes for the end of innocence.

Eventually she got back on her feet and our conversation continued, but I couldn't tell you what was said. It was just babble, an attempt to fill in the time before the Excedrin P.M. kicked in and we called it a night.

Sunday night is my least favorite time of the week. And the fact that this particular Sunday had started at 2 A.M. with the clock being pushed back an hour didn't help my mood. I don't get this daylight saving/standard time thing. And no matter how many people have tried to explain that it has something to do with farmers and the weather, I still don't get it. There are some places my brain just won't go. And then there are other places my brain just won't leave.

For weeks I'd been stuck on a couple of things. I was stuck trying to figure out at what point perseverance becomes counterproductive. Numerous times a day I considered giving up on the idea of trying to do this documentary. I was also stuck in a 24/7 sexual frenzy. It seemed like every minute of the day and night (amazing dreams) I was thinking about sex. I've never been a fan of sexual abstinence but the problem was I'm also not good at casual sex. What is casual sex anyway? For me the whole point of sex is passion. If it's casual, why fucking bother? I guess some girls can be passionate about the sex but casual about the guy. But if I sleep with someone I'm not crazy about, the minute after the orgasm—as opposed to men, who can make this transition in a second—I'm lying there thinking, How fast can I get this guy out of my bed? There's probably a gray area in all this but I'm not good at gray areas unless of course I've had a couple of drinks.

It was possible that the two issues were connected. If my work was going better maybe I wouldn't be so obsessed with sex. Or if my sex life was better maybe the zero velocity of my career wouldn't bother me so much. What had begun as a lull in the summer of '99 had become a dead calm by the autumn of '99.

I selfishly dumped all this on my friend Elizabeth. She'd just gotten back from a location shoot where she'd rewritten yet another action movie. "They made me take all the guns out and put in karate kicks instead." She rolled her eyes. "Sometimes I want to say to these guys, Did you ever consider creating a trend instead of just following one? But then I say to myself, 'This is the business we've chosen.'"

We both laughed, as we always did at our favorite line from *The Godfather: Part Two.*

Elizabeth had shown up unexpectedly and bearing housewarming gifts—flowers, my favorite verbena candles, and lunch. And as always she offered a theory or two while we sat at my kitchen table eating La Scala's famous chopped salad.

"You've gotten too good at living alone," she said. "And because you don't need daily intimacy with some-one—at this point you probably enjoy not having it—you can afford to be selective. And when you can afford to be selective, you set higher standards for the men you'll fuck. You see," she laughed, "if you were a little more fucked-up and codependent you'd be having sex all the time."

"So what are my choices here, sexual satisfaction and codependency or sexual frustration and independence?"

She broke off a piece of bread—just the crust, but added a slab of butter.

"Whatever happened to the guy you brought to my book reading? The cute research guy."

"William."

"Yeah, William."

"I like him a lot, I do. There's something there with us but I don't know what it is exactly. Doesn't matter because he's obsessed with Jennifer. Anyway, he and I are not a good fit."

"Why not?"

I got up to get another bottle of water out of the refrigerator and to work on my answer. "We're not enough for each other, know what I mean?"

"Sure, I do. I went through it all the time until I met Jake. Now I've got a man who's enough for me; the question is am I enough for him?" The second she said it, she laughed. "Obviously not, since he's got two other women in his life." Her laughter was hearty, no scarlet letter "B" for this girl. "You'll figure it out," she said. "You'll find a way to hold out for the 'enough' guy without having to starve yourself sexually."

"If only," I said.

She smiled. "Start a new trend."

★

"WANT TO GET some dinner?" Waz was talking to me from his cordless phone, even though with our windows open and apartments facing each other across the courtyard, we didn't need the hardware.

"Uh . . . sure."

"Where do you want to go?"

I caught a glimpse of myself in the mirror above the fireplace. It would take an hour for me to pull myself together enough to go to a high-profile hangout. "I don't care as long as it's low-key. Maybe something in the neighborhood."

"Italian?"

"Too many carbs in pasta."

He didn't point out other options on the menu. Nor the fact that my weight hadn't changed since he'd met me. What can I say in my defense? I have bad mirrors in my apartment.

"Swingers?" he suggested, knowing I loved diner food.

"Don't think so. I'll never be able to pass up their french fries. Maybe something a little healthier."

"Japanese."

I was about to say I hate sushi when I realized that at a certain point, hating all the options presented could result in eating microwave popcorn, at home alone. "Fine," I said.

Just then, our neighbor, the CAA agent, entered the courtyard. He was carrying a stack of scripts.

"Hey, Jeffrey," Waz and I both said at the same time.

Jeffrey stopped, looked at me, and then turned to Waz. "Oh, stereo, how weird." Then he did something that was beyond weird.

"Here, want a script? Here's one for you," he said as he tossed a script to Waz, and then as if flipping candy into trick-or-treat bags he tossed one to me. "And here's one for you." Then without another word he walked to the entrance of the building and disappeared inside.

Waz and I just looked at each other. A what-the-fuck-was-that-all-about look.

"This is what happens when the clocks get turned back," I said.

"Don't blame it on the clocks," Waz said.

"Better that than to think we're living next door to a wacko."

"Who isn't wacked?" he said. "We're all broken cups."

"Cracked, not broken," I replied.

"We'll see," he laughed.

There was something about his laugh that made me think a little mascara and blush wouldn't hurt.

★

"WOULD YOU LIKE some saki?" the waitress at Katsu asked. We were sitting at a small table in the middle of the restaurant. I'd forgotten that the decor was a little too sparse and white for my taste. Nothing like a Philippe Starck hotel room, but stark enough that the tuna sashimi and the edamame were the brightest colors around.

"Not for me," I said with conviction. I considered saki one of those drinks like ouzo and limoncello, drinks that temporarily separated you from your judgment.

Waz ordered a beer and adjusted his glasses. L.A. Eyeworks. Blue lenses. He then continued the conversation we'd been having on the drive over.

"Your problem," he stated, "is you don't have an ulterior motive."

Waz is one of the few people who can say your problem is this or that, and I don't get offended.

"That's my problem?"

"Lots of women can sleep with men they're not in love with."

"Or in lust with," I jumped in. I didn't want him to get the wrong idea. I wasn't chaste or anything like that.

"Okay, or in lust with, whatever. Point is it's okay to do things for a variety of reasons. It's normal. So what if some women fuck because they've got another plan. Because they want security, cash, a baby, the attention that comes with a celebrity boyfriend. So what."

"Oh please, those girls. Yeah, use his dick as a stepladder to more publicity. That's sexy? Being a media whore is sexy?"

"Calm down, kiddo," he said. "You're in a room filled with them."

I turned around and discovered he was right. One of the town's biggest media whores was present, a television star, notorious for blabbing the details of her sex life with celebrities. The running joke about her was that when she fucked an A-list actor, she had her publicist on the phone before the guy even had a chance to roll off of her. That night her long blond hair was pulled into a topknot and she'd taken a chopstick and stuck it through for decoration.

"I definitely don't want to be a member of that girl's club," I said to Waz. "Not that she would think I even qualify."

"All I'm saying," he said, suddenly sounding very much like John Lennon, "is give it a chance. It's okay to do something you're not passionate about."

Was this a pitch for me going home with him? If it was, it was the most inventive pitch I'd ever heard. Fuck me because doing something you're not dying to do will actually be good for you. Or maybe the idea was that once I did it, I'd be dying to do it again.

It was then that I noticed the waitress had not only brought Waz a beer but had placed a container of saki and a small cup in front of me before disappearing to the kitchen.

"I didn't order this," I said to Waz.

"Send it back."

But I didn't. I poured the cup full and drank it. Why not? I thought. Another one of those questions I should have spent more time considering.

★

I DIDN'T GET DRUNK but there's no way even one small pitcher of saki doesn't have an effect. Though it didn't separate me from my judgment, it altered it enough to make me wonder what the fuck was going on. To begin with, I ordered sushi even though I worried that parasites were hiding out in my California roll. I was living dangerously. More so when I found myself listening to Waz as if he were the Dalai Lama. Everything he said suddenly seemed brilliant. I found his stories about living alone and his "creative process" to be parables worthy of a congregation. For the moment, I ignored his preference for tall blond Danish models. I found myself asking him about his painting. I encouraged him to have a show even though I hadn't seen any of his new work and knew zero about the art business. I think I even offered to buy one of his paintings. I either did or was planning to when the blabbermouth actress stopped at our table on her way out. She was with her publicist. That's another thing about these girls—their best friend is often their publicist.

She stood right in front of Waz. "Hi," she said, with great enthusiasm.

He looked up at her through his tinted glasses. "Uh . . . hi," he said politely.

On second glance she stepped back in horror. "Oh my God. I thought you were someone else. I thought you were Sting." Her disappointment was palpable.

She grabbed her publicist's arm and pulled her away fast. Not wasting another word or moment.

Waz was unfazed by the slight. "That girl takes the refreshing out of refreshingly honest," he said.

★

WE WERE THERE for another hour but I couldn't tell you who else came or left the restaurant. Waz had my undivided attention. He started to remind me of Richard Gault, which is insane because, in spite of my exhaustive research, a clear picture of Richard Gault remianed elusive. So, I guess what was happening was Waz was starting to remind me of who I wanted Richard Gault to be. And that's when it dawned on me that maybe my new trend would have something to do with transferring your affections for one person onto another who, because of certain shared characteristics, acted as proxy for the original object of desire.

I imagined Richard Gault to be a real guy, someone who was physically fit from chopping wood and riding horses, not from obsessive, narcissistic working out. I don't get the appeal of a six-pack of abs. Give me a guy with a bit of a Buddha belly. It tells me that he's too busy taking care of business to spend half his life at the gym.

Obviously it's a different deal for women. In fact I think the woman of the new millennium is someone who should be able to have an orgasm while still sucking in her stomach. Surrender and control all at the same time. Give it up for your man but don't kid yourself that looking good isn't an important part of the mix.

Waz was definitely in good shape. Though he was wearing a jacket over a gray T-shirt, I'd seen his biceps and knew the guy was no slouch. I also know he worked out for health, not vanity.

Waz was also a thinker. So was Richard Gault, based on everything anyone ever said about him. And they were both artists. My intuition told me that Richard Gault had not retired his creativity when he said good-bye to Hollywood.

The clincher was when I dropped my napkin on the floor. When I reached for it, I noticed that Waz had paint on his New Zealand work boots. Not lots of paint. It wasn't like some artists who purposely wear their paint on their sleeve (shoes) to let the world know they're serious. These were just a few dots of color—blue and yellow. A mistake, not an affectation. In every interview, every snippet of conversation I'd ever heard about Richard Gault, that was the common thread—no affectation. Yes! The transference was complete. And who knows, maybe Waz was using me as a proxy for someone else. A tall Danish model? Uh . . . that might be too much of a stretch even for someone with a creative imagination.

I considered calling Elizabeth to tell her I had the beginnings of a new trend and then I realized I was a total moron. This is what actors do all the time. It's called having an affair with your costar while you're shooting the movie. You fall in love with the character but you fuck the actor. If that's what I was doing then I was ready for a one-night shoot. Let this night be the launch and the wrap party all in one.

"Let's get out of here," Waz said.

He didn't mean I'm ready to leave, dinner's over, end of evening. He meant let's go back to my place. "You want to?" he asked.

"Yes," I said.

"Yes?" he asked, surprised.

"Yes," I repeated. Three nods. I'm not sure what they added up to but it wasn't another night in front of the VCR.

★

FROM THE SECOND we turned the corner onto our street, we were in the middle of what could have been a location shoot for a police drama. Two squad cars, a fire truck, and a rescue van were parked in front of our building. Fire hoses ran from the hydrant on the corner right inside our courtyard. A burning smell hung in the air though no flames were visible. Waz pulled into someone's driveway and we both bolted from the car. I pictured his paintings, our documentary footage, and my favorite new brown suede motorcycle pants charred and ruined. We pushed past a throng of neighbors up to the front gate, where a cop stood guard.

Behind him, we could see that what was once our lovely apartment house garden was now blackened and scorched. At least a half dozen firemen were surveying the damage and checking through the rubble for burnt embers.

"Stand over to the side," the cop said. "No one's allowed in."

"We live here," I said.

"Which apartment?"

"101."

He looked at Waz. "You in 101, too?"

Waz kept his gaze on the devastation. "106." Finally, turning to the cop, he asked, "What happened?"

"Your neighbor up in 301 had some kind of breakdown."

"Jeffrey had a breakdown?" I was astonished. It was one thing to think a neighbor was a little nuts; it was another thing for him actually to be nuts.

"Something like that," the cop replied.

"So he decided to torch the place?" Waz asked with a detached sarcasm that reminded me of Kevin Spacey.

"Not the place," the cop corrected. "Though if firemen hadn't gotten here quick, who knows." The cop relaxed his stance. For whatever reason, he was warming up to us. "Your neighbor just decided he wanted to burn a couple of hundred movie scripts and decided to make his own bonfire in your front yard."

Scripts? I couldn't believe it. An agent has a breakdown and decides to take all the scripts in his apartment and set fire to them in the courtyard of his building. Why did I think this was going to end up as a *Vanity Fair* story about young stressed-out Hollywood. And then it occurred to me, Jeffrey would have to be dead to warrant that coverage. Then it hit me.

"Is Jeffrey okay?" I asked, panic building.

"Of course he's not okay," Waz replied. "He just symbolically committed suicide. I don't think he's going to be at the office tomorrow morning making a deal for some client to guest-star on 'Friends.'"

Waz's sarcasm had turned harsh. Unacceptably so, since I wasn't the one who struck the match or drove Jeffrey to do it.

"He's up in 301 with a couple of officers. They're questioning him before taking him in." The cop's tone was even and informative but he now looked at Waz warily.

"Can I get inside? I do live here," Waz reminded him impatiently. Clearly the Dalai Lama had left the building. This was a whole other side of Waz.

The cop stepped out of the way as Waz opened the gate with his key, neglecting to hold it open as I attempted to follow. It was the cop who kept the gate from closing in my face. "People react to things in a lot of ways," he said as he watched Waz disappear into the hallway of the building.

"It's been a strange day," I said. "All the men I know are moody and all the women feel bloated." In another situation the line might have been funny. Not in this one.

★

LATER, after Jeffrey had been led away in handcuffs (appearing thinner than usual, which is to be expected when all the life has been sucked out of you), my phone rang. It was Waz, and as I peered out my window, I saw him standing in front of his, looking my way. He smiled from across the burnt divide.

"Just wanted to say good night." He spoke softly.

"That's sweet," I said, knowing it was his way of apologizing.

For a moment nothing else was said. I finally filled in the blank. "Thanks for dinner."

"We'll do it again."

"Yeah," I agreed. "Soon."

Another pause. This time he wrapped it up. "Good night."

"Yeah, good night, Waz."

I hung up knowing that we wouldn't do it again. Not that way. Oh sure, we'd share a meal again but never one that carried with it the potential of a second act. The Jeffrey incident had killed our momentum. We needed a different kind of night to launch my new trend, which now appeared to be a saki-inspired folly. We needed a night filled with at least a couple of fiery stars, not a landscape of burnt embers.

One of the most seductive things about L.A. is that no matter how dark the night, the day often dawns bright and blue-skied and you get out of bed feeling better even if your circumstances are exactly the same. Or worse. My favorite memory of the earthquake of '94, which hit at approximately 4 A.M., was driving by Swingers just six and a half hours later and seeing people at the sidewalk tables, basking in the sunshine and having a late breakfast. The restaurant had not come through unscathed; certain equipment was out of order and a full menu would not be available for days, but no one seemed to mind. If that meant a beer instead of orange juice and cold cereal instead of an omelet, that was okay. And when an aftershock hit and the windows rattled a little, a few of the more nervous types reached for a cigarette, but that was the extent of the panic.

★

THE DAY AFTER Black Sunday, which is how I referred to the scorching of the courtyard, Jennifer insisted I meet her for an afternoon of lunch and shopping.

We sat outside at Café Med eating salads. Jennifer had made a big deal of "having to have the lentil salad," which was her "favorite thing in the world" and then ate only a few small bites. We got a fair amount of attention from passersby. It was one of the few areas along Sunset that gets heavy people traffic, mostly because of the popular stores in that block and more significantly the Coffee Bean that continued to be a major hangout—even after the incident with the would-be ax murderer.

Jennifer was wearing tight red pants and a black turtleneck. I saw two guys do a double take when she stood up to wave to a friend across the patio. The area between the low rise of her pants and her cropped sweater revealed her sexy navel, made sexier by a thin gold chain below her waist that sparkled in the sunlight. It was impossible for guys to see that and not imagine her wearing that chain and nothing else.

She'd brought along that day's *Hollywood Reporter* to show me a picture of Psycho Girl and her new manager taken at a premiere party. Poor James. He was going to have to pin his Julie Christie fantasies on someone else. I had no interest in the *Reporter*'s party page, but a front-page headline did catch my eye.

"Look at this," I said. "Here's an article about an executive who just got dumped by ABC."

"So?"

"So it says the guy recently inked a multi-year deal with the network leading insiders to believe there would be no restructuring for at least a year." I tossed the paper on the table. "That's insane."

Jennifer looked at me as if I were insane to care about some boring business item. "Do you know this guy?"

"No, but it's insane that a *multi-year* contract in this town means—at best—they might honor it for a year. And no one expects it to be otherwise."

Jennifer picked up the paper, but not to read this headline story. Instead she opened again to the photo of Psycho Girl and scrutinized it as if it were one of herself. The two had been spending a lot of time together but this was approaching *Single White Female* territory.

"I'm worried about her," Jennifer said. She then launched into a detailed description of Psycho Girl's latest drama, which had something to do with not being able to reach her dermatologist who was on vacation in Mexico and not trusting the doctor on call.

"Oh please, I have no patience for this," I said. "That girl is the anti-Robyn."

Jennifer looked stung by this remark but rather than strike back, she did a Jennifer. She took a detour. "Someone else was talking about an anti-Robyn the other day," she said. "Who came up with that phrase? I think it's catching on." She might as well have been talking about a new fashion trend that we were lucky enough to be on to early.

"I don't know who actually came up with it but I know at least five people who claim they did."

The "Robyn" in question was Robyn Wright Penn, one of the few actresses around who was into the work, not the publicity that comes with leading roles. She'd do press when one of her movies came out, but she didn't chase fame—and seemed uninterested in it chasing her. The anti-Robyn was any actress who was the complete opposite. Short on talent, big on self-promotion.

"The anti-Robyn," Jennifer repeated as if committing it to memory for future conversations. But not ones that involved Psycho Girl. Jennifer continued to defend her assiduously.

"But you have to admit it's scary to wake up and have a rash on your leg if you're in the middle of shooting."

"She's doing one scene in a movie for VH1. Besides, you get makeup. You get a body double. You wear pants. It's no big thing."

"What if it spreads to her face?"

I feared Jennifer could do a half hour on this topic so I calmly summed it all up. "Have you ever noticed how some people are addicted to melodrama? Ever notice how every single day, they have some drama going on and it takes precedence over everything? One day they've got a rash and they're frantically trying to get in to see Arnie Klein even though he's booked months in advance. But they just have to see him and no one else. Of course, the next day when you call them to see how the rash is doing, that's no longer the problem. Now it's their agent who's driving them crazy. And when the agent situation gets resolved, it's their housekeeper. Or their accountant. Or someone who was rude to them at the grocery store. And it doesn't matter what else is going on in the world. The Gulf War. Election Day. Armageddon. Nothing is more important than their dramas."

Jennifer didn't argue. Her ability to take a step back continued to fascinate me. More remarkable was the ease with which she could accommodate a new point of view. By not taking a stand, she alienated no one except, of course, those people who were offended by people who refused to take a stand.

"True," she said. She took a deep breath. "Why do you think I spend so much of my time worrying about her?"

"I don't know. Maybe because you don't want to think about your own life?"

The second I said it, I regretted it. It was so cliché. So amateur shrink. I felt even worse when Jennifer welled up with tears. She was not a crier. There was only one thing that could bring her to a public display of vulnerability. Trouble with her rock-star lover. She took another tiny bite of her salad and pushed her plate away.

"You really are upset if you're not eating your favorite salad."

"I never eat more than a few bites," she said, using the sleeve of her turtleneck to wipe away her tears.

"Why not? If it's your favorite."

"That's why not."

Obviously I wasn't getting it but I chalked it up to another one of those things that Jennifer occasionally comes out with that makes sense only in Jenniferland.

"I do this all the time," she explained. "Order food I really love and force myself to just have a few tastes."

"That's so crazy. So spartan. So G. Gordon Liddy."

"Who?" she asked and then dropped it. "I do it because it's important to control your appetites. Can't always give in to what you want at that moment. If you do, you lose."

Even an amateur shrink could figure that one out. It wasn't about food, it was about having the mental toughness to stay on the rock-royalty playing field—when you're not rock royalty yourself. The more I got to know Jennifer, the more I saw what was required of girls who were competing for the handful of eligible celebrities. I used to think it was about being young and looking good. Now I saw it was being young, looking good, and having the discipline and drive of a samurai warrior.

I don't know if she was tempted to take another bite of her salad or was just embarrassed by her tears, but suddenly she threw down cash for the check and said, "Let's go next door. I need to shop."

★

TRACEY ROSS is as much a clubhouse as a store. A clubhouse for Tracey's friends, which includes a lot of the young actresses and girls about town. You can always find something cool to wear there, my favorite being Tracey's collection of T-shirts. A white one with big red letters spelling RODEO GIRL. A sleeveless olive green one with a picture of Iggy Pop. And my all-time favorite, a black one with white lettering that read, "You don't have to lie to get me to fuck you."

Tracey, a tall, thin blonde who bears a resemblance to a young Farrah Fawcett, was on the phone when we walked in. She waved to Jennifer, who made quite an entrance. She was now all energy and bounce with a smile so appealing and exuberant it rivaled Jack Nicholson's. Was it her version of camouflage? If so, it was no surprise that she was copying Jack. He was the celebrity she most wanted to meet. In her obsessive search for the big protective umbrella of security, he was a nuclear defense shield. Even with the camouflage, it wasn't hard to see that Jennifer could use a little protection. She was working hard to keep the lid on the pain that comes with a rock-star romance. What else can a girl in that situation do but flash a smile, grab a few choice items, and head to the dressing rooms.

"What about you?" Tracey asked. "You looking for anything special?"

"I'm looking, hoping I won't find anything special. Lately I'm terrified to open my credit card bills."

Tracey laughed. "We all know that feeling. And yet," she said, "a girl needs to feel good."

"True. If you don't start with that you're not going to get anywhere."

She searched through a stack of T-shirts on a bottom shelf till she found what she was looking for. She tossed it to me. It was a short-sleeved, tiny blue one with a picture of Steve McQueen on it.

"From *Bullitt*," she said.

"One of my favorite movies." The comment was made by a woman who had been looking at some items in Tracey's jewelry case. She wasn't the typical customer. She was older, maybe early fifties. Dressed in plain clothes with a boxy brown linen jacket.

"Mine too," I said. "Who doesn't like *Bullitt*?"

"You should get it," she said. "You should wear it right now."

"Yeah. Well. Maybe."

She continued to stare at me in a way that was beginning to make me uncomfortable. I moved away to check out some shocking-pink G-strings. A moment later the woman followed.

"You're going through a lot of stuff, aren't you?" She handed me her card. Claudia's Psychic Predictions. A phone number and an e-mail address were listed.

"Everyone's going through stuff. We're all having system failures," I joked.

"A work thing isn't going as smoothly as you'd hoped."

That got my attention, though my cynicism was still intact.

"Most work things don't," I said.

"There's something else," she said, with growing seriousness. "There's a man that will be coming into your life. You haven't met him yet but he'll be very important to you. Already I see him coming down the road."

I looked at her with more interest now, though I still considered her just another pseudo psychic grifter working all the single Hollywood girls who are happy to pay for a little false hope. I wasn't immune. After James and I broke up, I'd spent two hundred dollars to see a psychic who told me that in the next two months lots of wonderful things were going to happen to me. Not one did, but at least for the rest of that day, I felt good. It was a two-hundred-dollar antidepressant. I wasn't rich enough to spend two hundred again for a two-hour break from the blues.

"How much do you charge?" I asked.

"Forty dollars for fifteen minutes."

It was probably a complete rip-off but I knew Jennifer would be detained for at least another half hour, and as Tracey said, a girl needs to feel good. So I went for the Steve McQueen T-shirt and the fifteen minutes of false promises.

★

CLAUDIA AND I went next door to the Coffee Bean, settling down with two cups of herbal tea (coffee didn't seem right for a psychic session) at a relatively quiet back corner. The only person within earshot was a guy who was sipping an espresso while hooked up to his Walkman.

Claudia took my hands for a minute, as if reading my palms. I felt like an idiot, and as soon as I politely could, I pulled them away. I stirred honey in my tea while Claudia took a pack of tarot cards out of her bag. She made me shuffle them and spread them out on the table.

"Pick one with your left hand and lay it upright," she said.

I picked a card, hoping it *wouldn't* be the nine of swords, a card that depicts a woman sitting up in bed, head in hands, sobbing her heart out. I couldn't handle a bad omen, even a bogus one. I wanted the Lovers card to turn up. What woman doesn't? But instead I drew the Emperor card.

Claudia smiled. "This man has a lot of power," she said.

"The man coming down the road?" I replied skeptically. Like I was going to fall for another man-coming-down-the-road story.

She then asked me to pick another card and lay it horizontally across the Emperor card. It was the eight of cups.

"You're on a journey," she said.

Oh great. I was so tired of being on a journey and so tired of being told to have patience. These were not good messages.

And the bad news continued as we went through the ten-card reading with me looking for the Lovers card and some immediate gratification, and Claudia gently lecturing me about character and faith. Maybe she wasn't the right lecturer because the more she tried to get me to think spiritually the more I dwelled on my need for some sexual sustenance. And then maybe because you can only preach to people in a language they understand, the gods answered my prayers with a physical manifestation. As if on cue, two hands gripped my shoulders.

"A little tense. What are those cards telling you?" It was William and his fingers were digging into the knots in my upper back and neck.

"Not what I want to hear," I said, as I grabbed his arm and pulled him alongside me.

"Come tell me about it when you're done. I'm sitting over there." He gestured to a table outside. An empty table. He was solo.

"Okay," I said, surprised to find myself excited by the invitation.

After he left, Claudia looked at me and said somberly, "He's not the one."

I looked at her with equal intensity and said, "It doesn't matter."

★

AS I SAT with William and took a bite out of his scone, I thought, Am I his proxy for Jennifer? She'd declined the invitation to join us. I'd gone next door to tell her William and I were having coffee but she was busy on her cell phone, having a quiet drama with her rock star. I understood. If I were in love with and having great sex with a celebrity who was also having great sex and in love with a lot of women who were leaking their stories to the press, I, too, would be having quiet dramas on cell phones. It seems there were lots of teary women speaking softly on cell phones all over Los Angeles. And lots of men whose moods fluctuated between flirtatious and unavailable. At the moment William was definitely in flirtation mode.

"I don't think you're getting enough sex in your life," he said.

"Who is?"

"Lots of people."

"Are you?"

"Not the right kind."

"Not the right kind? What does that mean? Is the right kind new pussy?" It was an old Hollywood joke:

What are the five things a Hollywood man needs to survive? Food, water, oxygen, pussy, and new pussy. An old, old joke.

William smiled, humoring me. "The right kind is . . ." Again his fingers dug into the knots in my neck. "I'd have to show you."

I have no idea why at that moment, on that day, William decided to ratchet up the sex talk, but I wasn't resisting. A girl can only feel good for so long, even when she's wearing her newly purchased Steve McQueen T-shirt. Really feeling good requires at least a little sexual attention.

"I think you could give me a few hints," I said.

"If I thought you could handle it, I would."

He wasn't being serious, which was why I, too, felt comfortable raising the stakes. "I am in the mood to be a little bad. I hear it's antiaging."

"Just a little bad?"

"I can keep up with you, don't worry."

"I don't doubt it. Guess that means I'll see you around midnight tonight. My place."

"Yeah. Count on it." I was kidding, of course. It never occurred to me that this was something I could or should do, until William looked at me the way he usually looked at Jennifer and said, "You have my address?"

★

HE LIVED IN a small house on a narrow road off of Beachwood Canyon. I'd never been there before, which was part of the fun. Unfamiliar territory was the name of the game. I was wearing a black leather trench coat. Underneath it I had on a short skirt, knee-high boots, thigh-high black sheer stockings, and a black sweater. I knew exactly what I was doing. I had a plan and it didn't include me drinking cosmopolitans and then going home feeling fucked and vulnerable.

He'd left the door unlocked as we'd agreed. He was sitting in the living room when I walked in. I didn't check out the room so much as I took it in. It felt like the kind of place someone his age with his history would live in. Nothing fancy, but comfortable. I did notice the fireplace. Couldn't help but notice it. He had a perfect fire going with plenty of wood stacked up to keep the blaze going all night. I know he didn't chop the wood himself, but just having it there and knowing what to do with it gave him a sexy, rugged edge that only made me want to accelerate the action.

"Hi," he said.

"Hi." I pulled a micro-cassette player with headphones attached out of my pocket and handed it to him.

"What's this?"

"I made a tape for you."

"On a micro-cassette?"

"Yep."

"You taped music onto this?" He wasn't complaining, just being a snob when it comes to sound systems.

"I didn't say it was music."

"Then what?"

"It's a bedtime story. One I wrote especially for you." I took off my coat and tossed it on the couch. Small talk was now officially over.

I sat on the edge of his bed, facing him, my skirt hiked up high. He was lying on his back watching me as I whipped off my sweater to reveal a lacy black push-up bra. He made a move to take my hand, pull me close.

"No, no, no," I said. "This is the deal. You just lie back, put on the headphones, and hit play."

He complied, with some reservation, until he heard my voice purring in his ears, telling the only kind of bedtime story I'm really good at. A cross between the *Story of "O"* and something from *Penthouse Variations*. I know how to bring a man along. I know how to seduce him into the mood, build to a climax, and deliver. And while William listened to my tale of lust with the proper stranger, I blew him.

★

MY PLAN had worked beautifully. Elizabeth would have been proud. I'd found my solution. This I could handle. It was passion without confusion, disappointment, or regrets. I got off on giving the best blow job of my life and now I was ready to put on my coat and leave. No penetration meant minimum vulnerability. Maybe that's all I could handle—passionate foreplay with orgasms. Maybe as the twentieth century was winding down, I and a lot of other girls I knew were finding that particular niche a valid alternative to the more conventional road that usually led to us crying into our cell phones. This was a much better system. I felt satisfied and strong. Connected but detached. My mistake was to sit around, talking to William instead of leaving immediately. Within five minutes he was hard again and I wasn't about to go home. The micro-cassette and headphones were tossed on the floor and William took charge. And stayed in charge until I left the next day.

There was one small interruption. Around midnight my cell phone rang. Only three people had my number. My ex-husband. My agent. And Richard Gault. Why any of them would be calling at midnight made no sense. I assumed it was a wrong number. And even if it wasn't, I wasn't about to get out of bed to answer it. Great sex has no competition. Well, almost none.

★

IT WASN'T UNTIL I was on my way home the next afternoon that I checked my messages and discovered that the midnight call was from Richard Gault. Ah, so he's a late-night guy, I thought. I liked that. I liked that he didn't worry about calling someone he'd never met at midnight. And I liked his directness. "I'm back in Colorado. You're welcome to come by."

That brief message brought an abrupt end to my post-sex serenity. The night spent with William had been surprisingly wonderful but it was twelve hours inside a bubble. Richard Gault was about life outside the bubble, which was riskier but more exciting. I didn't know if Richard Gault was actually more exciting or funnier or a better fuck than William. Or even more talented. Some of William's songs were getting damned good. And though Richard Gault had once been a celebrity, it wasn't as if magazine editors were clamoring to get him in their pages anymore. But a small group of loyal fans—including myself—still considered him God, and how can a normal guy like William who works at a newsstand compete with God?

Call it bad values or whatever you want, but bigger than life has a power that's hard to resist. Which is probably why Marilyn, Richard Gault's ex-lover, was still, twenty-five years later, sitting up in her Laurel Canyon house glowing every time she mentioned his name. It's why Jennifer was huddled in the back of Tracey Ross's store on her cell phone, trying to work things out with her incorrigible rock star. The celebrity world offers excitement at a high price: you may never ever be able to appreciate real life again. The only thing that beats bigger than life is being madly, passionately, wildly in love. And how often does that happen? I wasn't in love with William and he wasn't in love with me. Maybe if we could stay inside the bubble we'd fall in love. But Hollywood bursts bubbles and now William and I were exactly where I'd feared we'd end up. In a mess of mixed emotions.

Before I'd checked my messages, I was thinking about how delightful William was and how the word "delightful" was underused and underrated and that I was going to bring it back into use in the twenty-first century. After I checked them my only thought was whether I had enough Skymiles to get a free ticket to Colorado.

Christine was at the Coffee Bean with some crazy lady doing tarot cards. That's how it started. Stuff that had been
going on separately put both of us in the same place at the
right time.

The night before, Jennifer had called. Boyfriend prob-
lems. I met her for a drink. I wasn't looking to be the guy
she calls when she wants to get out of the house. I'm not
filler. But I decided I'd meet up 'cause lately she's been
saying stuff about how maybe we should go away to Palm
Springs for a couple of days. She described this bathing suit
she got in St. Barts and tells me desert sun is an aphro-
disiac. Sounds good but with girls like Jennifer you never
know. You can go to the desert, go out and get blitzed on
martinis, come back to the room you're *sharing*, grab her

and kiss her, and she'll say, "No, no, no. You know I have a boyfriend."

When I got to El Carmen, she was already there sitting at the bar, working one of the bartenders. It was like that old Stones song "Spider and the Fly." Jennifer wasn't "common, flirty, and thirty," but she could weave a web with a smile and a flash of cleavage. She was wearing a V-neck sweater and no bra. Didn't need one. She loved flaunting that. Why shouldn't she?

We were doing tequila shots. It didn't take long for her to start bringing up her celebrity boyfriend. If he even was a boyfriend. She still wouldn't name him but she had no problem telling me some other shit about him and how he wasn't treating her great. I know what that game is. If I put down the guy, she's going to end up defending him. The only move is to flatter her. Tell her how cool and special she is. My rule is make a girl feel special and you've got her. You may or may not get to fuck her but she'll be hooked. She'll need you more than you need her.

And it was working. Between stories about the bad-boy boyfriend, Jennifer starts telling me how much she and I have in common and how she's been tempted and if it wasn't for this other guy. You know. Usual stuff.

As she's talking, she's moving around on the bar stool, crossing her legs, uncrossing them. She's wearing a short skirt so there's a lot of skin showing. And suddenly she moves so that her right leg is spotlighted by one of the wall lamps . . . and that's when I see this thing. At first I can't believe it. I'm thinking, What is that thing on her leg? And I'm almost going to say something and then I realize it's a vein. The kind you see on old people. The kind my mother has. And at that moment I knew I'd never fuck Jennifer 'cause I no longer wanted to fuck her. In one moment, it was all over. I know this sounds fucked-up, but it happens. I wish it didn't but it does.

It happened to me once before when I met the most beautiful girl on a flight from New York to L.A. I swear I thought this was it. The perfect girl until, as we were walking to baggage claim, I saw that she had fat ankles. There are a lot of other things I can live with but there are a couple of things I can't. Fat ankles. A big vein. Can't do it. A flat chest, I can handle. A little extra weight can be sexy. Bad hair? Who cares? But all guys have their no-go zone and this was mine. What's crazy is the more time I spend around Jennifer the more I respect her. She's more interesting than I thought. And she's sweet. She is. It's not an act. But the other stuff was over.

I now had a vacancy on my to-do list and the next day I walked into the Coffee Bean and spotted Christine. She looked different. I've always liked her looks but that day she looked hot. Maybe it was the Steve McQueen T-shirt. Maybe the lesson here is that this whole desire thing is so fucking mercurial. One thing turns you off to a girl you've been after for months and another thing turns you on to a girl you'd never seriously considered before.

And when I went over to say hi to Christine, she grabbed my hand and held on to it. I could do a half hour on the different ways to read how a girl holds on to your hand and what it means. I don't need the tarot to tell me when a girl is looking for the Lover card.

★

SO WE HAD a good time. A great time. I always suspected Christine was one of those girls who loved to get wild sexually 'cause it was the only way to turn off her brain. Smart girls are the best in bed. A friend of mine once said that if you lined up a number of women and you wanted to figure out which one would give the best blow job, go with the IQ. 'Cause if a woman is that smart *and* she's down on her knees, she must really want to be there.

The other thing is that we get along great. An old girlfriend of mine once told me this story about why she married the guy she married. She said she could picture herself sitting next to him in rocking chairs on a front porch somewhere for the next fifty years and they'd never run out of things to say or get tired of being together. I kind of have that feeling about Christine, except when I think "girlfriend," I don't see it. I see myself with a different kind of girl—younger. But I'm going to see what happens. Let's just see.

This trip to Colorado is going to be something, even if it turns out to be nothing, which I just realized is a good line for the new song I'm working on.

How did I get here? That's what I thought all through the flight from L.A. to Grand Junction. There I was sitting between Waz and William—someone I'd contemplated sleeping with and someone I did sleep with—on my way to meet Richard Gault, whom I'd been dreaming about sleeping with even though we'd never met.

Where was Jennifer when I needed her? She was trying to get out of bed. She didn't say that when she called. She said she was a little sick and would take an afternoon flight. My instinct told me she was in a can't-get-out-of-bed depression. When I asked her about her rock-star boyfriend and if he was around she answered sullenly, "I'm not sure."

"I know what you mean," I replied.

"You do?"

I knew she doubted my ability to grasp her predicament. "Yeah, I do. It's like trying to follow a speeding Porsche down the freeway. A Porsche with no brake lights and no turn signals so you have no warning. You never know what's coming next and you can't react fast enough to prevent disaster."

She perked up. "That's right. How do you know that?"

"Because I've followed a few Porsches in my life."

The whistle on her teakettle sounded off. "Hold on a second," she said. I heard her running into the other room to turn off the stove and then run back even faster. "But every once in a while, it's cruise control for miles."

If I didn't have a plane to catch I might have asked what she meant by every once in a while. Once a month? Once a year? How little did this guy have to give to keep Jennifer in his rearview mirror? And what would she do if one day she looked up to find a girl in his passenger seat? I must have been communicating telepathically because she picked up on the general theme. "By the way," she added, "I think we should ask Richard Gault how he ends a relationship. I'm beginning to think that you find out everything about a guy's character by the way he says goodbye."

★

IF JENNIFER had been with us, the flight would have been a lot easier. Four instead of three. Three is a good number only when it's two girls and a guy. The Jules and Jim thing just doesn't work for me. Not that these guys were vying for my attention. Waz was reading another detective novel by John Simmons. He was into these books the way he used to be into Paul Auster novels. Complete focus. Meanwhile William had his earphones on the entire time though he did occasionally touch my leg suggestively. It felt good but it also added to my confusion.

I shut my eyes and tried to nap, but a stewardess's voice over the sound system snapped me out of any reverie.

"Will those passengers in coach who have thrown their trays on the floor pick them up and wait for someone to retrieve them. You wouldn't throw your dishes on the floor at home. Please don't do it on our aircraft."

Whoa, I thought, air travel isn't what it used to be. What is? Sadly, I knew the answer. The whole man/woman thing. That never seemed to change. Insights. Information. Education. Epiphanies. Experience. Add it all up and it still equaled—what? Huh? How? How come? What was that about? And—how did I get here?

★

TEN MINUTES after checking into my room back at the same low-rent roadside inn we'd stayed at before, there was a knock on my door. I opened it to find William, who walked in like I was expecting him. He was drinking a bottle of Beck's.

"Your room's nicer than mine," he said as he sat on the bed and offered me a swig.

"Uh, no. I don't like beer. I have a lot of boy in me but not that much."

He put his bottle down on the table and grabbed me. In a second he was on top, kissing me.

If I let this happen it'll be fine, I thought. It'll be great. Sex with William would be a whole lot better than the nap I was planning on taking. But I could not turn off my brain. What if this? What if that? And then he surprised me. He stopped, rolled off, and lay there for a second, our bodies still touching, legs intertwined.

"I even like the pauses," he said.

Coming from an L.A. guy, who, like myself, was conditioned to feel that immediate gratification wasn't immediate enough, that declaration was almost bigger than an I love you.

"Me too," I said. At that moment I wished things could be simple. I wished I'd never heard of Richard Gault. I wished I didn't live in Hollywood. I wished pop culture didn't exist. I wished magazines were extinct. I wished celebrities, even ones from decades past, had no hold on me. But things weren't simple. And as nice as it was to cuddle up next to William, I knew he wasn't enough for me, and I'd never be enough for him.

★

AND THE SURPRISES continued. Jennifer arrived, early evening, with Psycho Girl. Footsteps in the hallway and Jennifer's giggle had me opening the door before they even knocked. There they were: Psycho Girl with her hands in a fur muff and Jennifer wearing the matching hat. If William had been there, he might have pointed out their matching furs as another example of the symbiotic thing girls get into when they first start becoming friends. It flashed through my mind that James once mentioned that Psycho Girl was an avid supporter of PETA. But then she was once also an avid supporter of James. I was mildly curious about her definition of ethical treatment but it was two against one and, at that moment, these girls were in no mood for definitions. Jennifer's mood had picked up considerably since our morning phone call. Now she had a giddiness often found in girls as they anticipate a big Hollywood party. Something was definitely up.

"You don't mind, do you?" Jennifer asked, referring to Psycho's presence.

I wasn't thrilled. But I only had two choices. Drama or velocity. I'd come too far to let this girl slow me down. "Welcome to Silt," I said.

Psycho Girl looked around the room. "Is that where we are?" She checked her watch and looked at Jennifer. "It's already six."

Jennifer lit a cigarette and then handed it to Psycho, as if the two of them were so in tune, words were unnecessary. After Psycho exhaled, she gave Jennifer a kiss. They were definitely displaying a lesbian vibe. I say "displaying" because I doubted they'd gotten together for real. My intuition told me this was for show. Or as they say in cowboy country, it was all hat and no cattle.

"Where are the guys?" Jennifer asked.

"In their rooms, I guess. Or at the bar. I don't know."

"What's the plan?"

"The only plan is that Richard Gault expects me and Waz at his house at eleven tomorrow. He hasn't agreed to anything though. We're just going to present our case."

"Then what are you here for, Jennifer?" Psycho teased. "To take notes?"

Jennifer laughed. A laugh that was slightly manic.

"She's coming, too," I explained. "I'm bringing the whole crew. I just haven't mentioned that to Richard yet."

"What if he says no?" Psycho asked, as if she were Jennifer's agent negotiating a deal.

"Then we'll shoot Jennifer and William at locations in town, asking the questions we would have asked had we been able to interview Richard."

Jennifer perked up. "You want me on camera?"

"And you, too," I said to Psycho. "If you want," I offered, knowing she'd turn me down.

"I don't think so," she said. "I don't do digital unless it's with a major director." She checked her watch again. "Jennifer, we should leave by seven."

"Where are you going?" I asked.

"You should come with us," Psycho said.

"It's going to be a fun party," Jennifer said as Psycho Girl pulled a vial of coke out of her pocket and handed it to me.

That explained a lot. It explained Jennifer's mood and Psycho's friendlier attitude. Guess she'd switched her drug of choice.

"You just got here and you're invited to a fun party? You move fast."

"Wait till you see how I drive," she said, as she handed me a straw.

★

HAVING A GUY in common is the easiest way for two girls to become fast friends, even if they once were fierce enemies. And though Psycho Girl and I were never fierce rivals over James, we were natural adversaries. Yet in a mere half hour we covered some kiss-and-make-up ground. By six-thirty we were in striking distance of an armistice. Like two countries who don't really trust each other but sign a truce for pragmatic reasons, we, too, were going along with the protocol of being on the same side. It was the protocol that came with partying together. The drugs facilitated the semblance of camaraderie. I'd even confessed my dalliance with William.

"Ice it," she said. That was Psycho Girl's advice. And she offered it standing in the middle of the room, as if she were delivering a lecture from behind an invisible podium.

"It's complicated," I said. "William and I have some kind of connection but . . ."

"There's someone else," Psycho guessed.

"Not exactly." No way was I going to share my Richard Gault fantasy or my theory about God versus the cute newsstand guy.

"I don't know," Jennifer said, "maybe it's all a lot simpler than we think. Like with my rock-star boyfriend."

"Oh come on, Jennifer, you can say who it is." I was teasing. It didn't really matter who it was.

"All I'll say is, he's not married and he never should be."

"Jennifer's right," Psycho Girl said as she stretched

out on the bed as if she owned the place. The dirt on the soles of her Ralph Lauren riding boots left a smudge on the off-white bedspread but she either didn't notice or didn't care. "It is simple. Here's how you handle guys: First you decide whether they're worth the effort. If they are, then you create a need in their life and fill it. It's that simple."

"Sounds a little cold."

"It works," she said.

"What need did you fill with James?" Actually I could think of a half dozen but I wanted to hear her version.

"He's in love with love," she said. "He needed to be reminded of that need and then I got him to think I was the only person who could satisfy it." She flicked a loose eyelash off her cheek. "But then I got bored."

"So what is it that *you* need?" I asked.

"I need a guy who can take me higher," she said. She wasn't talking drugs. Or sex. She was talking a three-picture deal.

"But what I really need right now, at this minute . . ." She paused for a second as she leaned over and rubbed Jennifer's shoulder. I fully expected her to say something provocative and sexual. "I need to get to Aspen." She then grabbed her vial of coke and tossed it into her Gucci bag. "You coming or what?"

★

I WANTED TO. I had been seduced into their party mood and couldn't imagine a quiet evening spent at this roadside inn, eating bad food and watching TV. Jennifer and Psycho Girl went back to Jennifer's room to change their clothes and had given me till seven to make up my mind. It wasn't an easy call. As the director and producer of this documentary, I thought I should set a better example. Running off to Aspen for a party with the girls made the whole project seem more like a hobby than a mission. Another problem was that it was a girls-only proposition. Psycho said she couldn't bring the guys. Another argument for why I should stay. I shouldn't desert the rest of the team. It wasn't considerate. It wasn't respectful. And then there was the William question. What do I do if he shows up at my door at midnight with a beer and a smile? There wasn't enough time to figure all this out, I decided, when Waz turned up.

"Good news," he said. "I just talked to Carl and—"

"Who's Carl?"

"The kid at the front desk. He said if we drive to the next town, there's a bar there with a Sony wide-screen TV and Pay-Per-View."

I guess I didn't look sufficiently excited.

"They've got the fight," Waz exclaimed. "The heavyweight fight that's on in Vegas tonight. Sweetcakes, you're going to lose your honorary guy status if you don't keep up on these things."

"My idea of a good fight would be my therapist and my ex-husband's therapist in the same room, going ten rounds. That would be better than a Tyson match."

"Get over it," Waz said.

"I am over it," I said, "but I think I'll pass and hang with the girls."

He picked up on the plural. "Girls? Who's here?"

"Jennifer brought Psycho with her." I could have said Jennifer brought Giselle. He was curious. That's all. Nothing, not even a supermodel could distract him. That's what an exciting heavyweight fight can do to a guy.

"You think William will care if the girls go out without him?"

"William's the one who's been working Carl. It's a heavyweight fight," he said, dancing around the room. "And that's not even the best part. The first fight on the card is . . ." He rattled off the details the way Jennifer rattled off the names of VIPs at a party. While I listened, I grabbed my leather jacket and dug my favorite sweater out of my suitcase. It was five to seven, and I didn't want to miss my ride.

We traveled to Aspen in style. When she'd arrived at the Grand Junction airport, Psycho Girl had rented a Jeep—the kind that comes equipped with everything you'd need in a blizzard. It didn't matter that it was only late November with no snow in the forecast. By L.A. standards, it was freezing. Which was why we insisted Psycho park as close as possible to our destination, a Victorian-style house just a few minutes from town. Psycho took that to mean on the lawn.

"I like creating my own parking spots," she said as we tumbled out of the car.

"Whose house is this again?" I asked.

"It's Cassandra's," Jennifer replied. "You know Cassandra. Everybody knows Cassandra." Her pace quickened, she couldn't wait to get inside.

Psycho was just the opposite. She slowed down. It was very deliberate, as if it were part of a pre-party ritual. "Players in a prayer huddle before a big game" was the image that came to mind. But this was a huddle of one. When she refocused, she smiled at me and then unexpectedly took off the beautiful midnight-blue cashmere scarf she was wearing and put it around my neck. "You should wear this," she said. "It looks cool on you."

Jennifer was already at the front door when she turned back. "What are you two doing? Are you coming or what?" She might just have been impatient but I think she was also a little jealous.

★

OF COURSE I KNEW who Cassandra was. The daughter of a well-known producer and the stepdaughter of a former TV sex symbol, she grew up a wild child in Beverly Hills, Aspen, and New York. This party was for her thirtieth birthday, and though she'd chosen Aspen instead of one of the coasts to celebrate, her promise of a weekend of nonstop fun attracted plenty of people. Many who would get on a plane for any distraction and would certainly get on a plane if there was nonstop Cristal and a number of other sinful pleasures awaiting them on the other end.

Over the last decade, Cassandra had tried being an actress, writer, music supervisor, and producer. She'd also launched her own PR firm (which lasted six months), was briefly a talent manager, as well as a jewelry designer (one season of beaded bracelets sold to Fred Segal), and was now declaring herself a photographer. She was generally considered to be a good person. A big heart but a little off balance the way a lot of children of Hollywood royalty are when their sense of entitlement mixes with a growing awareness that the castle has been rented, not bought. In Hollywood, when the king is dead, the king is dead.

Though on that night, Cassandra floated through the party like a princess, complete with a velvet gown created for the occasion by an up-and-coming London designer. Problem was, Cassandra is one of those big-boned athletic girls who looks best in jeans, a T-shirt, and no makeup. Velvet gowns, heavy mascara, and bright red lips make her look like a transvestite. As for her beautiful long blond curly hair, it had been given a professional blow-dry to make it stick straight, a style the fashion magazines were raving about but what do fashion magazines know or care about big-boned athletic girls.

★

FROM THE SECOND we walked in, I knew I'd made a mistake. I felt as if I'd crashed a stranger's high school reunion. The room was filled with a large, seemingly tight-knit group which would, no doubt, be polite to outsiders but not particularly interested in them. In situations like this, it helps to arrive with your own posse, but mine quickly disbanded. Jennifer spotted a guy she knew and ran over and gave him a big hug. She hung on to him in a way that made me worry. Public display of desperation. I'd done the same thing myself. In the weeks after James and I split up, I'd exhibited the kind of forced frivolity that comes from having a bruised heart. I knew the signs. But the last thing a girl in that state needs is someone telling her that her bruises are showing.

Across the room, Psycho Girl was so bubbly, her personality seemed more suitable for someone wearing a multi-tiered pink party dress. She was laughing girlishly and talking up the West Coast editor of a weekly entertainment magazine.

I made an effort to mingle—with a minimum of success. Part of the problem was the room was decorated a little too preciously. All those Tiffany lamps and Lalique vases. You don't want to get too tipsy and knock over one of those. I found myself being careful with my words, my actions, and the amount of alcohol I consumed. I did manage to strike up a brief conversation with a good-looking guy who was a chef at a popular Aspen restaurant. He was the one who pointed out that it was an odd gathering because half the people there were die-hard partygoers and the other half were in the program.

I checked his glass. "Is that vodka or water?"

He laughed. "I could never do the AA thing," he said. "I tried it once. I got so boring, *I* wouldn't fuck me."

He made me laugh and he was sexy and attentive. It's not a combination I normally walk away from. But rather than find it flattering, I became depressed. I had Richard Gault on the brain the entire time we talked. If a stranger's flirtatious attention was making me miss a man I'd never even met, I was in trouble. I used the cliché exit line "Got to get a drink" and moved on.

Back in my James era, I used to say it was either him or a convent. It wasn't a healthy way to live and now I was approaching the same myopia, only worse. This time around my choices were a convent, Richard Gault, or maybe another night with William. What a selection. Celibacy. A man who was little more than a figment of my imagination. Or a newsstand guy who though delightful had the bad timing to hook up with me just as I was about to meet God. And yet it beat the hideous dating game. I was reminded of that as I eavesdropped on a conversation between a man in his late thirties and a woman in her early twenties.

"You can't set out to get someone," he said. "That never works."

"You can't? I know a lot of girls who do. They have a book of rules and it seems to work."

"Strategy. Manipulation. No. Doesn't work. I can sense it the second a girl is operating from that place. I can feel it."

The woman seemed to perk up at this news. It was easy to imagine her thinking, Maybe this is a different kind of man. One you don't have to play games with. "So you never get involved with women like that?" she asked.

"I didn't say that," he replied. "If their manipulation taps into one of my weak areas . . ." He stopped and smiled. These were weak areas he was proud of—a weakness for beautiful, manipulative women didn't affect his male ego. "Then, I can't help myself." He grinned. "What guy could?"

She looked at him, hurt, as if she'd been blindsided. "So operating from a game plan doesn't work for a girl unless the guy has a weakness that is compatible with the game she's playing and in that case you can't resist?"

He nodded, pleased with himself.

"So I guess Lady Macbeth in a G-string is your dream girl," she said and walked away. So did I.

Thank God for fireplaces. If I'm alone at a party, I feel much less like a conspicuous outsider if I can hang out in front of a roaring blaze. It's acceptable to stare at a smoldering log as if it were a TV and you were tuned to your favorite show. Or, people can assume the room's a little chilly for your taste and you're just trying to get warm. You tend to fade into the background when you're log gazing and people carry on their conversations as if you weren't there. This was definitely the case with Psycho Girl, who was still doing her best to charm the West Coast editor.

"Everything goes into my work," she said. "Everything. Any guy who's going to be involved with me better know that. I have to be that focused if I'm serious about my career. If a guy can't handle that fact then I can't handle him. If that sounds selfish, so what. I give back to the world by being an artist."

I'd never heard that particular justification for narcissism before. "I'm selfish because my selfishness is good for mankind" was an interesting approach. Horrifying but interesting. Unless, of course, you really are Picasso. Not that any of this interested the editor.

"So who are you dating?" she asked.

Eventually I went looking for Jennifer and when I

couldn't find her, I got concerned. Over the last couple of weeks, I'd watched her struggle to attach to a man who would never attach to her. It ignited a protective instinct in me. Maybe in lieu of having children, my nurturing instincts would now be channeled into playing big sister. Whatever it was, I suddenly had to make sure she was okay. And she wasn't.

I found her outside. The temperature had dropped another ten degrees, and by L.A. standards, it was fucking Antarctica out there. She and I sat on the back steps, shivering as she finished her drink and had a cigarette. Her manic energy had given way to exhaustion and fragility.

"You know what gets me?" she said. "He doesn't even think he ever has to explain anything."

"I know. I know," I replied, though I didn't know, not having ever been involved with a big-time celebrity. "Where's the line between privacy and manipulation?"

"The worst thing though, the very worst thing . . ."

I waited for her to confess to some hideous thing he'd done.

"The worst thing is he's a really great guy."

I couldn't come up with anything to say, nothing to assuage her anguish. So I took off the midnight-blue cashmere scarf and wrapped it around her neck.

★

I WENT BACK into the party and did another hour and a half of log gazing, eavesdropping, and brief conversations, including one with Cassandra.

"Thirty is a great age," she said.

"Yes, it is."

Cassandra used her finger to stir her vodka/cranberry. "My stepmother always said her life began at thirty." She took a big gulp of her drink and then placed her empty glass on the fireplace mantel. "Just happened to be the year she met my dad." She paused and then with a light touch added, "And the year she got her tits done."

Her delivery was flawless. Like a true second-generation company town girl, she knew how to vent and titillate without getting too sloppy.

★

I COULDN'T FIND a clock but I knew it was late. The AA crowd was leaving and the drinkers were now talking to strangers. Jennifer and I were certainly ready to go but I feared Psycho wouldn't cooperate and it was her ride, not ours. We were hostage to her mood.

"I'll find her," I told Jennifer, who looked like she didn't have the energy to do a walk-around. I checked all the party rooms, the bathrooms, and even the upstairs, where I found two guests rolling around on a brass bed, the girl wearing nothing but her underwear and Apres ski boots. But Psycho Girl was nowhere to be found. I wandered down the hallway and into the kitchen, where, to my complete shock I found R.D. sitting at the table eating a piece of pie. He was alone except for Cassandra's housekeeper, who was over by the sink washing some wineglasses while keeping an eye on an old Burt Reynolds movie on the countertop TV.

"Have you been here all night?" I asked R.D.

"About a half hour."

I was thrilled to see him. I suspected I owed him a big thank-you.

"So tomorrow morning?" he said. He pulled a chair over. "Sit down, have some pie."

I took a seat and eyed the apple pie with caramel sauce on it. It was my favorite dessert but being one degree away from the main man put my appetite on hold. "You got Richard to call, didn't you?"

"Yep."

"At midnight. Were you guys smashed?"

"Figured I'd take advantage of the situation," he chuckled. "But," he added soberly, "you know he's not going to do it."

"Don't tell me that. I brought my whole crew."

"I warned him."

I tried to read R.D.'s face to see if he was kidding or not. He washed some of that pie down with a glass of milk, oblivious to my scrutinizing.

"He's not going to throw us all out when we show up, is he?"

"Hell, no. He'll probably invite you to stay for lunch. He'll grill one of his steaks. From one of his cattle. He likes to show off a little."

"His cattle?"

He laughed. "I'm not going to say anything more."

And I didn't push it. Time for a topic change. "What are you doing at this party anyway? In your stepping-out clothes." This time he was wearing a burgundy-colored shirt with silver buttons.

"Cassandra's practically my godchild."

"Where's your wife?"

"She hates these kinds of things."

"She's not worried about you out at parties with all these pretty girls around?"

"If she is, she doesn't show it."

"Damn. Why can't I learn how to do that?"

Just then, a young girl, maybe seventeen, entered the room. Fresh-faced with Botticelli hair and a tiny gold nose ring.

"Can I have a taste?" She leaned over R.D.'s shoulder, breaking a bite of crust off his pie.

He broke into a big grin. "You're one of those girls, the ones who just eat the crust."

"That's me," she said, as she popped the piece into her mouth and then reached for another bite.

"Hey." He playfully slapped her hand away. Clearly, he would have given her the beautiful burgundy shirt off his back—or anything else she needed.

"I'm going to get all big and fat now that I can't do drugs anymore." She said this lightheartedly because she didn't have to worry. She was all of a hundred pounds—maximum.

She turned to me." Hi, I'm Isabella Gault. I just got out of rehab. R.D.'s making sure I don't get into trouble." She said this as if part of her therapy called for making declarative sentences to strangers.

"I have spies everywhere," R.D. teased. "Remember that."

She gave him a kiss on the cheek, broke off another bit of piecrust, and headed back to the party.

"She actually *is* my godchild," he explained.

"So God has a fucked-up teenage daughter who just got out of rehab?" It wasn't what I expected.

"God?" R.D. raised his eyebrows. "Slow down," he said.

I knew what he meant but I raced right over those speed bumps. I didn't even stop to ask the question that logically followed. I didn't ask if he was married. It would fuck with the fantasy and I'm too much of a Hollywood girl not to understand that you can get a lot of mileage out of suspension of disbelief.

★

I ENDED UP getting R.D. more pie and listening to more of his stories about L.A. in the good old seventies. I'd forgotten about making an early exit until Psycho Girl strolled into the kitchen as if she were looking for someone in particular. My guess was it was either a guy or the West Coast editor. Not finding them, she rested her elbows on the table and peered at R.D. "You were at Frankie's party."

"Good memory," he replied.

"This is R.D. He's a friend of Richard Gault's," I explained. "He was just telling me about the time Richard was seeing Julie Christie."

Psycho Girl perked up. "This Richard Gault guy went out with Julie Christie?"

"Julie was crazy about him," R.D. said.

"She was? Tell me more. Tell me everything. She's one of my role models. I like the way she shot that guy in *Doctor Zhivago*. Bam!" Psycho Girl laughed uproariously. It was the most fun I'd ever seen her have. The girl knew how to get attention. Cassandra's housekeeper switched her focus from Burt over to the girl with the big laugh. But the good times didn't roll for long. The kitchen door swung open again. In strolled a striking woman, looking for a clean glass. She helped herself to one of the wine goblets but filled it with water. Though older than most of the other women at the party, her thick auburn hair and deep green eyes earned her second looks. If not third.

Psycho yanked me close to whisper something in my ear.

"What?" I couldn't understand what she was saying.

She looked over at R.D. "Excuse us, this is a girl-thing," she said and this time spoke up loud enough to be heard across the room. "That woman over there hates me."

"She does?" If she did, she wasn't showing it. She was minding her own business while slowly drinking her water. "Why does she hate you?"

"Because of Joey, a guy who's here at the party. We go out sometimes. She's always after him and he's so not into her. Hello? She's forty. Why would he be?"

It was not the thing to say to a woman of thirty-five, but it wasn't my job to teach her manners.

The older woman looked over at us, nonplussed by Psycho's slurs. She carefully rinsed her own glass and put it on the drying rack.

"Thanks," the housekeeper said.

Suddenly it got very quiet except for the sound of the woman's cowboy boots on the wooden floor as she walked toward the door. The silence was oppressive but I preferred it to any kind of confrontation. I thought we were safe until the woman passed a few feet in front of us. That's when Psycho Girl snapped, "He's not into you. Why don't you get it?"

The woman stopped. She calmly faced Psycho, her hands on her hips. She had twenty pounds and three inches on her and you got the feeling she could level Psycho with even a mediocre punch. Instead, she laughed. "He isn't? You better tell that to his dick." With that, she turned and left the room. The kitchen door swung back and forth a couple of times before coming to a stop. From outside could be heard the sound of a truck spinning its tires in a rut. From the living room came a shriek and giggles as if someone had delivered a punch line to a pleased audience.

Without warning, Psycho Girl sprung out of her chair and dashed off. I followed, mostly because I thought she was capable of driving off and leaving Jennifer and me stranded.

By the time I caught up with her, she was in the hallway near the front door. Along the way she'd grabbed someone's full glass of champagne and was now approaching a young man who turned out to be Joey. Without a moment of hesitation, she threw the contents of the glass in his face and ran out of the house.

It happened so fast, it took a moment for people to react, but I remember seeing Cassandra standing there aghast while a couple of guests offered Joey cocktail napkins to soak up the bubbly. I knew I needed to chase after Psycho but the sight of Cassandra captivated me.

There she was, the birthday girl, losing control of her own party. She watched as Joey became the center of attention. Again, I took note of her blown-out hair, which probably took at least an hour to get as straight as Jennifer Aniston's. This is what I thought. Poor Cassandra. All blown out and no one to blow. I could relate.

★

ON THE DRIVE BACK, Jennifer was quiet and in no mood for conversation. I was exhausted but wouldn't think of dozing off because with Psycho at the wheel we could end up in a ditch or dead or at the Denver airport. I also have to admit, I really wanted the answer to the key question of the night. "Why did you do that?"

"He'll be calling me ten times a day now," Psycho said. "They all love a stiletto on their chest from time to time."

She amazed me. I had to remind myself she was only twenty-two. That was quite young to be so hard. Even if it was all an act.

"Where did you get this attitude?" I asked. "You're so tough."

"You should meet my mother," she said. A tear rolled down her cheek. She let it roll. And then another. It moved me but I had to consider that she was an actress. Was it real? Was she just milking the emotion so she could access it for an upcoming casting call? While I debated this issue, she reached up and turned the rearview mirror in her direction. And then with one eye on the road and one eye in the mirror, she watched herself cry.

When big sky country gets gray, it gets cobalt. We all piled into Psycho Girl's Jeep for the short ride to Richard Gault's Spring Creek Ranch. No one was in a good mood. The heavyweight fight had been stopped in the second round on a judgment call that showed little judgment. For that reason or a dozen others, William had not shown up at my door in the middle of the night and had barely said a word to me all morning. He sat up front and fidgeted with the radio, trying to find a station that wasn't country or easy listening. Jennifer sulked in the backseat, doing her best to climb out of the dark hole that had gotten even darker after she'd called her rock-star ex-boyfriend at 2 A.M. He said he'd call her right back and never did. Waz seemed increasingly bored by the whole Colorado excursion. Psycho Girl had on dark glasses, which made me consider questioning her ability to drive, seeing as the sky was dark enough. But I said nothing. My thought was just get us to the ranch, get me face-to-face with Richard Gault, and from that point on whatever happens I can live with.

★

AS WE PASSED beneath the arched sign for the ranch everyone's depression seemed to lift a little. No matter what had gone on before, I think we all understood that this was a new page.

As we headed down the quarter-mile road that led to the main house, passing over a tiny bridge that could have been built a little sturdier, I gazed out at the magnificent expanse of land. In the distance was a vision—a beautiful woman, on horseback, her blond hair flowing in the wind. She was gone in a flash, heading in the opposite direction, but it was now impossible to ignore what I'd always suspected.

"I guess God has a twentysomething gorgeous blond girlfriend," I said.

"Wife, not girlfriend," William corrected with some noticeable hostility.

Suspension of disbelief was now no longer an option. Thank you, William, and fuck you, William. I now understood why the messenger is such a high-risk job.

A minute later, we pulled up in front of a two-story white house with a huge front porch. As we poured out of the Jeep, the front door opened. It was him. And as I got closer, I saw that he was everything I'd hoped he would be. He was tall, dark, and still handsome. His face, which had once been devastatingly beautiful, had aged honestly. Though lined, weathered by Rocky Mountain winters, his eyes were bright and alive and his smile dispelled any fear that he'd lost his spirit. He was dressed in the standard Colorado uniform: jeans and a flannel shirt and, just standing there, conveyed a sexiness that suggested he loved women and knew what women loved. There he was. My version of the perfect man. Problem was, in that first moment of contact, when we shook hands warmly and gazed into each other's eyes—there was absolutely nothing there. No juice. No hookup. No electricity.

★

WE HUNG OUT in the kitchen. Awkwardly at first. Lunch was offered even though it was only eleven-thirty in the morning.

"We get up early around here," Richard said.

Waz spoke up first. "I'll take some coffee."

"Got an ashtray?" Psycho Girl asked.

I slid one that was on my end of the table down toward her.

"Got a match?" Her gaze locked steadily on Richard.

He pulled a Zippo out of his pocket and lit her cigarette.

It worked. She had his full attention until Jennifer squealed. A big chocolate Labrador retriever had raced into the room and Jennifer was hugging it and talking to it as if she expected it to answer.

"That's Waldo," Richard said.

"Waldo. Cool name," William said. And it wasn't until he'd spoken that I remembered he was even there. Oh no, I thought, my options were being eliminated with a one-two punch. No Richard Gault. No William. I was on the fast track to a convent.

Shell-shocked by my disappointment that God and I were not an item made in heaven, I said very little and observed even less. I was vaguely aware of Psycho Girl conspiratorially whispering something to William and made note that Jennifer was uncharacteristically not trying to bond with the most important person in the room. Maybe this anticlimax is a good thing, I decided. Probably better for the work. I consoled myself by imagining the chaos that would ensue if Richard Gault and I did have a lust link. Pursuing a married man is a major taboo. If you cross that line, you become one of "those" women. No one wants to be perceived as one of "those" women even if they are exactly and precisely one of "those" women. Even the most predatory women proclaim themselves to be the type that "would never go after a married man." But I don't know many women who, on meeting a man who is a door into a whole new exciting life, don't have a moral dilemma. And since in Hollywood being consumed with a moral dilemma is considered a sign of aging, not maturity, most women chuck the debate and step over the threshold, on the condition that it be kept secret.

I'd been the victim of such a deal. When my best friend Remy fucked my husband, she insisted on secrecy until her desire for drama exceeded her need for privacy. Had I been tempted by Richard Gault, would I have fared any better than Remy? Would I have justified this indiscretion the way she did, claiming the marriage was in trouble to begin with? There is no faster exit off the guilt highway. But I was spared that test even though I could appreciate this extraordinary man who was half artist, half cowboy, and not a bad chef.

He'd made the soup himself and it was damned good. The homemade bread had been baked by his wife.

"What's her name?" I asked.

"Lucy. She'll be back soon so you'll meet her."

My intuition told me he had a pretty good marriage. Maybe even great. It was the way he mentioned her name. I got the feeling he enjoyed saying "Lucy." Adored saying "my wife." But that's all. He didn't describe any kind of domestic bliss. He didn't extol the benefits of marriage. I'm always suspicious of men who try to sell you on their happy home life because they're often the very guys who are trying to fuck Elizabeth Hurley.

I was slowly picking myself up off the floor, gearing up to make my pitch for why Richard Gault should let me turn on the camera, when he did something that caught everyone by surprise, more so because it was done in such an offhanded manner.

In the middle of lunch, Richard sprung out of his seat, went to the foot of the stairs, and called out the name of a houseguest who had been ensconced upstairs. And then bellowed, "You coming down?"

The name alone didn't trip off any alarms. There are

lots of people with the same first name. But the voice that answered definitely woke us all up.

"Yeah, Richie," the guest replied good-naturedly. "Keep it warm, I'll be down after I finish up this call."

It was a voice I'd heard in countless movies. Though only thirty-eight, this actor had already become an integral part of the culture. So many of his roles had been in movies that served as flash points for issues that defined his (my) generation. He was also a guy who did everything he could to stay out of the spotlight. And because of that, he deserved his privacy. Doesn't mean he wasn't occasionally spotted at Da Silvano in NYC or Les Deux Cafes in L.A. Doesn't mean he didn't have to do the obligatory magazine interview when one of his movies came out, but even when he was public, he kept his personal life extremely personal. I knew he'd been married once, a decade ago to his high school sweetheart, and had a son. He'd grown up a Southern California surfer boy, but somehow along the way he'd acquired the style of a young Jean-Paul Belmondo. It was easy to imagine him with a Gauloises dangling out of his mouth. There was also something a little dangerous about him. I'd seen him once at a restaurant, passed by him at the bar. He had a look about him that made me think, I can imagine talking to this guy and not knowing whether he wants to slap me or kiss me. He was also known for being a bit of a tortured soul. He was on a search for authenticity. Made sense he and Richard Gault were buddies.

No one wanted to say, *Do you know who that is?*— which is what we were all thinking. Not a word was uttered until Richard rejoined us at the table.

"You know him, don't you?" He said this nonchalantly, as if it were no big deal to have a movie star in
your house.

"I've seen him around," I said.

"Read about him," William said.

"Once saw him standing in line to get a hot dog at
Pink's," Waz said.

"He's friends with my ex-boyfriend," Jennifer said.

The only one who remained silent was Psycho Girl,
who looked stricken.

"You okay?" I asked.

"I have a headache," she stated. "I'm going for a walk."

"Want some aspirin?" I said. I was the aspirin queen.
Especially when traveling. "Excedrin. Aspirin-free Excedrin. Bayer. Tylenol. Extra Strength Tylenol. Aleve."

"No thanks," she said. Quickly she got up, buttoned
her coat, and made an even faster exit than she did at
Cassandra's party.

"What's that about?" Waz asked.

William watched her through the window. "You think
someone should go with her?" Was he being chivalrous
or was he smitten? I think Jennifer was wondering the
same thing.

"She'll be fine," Richard said. "As long as she doesn't
get too close to Lucifer."

And that's when I remembered that R.D. had mentioned the Lucifer thing. Was it Lucifer as in the Devil?
Was there a dark side yet to emerge in this rural won-
derland?

"Who's Lucifer?" Jennifer asked.

Richard grinned mischievously. "Lucifer is our bull."

★

EVENTUALLY, there was no way to delay it. It was time for me to state my case. I silently gave myself the pep talk Elizabeth would have given me: *Trust you know what you're doing. Know where you're going. And always remember that your brain is your second pussy. Seduce him with your intelligence.* She and I both believed that good storytelling required a certain amount of seduction even if it's only seducing the listener into your world. Which reminded me. I pulled a copy of her book out of my bag and offered it to Richard.

"A present for you," I said. "My best friend, Elizabeth West, wrote it. I thought you might find it interesting."

He took the book and held it as if it were a treasure.

"Did you know that I . . . ?" He stopped. "Maybe we'll get into that later." He sat back and waited for me to dazzle him.

I started by talking about the lull of '99. "No wonder everyone I know is in a slump," I said. "No one's calling it like it is. We have all these people living off the soft lie."

"The soft lie? Did you just come up with that?" Waz said.

"You know what I mean, those lies that have just enough truth in them so they seem legitimate. It's like when you buy something that's cotton blend. What does that mean? Fifty-one percent cotton and forty-nine percent everything but? You ask the salesperson, 'Is this cotton?' and they shake their head yes and then say cotton blend. As if the two are the same."

Richard Gault smiled. "Soft lie, cotton blend. I get it. Okay. Go ahead."

"So, I thought it might be interesting to track down someone who was known for calling it like it is to see if he's still saying it like it is."

"If he's cotton in a world of cotton blends," Jennifer added as she moved into the seat next to William that Psycho Girl had vacated.

It was turning into a cozy gathering. Just the five of us. The sky had grown considerably darker since we arrived, making our corner of the warm and homey kitchen even more inviting.

"Telling people what is or isn't, is not a job I want," Richard replied.

"What if we just asked you your thoughts on certain subjects? I'm not trying to turn you into a guru or anything."

"Ask what you want. Right here. But I'm not interested in being the subject of a documentary."

His tone, though sympathetic, was definite. As I scrambled to find some fallback position, William took him up on his offer.

"Do you think rock and roll has lost its relevance? Back in your day, it stood for something."

Richard reached for the red wine on the table, poured some in his empty water glass, then passed the bottle to me. I placed it on the table, within everyone's reach, but there were no takers.

"Shit, if we're going to start talking about my day . . ." He took a sip. "I'll tell you this. I'll tell you when rock and roll lost a lot of its meaning for me. It was about thirty years ago and a band from London had come over to promote their record. Their whole thing was rebellion. Fuck you. I'll piss where I want. That's what they advertised. They arrived on a Thursday night. Their record company put them up at the Beverly Hills Hotel. By Sunday they'd already gotten so comfortable with room service and champagne and eggs Benedict with hollandaise sauce, specially made with each order, that they weren't ever going to go back to pissing wherever they wanted. It only took three days for them to lose the best thing they had going."

William thought about that for a second. "Who the fuck would give it up for hollandaise sauce?"

Jennifer laughed like it was the funniest thing she'd ever heard.

"I got a question," Waz said. "What's the deal with the whole Bonanza thing?"

Richard laughed. "I don't know, I ask myself that every time I'm up at dawn mending fences."

"Are you trying to torture me?" I said. "This is exactly the stuff I'd love to have in this documentary." But I didn't look tortured. I was enjoying every minute of it even if it turned out to be the end of my road.

"My question next," Jennifer said. "How do you say goodbye to a woman when you break up with her?"

She'd moved even closer to William and was being more attentive to him than she'd been in a while. William didn't seem all that thrilled. He kept looking out the window at the road.

"This is not an area I ever had a lot of good sense in," Richard replied. "Sorry to disappoint you."

Jennifer persisted. "I'm not asking if you do it well. Who does? I'm just curious how you do it."

"Like most men, badly. I guess 'cause I'm afraid if I tell the truth she'll stop loving me."

"Won't she stop loving you anyway?"

"You would think so, but that hasn't been my experience."

"Why do you want them to love you if you're not into them anymore?" I asked.

"Who voluntarily gives up love or power?" he said. And that's when the rains began.

★

IT RAINED HARD. An early snowstorm would at least have been beautiful and put everyone who was hoping for a good ski season in a better mood. The appearance of the movie star might have brightened things up but he had yet to come downstairs. "That must be some call he's on," Jennifer said. Richard just nodded and kept the soup hot. For an hour the rain pounded the roof relentlessly. I started to worry about Psycho Girl out there somewhere in the storm. William was about to go looking for her when the phone rang. It was the foreman calling from his house, which was only two hundred yards up the road. William was at the door when Richard took the call in the kitchen and signaled to him to hold on. We all listened attentively to his end of the phone call.

"Good. I'm glad. Why not? Don't tell me that. What can be done? Fuck. How long once it stops? Okay. Nothing we can do about it now."

When he hung up, we looked to him for a translation.

"Part of our bridge washed out. Your friend is fine, she's up at my foreman's house. You might as well make yourself comfortable. No one's going anywhere till the storm lets up and we can get that fixed."

There were a dozen questions I wanted to ask. "What if it doesn't let up till it's dark? What if it rains till morning? Are we spending the night? Where? How? How was Lucy going to get back? Was Psycho Girl on her way over? And what would we do about dinner?

The movie star suddenly made his appearance with the genius timing of a professional. Smiling. "Anyone interested in a weather report?"

★

MOVIE STARS do come with their own inner wattage. The downside is that they can make everyone else hyper-conscious. It was impossible for me not to be aware of him and what he was doing, what he said, who he responded to—or didn't. I know I lost IQ points trying to impress him. I found myself saying things like "wow," "super," and "beat." As well as a couple of phrases I'd picked up from some South Boston felons—"ace kool," "benzo," and "boned out." What was I thinking?

Richard, of course, was unfazed. He went about his day and his chores as if he didn't have five strangers and a celebrity in his house. Yes, five. Psycho Girl had returned. She spent the remainder of the afternoon quietly

talking to William when she wasn't on the phone screaming, trying to get the National Guard (only a slight ex-
aggeration) to get her the fuck out of there. The rest of
us read, talked, and played some pool. Richard had a
table set up in a spare room and the movie star and Waz
played a few games. I was too insecure to bring my amateur talents to the table and Jennifer was too manic to
do anything other than continually check her voice mail
to see if her rock star had called back. I welcomed a task.
Any task. And since Lucy couldn't get back and was
staying with friends in town, I was happy to volunteer
my services in the kitchen.

Dinner was, indeed, steaks from Richard's own cattle, though he wanted us to understand that having a
hundred head of cattle does not make one a rancher. Jennifer threw together a salad that was as good as anything
at The Ivy. I contributed the mashed potatoes, which
Jennifer confessed was her favorite food—so therefore
only allowed herself a bite. Psycho Girl remained aloof,
at times conferring with William as if he were her con-
sigliere. I really didn't get it. I would have guessed she'd
be loving every second of her proximity to the movie
star and a secret celebrity like Richard Gault. But she
made no move in their direction, especially not the
movie star's, even when he asked her if she wanted a
glass of champagne. Richard had decided that a rain-
storm was a good reason to break out the good stuff.
One glass of that stuff and things started getting interesting. The movie star talked about how he'd been
spending too much time on the phone, trying to finish

up some L.A. business. "Entitlement, paranoia, and stupidity. The combination I hate the most."

That comment inspired a conversation about combinations we all hated. Waz said it was polka dots and red hair. "Redheaded women should not wear polka dots," he said. "It's like wearing too many bows."

William said he hated people with expensive seats at the Staples Center who didn't have a fucking clue what the game of basketball was all about. I think he was surprised when Richard disagreed.

"I used to think that a real fan should know the game but I've got to tell you, lately I think it's mainly about enjoying it on whatever level you can. I've been watching the Clippers games and there's something about those fans. Cheap seats. Floor seats. Doesn't matter. It's about the level of your involvement. These Clipper fans love their team. I don't know if they know the game or not but to be devoted to the Clippers in Laker territory is something. Or maybe I've got a soft spot for underdogs and their underdog fans."

Jennifer said the combination she hated most was rich L.A. girls who hired spiritual advisors.

I wanted to come up with something smart to make up for the preteen street lingo I'd been mouthing earlier, so I used the spiritual advisor mention to get into my theory of alchemy. "I think you can spend a lot of money on these things but what it comes down to is you've got to learn how to take any experience, even a bad one, and turn it into something useful. Lead into gold."

The movie star smiled. For a second I thought he was intrigued. "You know I've done a little reading on this," he said. "This lead-into-gold business you're talking about?"

I nodded, reasonably sure he was about to back me up until, with the same smooth delivery he'd used playing so many wild men on screen, he added, "It takes about thirty years."

"It does?"

"It does."

That shut me up as he turned to Psycho. "What about you? Any spiritual philosophies? Any combinations of things you don't like?"

She didn't look as if she'd even heard him until she suddenly leaned forward. "Yeah. Okay. Here's a combination I hate: PMS, a monsoon, and a four-wheel-drive Jeep that doesn't come equipped with pontoons."

I had to give her points for that one.

★

AFTER DINNER, we sat in the living room with the fire blazing. Everyone looked beautiful. The men looked rugged and the women looked creamy. If I could package that lighting I could sell it to Ralph Lauren for millions.

Waldo, the dog, lay on the floor either at Richard's feet or at Jennifer's. A video of Peter Sellers as the Pink Panther played on the VCR, but my attention wavered, more so when William left the room and then, moments later, Jennifer followed.

I let a few minutes pass before I got up and wandered out to the kitchen. No sign of them. But there was something outside the window that startled me. It was a deer feeding off pieces of bread that had obviously been left there by Richard. I'm not a pet person. I'm only good at unconditional love when it comes to loving guys who are destined to break my heart. But a pet deer was a whole other thing. And then a crash startled me even more and sent the deer running.

I turned toward the pantry and saw a couple of cans had fallen off the shelf. When I went to pick them up I realized I was not alone. William and Jennifer were having a private talk in the back corner of the storage area.

"Sorry," I said as if I were trespassing. I put the cans back in their place. I noticed Jennifer had one hand slipped inside the waist of William's jeans. It didn't appear as if he were resisting or encouraging.

"I was looking for a beer," he announced.

"Try the refrigerator," I replied.

Jennifer pulled her hand out of his pants. "He was about to but I waylaid him." And then she giggled. "Waylaid. What a fucking funny word that is."

William grabbed himself a Coors and went back into the living room. Jennifer's giggle died with his departure. In its place was a remorse she rarely displayed.

"I'm sorry. I know you have a thing for him, but—"

I cut her off. "Don't worry about it. I *had* a thing for him. It's gone. It wasn't something I planned on. Didn't plan on getting it, didn't plan on losing it."

"Whatever. I know I shouldn't be grabbing his dick but I couldn't let *her* get away with it—without a fight."

"Her?"

"Psycho Girl." It was the first time Jennifer had ever referred to her that way.

"I was just playing," she said. "She'll fuck him for real."

"I don't know about that. I don't think she's that into sex." I didn't add that I wasn't so sure Jennifer was just playing.

"She's into it, her way. She doesn't mind lying there and letting you do her, but that's all."

Jennifer sounded as if she were talking from experience but I didn't bother with a pop quiz.

"Now what are *you* going to do? You grab a guy's dick, he's got the right to expect you to fuck him."

Jennifer leaned against the wall, defeated. "I'm going to tell him the truth. I can't fuck him, or anybody. I'm in love with my rock star except he's not mine. What am I going to do? Where did Jennifer go?" she asked. "Look at me. I'm marooned with a movie star and I don't even care. Me. Jennifer. I guess that means I'm in love. If that's not love, what is? And if it is love, I hate it."

"We're in great shape, the two of us," I said. "Might as well just take a vow of chastity right now and get it over with." I figured commiserating was the best Band-Aid available.

"I don't think I'm going to fuck anyone again. Ever." She paused. "Not for another month at least." She tried to giggle at this attempt at levity but it got caught in her throat and she sounded like a kitten choking.

I suspected I was hearing a lot of soft lies, but you

can't let a kitten choke even if they're choking on hard lies. "You know what I respect about you?" I said. "I respect that you never told anyone who he is. Most girls would be trading on a rock star's name all over town."

She started to cry. "I really love him and I thought I could hold on to him longer this way."

I gave her a hug, thinking life is so strange. Here I am comforting a girl who, seconds ago, was coming on to a guy she thought I was in lust with. And stranger still, I genuinely liked her.

"What are you girls doing in there?" It was Waz, who had come looking for us. "Are you having sex?"

"Kind of," I said. That got Jennifer's real giggle back again.

★

IT WAS GETTING LATE and no one made a move to toss another log on the fire. I thought the night was winding down until the movie star unwittingly came up with an unconventional but award-caliber finale. He was sitting in the corner, the light from the fireplace flickering across his face. He appeared relaxed. Comfortable. Home on the range. No one had said a word for a few minutes when he punctured the silence. "Are you still seeing . . . ?" And then he mentioned a name. A name that woke Jennifer up even though the question was addressed to Psycho Girl. "That was a strange dinner party, wasn't it? But you two looked like you were having fun."

Psycho Girl gave him a look meant to stifle him but movie stars don't intimidate easily. Especially not this one.

"What? I don't know what you're talking about," she said. "Who? What?"

He repeated the question.

Jennifer winced in pain as if she'd just been shot. "Who was at what dinner party?"

The movie star filled her in and only then did I realize he was talking about Jennifer's rock-star love. She turned to Psycho Girl. "You saw my boyfriend?"

"He's not your boyfriend."

"Whatever he is, you saw him?"

"Yeah, I saw him. And your problem would be . . . ?"

"Did you fuck my boyfriend?"

I noticed Jennifer's right eye had started twitching again.

Psycho glared at the movie star. "This is nice. Is this what you wanted?"

"Answer the question," Jennifer insisted. "Have you been fucking my boyfriend?"

Psycho straightened the cuffs on her sweater and smoothed out a crease on her Prada pants. Then she spoke softly, but defiantly. "He's not your boyfriend."

"Whatever the fuck he is, he's off limits to you."

"Nobody is off limits to anyone else," Psycho Girl replied calmly.

It was the kind of remark that generally set off my South Boston fuse. Usually I'd be up and in her face, but instead I felt immobile and sad. She was only twenty-two.

And even if I suspected that was the way of the world, I couldn't stop trusting. I hardly knew Richard Gault but I trusted he would guide us all out of this wilderness.

"That's a scary way to live," I said to Psycho. "And I think I know what I'm talking about."

"It's not her fault," William argued. "How was she supposed to know? Jennifer never mentioned his name."

"I mentioned it to her," Jennifer screamed. "She was the only one who knew."

I looked over to Richard Gault, expecting him to do something to control these emotional pyrotechnics, but he let it play out without interference. I trust he had his reasons. And I could guess why the movie star remained silent. Although his reputation warned that he could be a bullshit buster, I took him to be the type that was only interested in the information, not the argument. It wasn't his job to referee.

"It's the Jerry Springer show live from Silt," Waz joked.

No one laughed.

Psycho Girl had had enough. "Shit happens and there are so few great guys in the world," she said. "And anyone who pretends otherwise is lying." She got up and walked out.

Her exit created a vacuum. For a second I almost missed the drama. William must have, because he quickly got up and followed her.

"Where are they going?" Waz asked. "That kind of exit requires jamming a car in reverse, then throwing it in drive and leaving at least twenty yards of skid marks."

"I think they're in the kitchen," Richard Gault said as he peered down the hallway.

"I'm sorry for all this," Jennifer said. "I've been sorry since I got here." She looked at Richard. "Not here in your house. Here in Colorado. I'm making all the wrong choices. That ever happen to you?"

"A cosmic reversal," Richard replied. "And as cosmic reversals go, this one isn't so bad."

"You want to hear about some bad cosmic reversals," the movie star chimed in. "Richie and I have some stories."

"You've both seemed to weather them pretty well. What's the secret?" I asked.

"Learn to love your scar tissue," Richard said. "Hope that doesn't sound too profound."

"Not too profound at all." Jennifer seemed grateful for any advice at all.

"Not too profound," I agreed. "But I think it might be easier for men to love their scar tissue than it is for women. Battle scars don't get you a lot of dates."

"If you love your scars, they disappear," Richard said, tongue in cheek. "Didn't you know that?"

"Alchemy. Lead into gold," the movie star reminded me.

"Thirty years," I reminded him.

"I might have exaggerated the number," he laughed. "Maybe it's thirty years if it's all hard labor. Some say love can accelerate the process. Not that I know a lot about that."

"Since when does love make anything easier?" Jennifer asked. And then, showing her trademark recuperative power and spunk, she added, "but I love you for saying that." She rubbed her forehead. "I think I should go to bed. She looked to Richard. "Guess I need a sleeping bag and a sleeping pill."

"We're very equipped around here. Equipped for all emergencies and circumstances."

★

THE MOVIE STAR GRINNED. "I think the reason you keep that bridge in such bad shape, Richie, is so this kind of thing will keep happening. All writers manipulate their world for a better story."

"Are you a writer?" Waz asked.

Richard got up and walked toward the staircase. "Only by default." He started up the stairs. "Anyone want to know where they're sleeping?"

Jennifer and Waz followed his lead with Waldo trailing behind. That left me and the movie star.

Until that moment I hadn't realized that one of the advantages that comes with being famous is that you can skip the preliminaries.

"Shall we finish this?" the movie star asked, holding up the bottle of champagne.

"Yes," I said.

He picked up the bottle and our two glasses. I followed him to his room.

chapter twenty-six

I wouldn't have fucked him if he wasn't such a great kisser. This was risky territory for me. For any girl. It was risky because he was so sexy and smart and FUNNY and I knew long after he was gone I would ache for him. And the year had gone on too long and there'd already been too much pain. But those kisses made it impossible for me to walk away. Whether he was famous or not, he owned me from the first touch. But I can't deny, his fame offered a bonus. For months I'd been trying to find a way to rise above the mundane. Everything had become a task. I needed to be reminded of the existence of a higher force. I needed something or someone to bring me into the "power of now." Forget the past, ignore the present. That's what I wanted and that's what I got. Me and him in a room with no time clock.

We weren't completely alone. There were at least a half-dozen characters he'd played on the big screen in there with us. He didn't break into dialogue or accents or anything silly. But being with him triggered those images in my mind. It was like having group sex but all with one guy.

If that makes me a star fucker, that's okay. Making love to the movie star cracked open my heart and expanded my vision—and isn't that what every religion in the world (and any drug worth taking) is all about? It's not like I was fucking him for a new Mercedes or to get my picture in *Us Weekly*.

Would I betray a girlfriend to experience it again? I wish I could say no. Absolutely not. I would never do that. But I might. Not that I counted on the movie star to call again and as far as I knew he didn't have a serious girlfriend and if he did it wasn't a close friend of mine. But all roads lead back to the same issue. Where's the line between loyalty and living your life? And thinking about that, it suddenly all became so clear. I still hated Remy, maybe always would, but I could no longer blame her.

When I woke up, the sun was shining brightly through lace curtains. My first thought was something is missing. My second thought was—the lull is gone. It had disappeared completely and already felt like a distant memory. It would have been nice to turn to the movie star and give him some of the credit for this achievement but he, too, was gone. Really gone. And that was okay. And it was more than okay when I went into the bathroom and saw that he'd left me a message on the bathroom mirror. "You're beautiful." I definitely was going to ache for this guy but it was all worth it.

Richard was at the kitchen table with Lucy. I was startled to see her there and more shocked that at close
range in the brilliant daylight she was obviously not
in her twenties. She was a woman in her forties. A gorgeous woman, but not a kid and not trying to look
like one.

Richard introduced us and she offered me some
coffee.

"Where's everyone?"

"They all left," Richard said.

"They left? Without me?"

"The bridge was fixed by seven. William and the actress were gone by eight. Waz and Jennifer are back at
the motel. They got a lift in from my foreman."

Lucy anticipated my next question. "We can drive you over there whenever you're ready."

"I guess I'm ready now."

"Let's you and me take a little walk first," Richard suggested. "You want to meet Lucifer, our bull, don't you?"

"No. I really don't." But I was pleased to have a parting conversation with Richard and grateful that neither he nor Lucy had mentioned the movie star.

I checked out the bull from the other side of the field. "I'm a wimp when it comes to the great outdoors," I said.

"I can see that."

The bull stared at us as if he might charge at us at any moment but Richard hoisted himself up on the fence and sat with his back to the beast.

"Lucifer? Is there a message in that name? R.D. told me to ask about the whole Lucifer thing. To figure it out and get back to him."

Richard smiled. "Of course he would." He took a minute before offering any further explanation. "R.D. and I have a running argument about who 'the enemy' is. By argument, I mean what we sometimes get around to talking about when we're on our second vodka and it's been a slow news day. He thinks the enemy is out there. You know. Corporate conglomerates. Five companies controlling the world. That's his enemy."

"I think I've heard that argument before. I think I've been the one arguing it."

"Yeah, well, I'm no fan of corporate conglomerates but I like the convenience of a DSL line. No, I say the

enemy is in us—part of our wiring. We're all children of
Lucifer. Creative and demonic. Who hasn't challenged
the gods now and then? There've been times when I
would have sold my soul for a little justice. In the end,
all you can do is do whatever you can to help the species
evolve up a notch, score more points for the creative
side. And have as good a time as you can while you're
doing it."

"Sounds good."

"As long as you don't make the mistake Lucifer
made. He got stubborn. And greedy. Had fifteen, wanted twenty."

I had no idea what he was talking about and glanced
over to the bull as if that would help me decipher
Richard's shorthand.

"You know, minutes," he explained. "Andy Warhol's
fifteen minutes of fame. Most people fuck up when they
try to stretch it to twenty."

"Weren't you even tempted? You *are* the guy who
said no one ever voluntarily gives up love or power."

"Nope. I had fifteen and would have been happier
with five. Besides," he said as he jumped off the fence,
"fame ain't power. And it sure ain't love."

★

WE TOOK the long way back to the house. And though
my idea of a hike is doing twenty minutes on a tread-
mill at a level-fifteen incline, even I had to concede that
a walk in the country is as good for your butt and even
better for your spirits. I didn't even get depressed when

Richard delivered the inevitable bad news. "You understand why I can't do your project?"

"I do. And I don't."

"Once you start selling yourself to the media there's no self left. They're savages." Unexpectedly he put his arm around my shoulder, a protective gesture, as if at that moment members of the media might attack from the bushes. "Ever wonder how birds who eat bees can swallow their prey without getting stung? You know how they do it? They pound the bees on a branch until their venom is gone and the stinger's destroyed."

"There's the media and then there's me. I hate the media. I just want to do a documentary for all the people like me who are tired of getting their information from magazines that don't know the real thing from an impostor with an expensive publicist."

"Look," he said. "It's one thing for you to make a documentary. It's another for me to agree to be the subject of one. You know what I'm saying. It's a very different risk. Different exposure."

"Yeah. I know. I get it. So why did you let us come out here?"

"Because I'm never sure I'm right."

★

AS WE DROVE into town, I tried one more time. "You've got a daughter, right?"

"I do."

"She's the reason you canceled the last time we were out here, right?"

"How'd you know?"

"Guessed. Doesn't matter. She's seventeen. You know how hard it is to be seventeen these days? And twenty-seven? And thirty-seven? People need all the help they can get. All I want to do is correct some of the misinformation out there."

"I'm not your guy," he said.

★

WHEN WE PULLED up in front of the motel, Richard took a book from the floor of the backseat and handed it to me. "For you. A going-away present."

It was the new detective novel by John Simmons.

"Oh, are you into these books, too?" For some reason I flipped immediately to the back cover, where the author's picture is usually found, but there wasn't one. Just a one-line bio saying John Simmons lives on his ranch in Colorado. I gasped. "Oh my God, you're John Simmons."

"How else could I afford life on the Ponderosa?"

"That is so great, so fucking great." I looked on the floor of the backseat. "You happen to have another copy with you? It'll make the best Christmas present for Waz."

I felt bad for her. She blamed herself. She said, "William, I should have just pulled the movie star aside and said, 'Look, this is the situation.' If I'd confided in him from the start, he probably wouldn't have said anything and Jennifer wouldn't have found out and then the trip to Colorado would have been a nightmare instead of a disaster."

I reminded her that we got to know each other on that trip, so it wasn't a total nightmare. She got all nervous and said, "Yeah, I know. I didn't mean it that way." This girl hates to make a mistake. She wants to do everything right. Exactly right. All the time. But it's got to be her version of right, which sometimes is fucking nuts. As hard as she is on everyone around her, she's harder on herself. The girl can't let go and it doesn't make for a good time. We did sleep together that first night in Silt. She came to my room after she got back from what she said was a disastrous party in Aspen. She told me all this stuff about Christine and how she wasn't into me and was going to ice the situation. I didn't figure Christine to be like that. Talking that shit to her girlfriends. Anyway, it put me in a weird mood so when this twenty-two-year-old crazy actress says, "I'm depressed, too. Let's just fuck and forget about everything else," it sounded like a good idea. Now I'm thinking that she might have made up that stuff about Christine. Very possible. She's an actress. She makes it up as she goes along.

We still hang out a little and sometimes when she's in a reckless mood, she'll say, "Maybe you should be my new boyfriend." Yeah, right. She's never going to be with a guy who works at the Centerfold. The perfect guy for her is someone who has money, a low-profile career, and doesn't mind taking care of her twenty-four hours a day. A high-profile guy would get too much attention. The rock-star thing was a fling. I think she occasionally sees someone named Joey who lives in Aspen. Doesn't matter. When she's in L.A., I hear from her. The other night she called and said, "I'm flying in tonight. New York was a nightmare. The plane arrives at eight. Can you pick me up and bring me a Xanax?" I take care of her and I get three songs out of it. Works for everyone.

Meanwhile, Sarah's been around. She came up with a great second verse for my new song, "Little Miss Perfect." We worked all night and fucked all day. Life is good.

Haven't seen much of Christine but the last time she came by the Centerfold she seemed happier. I've noticed that things seem less obvious to her and she never says "hideous" anymore. What that means, I don't know. What can I say? Merry fucking Christmas!

How much longer will I be able to spend fifty dollars a week on magazines? The thought crossed my mind as I loaded up on my usual weekly fix at the Centerfold. But because New Year's Eve was just a few days away, I decided to put all questions about my nonexistent career and shrinking bank account on hold until I got through the holidays. It was hard to feel too panicked at that moment because it was one of those L.A. December days that is so bright and clear and invigorating (yes, good air quality, for a change), you can't imagine why any transplanted East Coaster would be nostalgic for snow and chestnuts roasting on an open fire. You can have Jack Frost nipping at your nose. Give me sunlight on my freshly pedicured toes. Nars tomato-red polish.

Even William took a break from listening to KCRW's morning show to catch some rays. He brought two folding chairs out of the Centerfold's teeny office and set them up in the adjacent parking lot. We sat side by side, flipping through magazines and newspapers, doing our usual commentary.

William pointed out an item about a brilliant filmmaker who was currently dating a mediocre sitcom actress.

"I can't get my head wrapped around that one," I said.

"It's the age thing," William replied. "He's fifty-five and she's twenty-five."

"I still don't get it. I mean I get it. I know why older men seek out young women but this particular case doesn't compute. It's like if Picasso were alive and he was dating Anna Nicole Smith."

"Good one," he said, giving me a playful nudge. Then he leaned back in his chair, basking in the sunshine, and said the strangest thing. "Not exactly two rocking chairs on a front porch but it's pretty close, you know what I mean?"

I didn't, but I guessed someday I would.

chapter thirty

Neither one of us had made plans for the big night. I just happened to look out the window around eight and saw Waz arriving back at his apartment with a bag of groceries.

I stepped outside. "Having a party?"

"Should I?"

"I've got some champagne and party hats."

"Get on over here," he said.

It seemed appropriate that he and I were together at the end of the millennium. All year long we'd been vocal about how much we hated the whole drumroll to the big moment. "Countdown to more delusion," we called it. But when the night finally hit, neither of us was in a cynical mood.

We ended up ordering in and watched TV, flipping the channels. I made him stop on some entertainment news show. They were doing an on-location piece from the set of the movie star's latest film. They didn't get to interview him but seeing his face on this particular night inspired my one and only resolution for 2000.

As much as I loved how bigger than life he was, and as much as I believed that a bigger than life experience was occasionally necessary in order to keep life vital, I was beginning to realize that putting someone on a pedestal (my code name for him was Zeus) denies them their humanity. That can't be good. Not good for them. Not good for anyone. My resolution was that if I ever saw him again, I would kick over the pedestal. He didn't need it. And neither did I. He was tall enough on his own. And though it was scarier to deal with a man than a god, I was ready to take it on. It was a silent resolution but Waz picked up on it.

"What are you so happy about?"

"1999 is over."

"One more hour," he said.

★

RIGHT BEFORE MIDNIGHT, I went into Waz's bedroom, looking for a match to light the good-fortune candle I'd bought at a Mexican drugstore. His closet door was open and there—among dozens of black or gray pants, a couple of black suits, and a brown L.L. Bean jacket—was a bright red dress. I walked back into the living room holding the dress on its hanger. "Jennifer?"

"I can't believe you." He had this adorable look on his face. I'd discovered the secret he was dying to tell.

"That's not a denial. Where is she? Why aren't you with her tonight?"

"We're taking it slow. We're purposely not spending the holidays together. We don't want to get into that thing where you're accelerating a relationship because the calendar says it's December thirty-first."

"I think it's great."

"It was completely unexpected. For both of us. She jokes that I'm the first renter she's ever dated. And I tell her that I usually only go out with girls who read. Truth is she's a closet reader. I caught her hiding a copy of F. Scott Fitzgerald's short stories inside her copy of the *Enquirer*."

I giggled, as if channeling Jennifer. "You and her. I love it."

"You do?"

"Yeah, just don't take it too slow."

★

FOR THE LAST MINUTE of the year we turned on the TV. Every station had millennium coverage. Our favorite was channel seven's local news—live from Disneyland.

"That is so cheesy," I said. "ABC is owned by Disney so basically they're starting off the millennium by self-promoting."

"Vile," Waz said

"Disgusting," I seconded.

We started laughing because it was so typical and because I think we both believed that, in spite of the hype and the bullshit and all the hard and soft lies, somewhere out there, another force was growing—a force of people in search of a smarter, cooler playground. Where this crazy optimism came from I don't know.

Ten, nine, eight, seven six, five, four, three, two, one. Blastoff.

A few cars driving down our street started honking their horns. At the same time someone was at the entrance gate to our building trying unsuccessfully to ring through to an apartment. They couldn't get beyond the dial tone. I could relate.

"Shall we help them?"

Waz looked out the window. "Oh yes," he said smiling. "I definitely think we should."

I followed him out. Unexpectedly he stopped and pushed me ahead.

"What are you doing," I laughed, "I almost tripped over you."

"Yeah, what are you doing?" It was Richard Gault.

Nothing could have prepared me for that voice. For that vision of Richard Gault at my front gate at a minute after midnight, January 1, 2000.

"What are you doing here? What does this mean?" I unlocked the gate but he didn't come in. Instead he gestured to the street, where a Toyota Land Cruiser was double-parked, Lucy at the wheel. She waved as he handed me a piece of paper with a phone number.

"Call me there tomorrow. We should talk. Happy New Year." He took a few steps toward the street and then stopped. "Almost forgot." He pulled a large tin of caviar from his jacket pocket and tossed it to me.

"You do like caviar, don't you?"

"She loves it," Waz said, filling in for me as I stood there in a mute stupor. A caviar-bearing cowboy who had something to say. It was going to be an interesting millennium.

When Richard got to the street, he looked back and said, "We'll handle the savages."

Carol Wolper is a screenwriter and the author of the novel *The Cigarette Girl.* She lives in Los Angeles.